Seized Assets

Samara Black

ISBN 979-8-9898465-2-8 (eBook)

ISBN 979-8-9898465-3-5 (paperback)

Library of Congress Control Number: 2024920254

Printed in the United States of America

Book Cover Design by Cheshire Gato Media

Front cover:

Photo by: Samara Black

Cover model: Karolina Faler

Back cover photo credit: Gilbert Cayamo (via Pexels)

First edition 2024

This book is dedicated to Corrine.
Thank you for the name borrow.

Contents

Author's Note

This is the second book in a series. It's highly recommended you read the first book (The Asset) before continuing.

This book ends on a cliffhanger. You've been warned.

The following story includes the following content that may be inappropriate for readers under the age of 18:

- Cursing, profanity, dirty words

- Violence, sometimes graphic in nature

This story also contains the following content that might be sensitive or triggering for some people:

- Self harm (takes place off-page, partially described)

- Suicide attempt (takes place off-page, mentioned)

- Pregnancy loss (takes place off-page, mentioned)

- Graphic violence, including against women (multiple, described)

Chapter One

Roman Holiday

Rome

January 18

Larissa

Avvilire's line wrapped around the block. Thankfully, I befriended a group of drunken party girls on the VIP list. It was worth the cost of a round of drinks and listening to stories about Marcello and his cheating ways. Honestly, the guy was a pig who totally didn't deserve Viviana's affections. Unfortunately, we all knew she'd take him back. Again.

I moved away from the crowd and leaned against the rail separating the bar from the dance floor. The liquor was top shelf, and my third Bellini was strong enough to diminish even my high tolerance for alcohol. I tuned out the world and surrendered to the music. After swaying a little too close to the edge of the rail, however, it was time to slow down on the booze. Drunken Larissa was an emotional wreck whose mind traveled to places it shouldn't. It had been two goddamned years, I reminded myself. Time to move on. I needed a night away from dark thoughts and darker urges. A night to finally enjoy myself, free from my demons of the past. That was the goal, and it was time to make it happen.

The floor before me was a sea of bodies dancing and writhing around, far too dangerous for a spy who traveled in the shadows. After being away from the life for so long, the long, dark blonde wig and brown contact lenses felt strange at first. By the time my stilettos stepped inside the club, however, they felt like just another mask. Smoothing the short red dress that clung to me one last time, I joined in the chaos.

A pair of dark eyes met mine after the second song. I did my best to play it cool, giving him a small smile and rejoining Viviana's group. I closed my eyes to absorb the fast beat of the next song. Blissfully numb, my body swayed and moved without a care until my senses prickled. When a muscular arm snaked around me and grabbed my hip, I stilled.

Turning, I looked into the dark eyes of a sinfully attractive man. His black hair was longer on top and slicked to the side. My fingers twitched with the urge to feel if it was as silky as it looked. His chiseled jaw was peppered with stubble and just begging for my lips to trail kisses across. He stepped closer and smiled.

"May I have this dance, *bella*?"

His voice was deep and raspy, the kind you wanted to whisper dirty things in your ear while he did even dirtier things to your body. He oozed sex from his pores, making him the perfect distraction for the night. When his large hand enveloped mine, his fingers caressed the skin, causing a shiver.

My dance partner gripped my hips against his, holding me in place as we moved to the heavy techno beat. I wrapped my arms around his neck and closed my eyes. At the feeling of a warm breath on my cheek, I looked up and found his lips hovering over mine. Holding his gaze, my hand moved to his chest and slid lower. As soon as our lips came together he probed my mouth with his tongue.

We broke apart, and his eyes shifted to something or someone over my shoulder. With the smallest of nods, he led us away from the floor and followed two men toward the back of the building. We came to a metal door around the corner, which led to the stairs. The door closed with a loud bang behind us, quieting the music but not the drumbeat that still pulsed through my veins. He pushed me against the wall and assaulted my neck with his mouth and tongue. I confirmed the silkiness of his hair when my fingers grasped the back of his head and pulled him into another kiss. He pressed his erection to my stomach, groaning when my fingers stroked him through his pants.

His hand caught mine. "I've wanted you since I first saw you watching me the other night. I'm going to have you right here against this wall."

"Upstairs," I whispered before trailing kisses along his jaw.

"An adventurous one. I approve."

The stars twinkled against the black sky. The air was chilly, but I knew I'd be warm soon enough. He led me to the edge of the roof and stopped at the front of the building. The Tiver River glittered in the distance. I clutched the railing in front of me as he pressed my back to his front.

"I'm going to bend you over this rail and fuck you under the night sky." He pulled my dress higher, sliding his fingers close to my core. "When you come, I want the crowd below to hear you." At my shiver, he turned me to face him and smiled. "Do you want that?"

I cupped his face with both hands and trailed soft kisses against his lips. "You have no idea."

It took less than five seconds. My fingers flexed, exposing the small but sharp blade hidden inside the black jointed ring that extended the length of my index finger. Judging by his wide eyes, he didn't feel me slice his jugular until it was too late. Blood gushed from his neck and all over his beautiful and expensive suit, staining the gold pin on his lapel in the shape of an "S," the mark of a high-ranking member of the Sardi family. He opened his mouth, no doubt to scream, but nothing more than a choked, wet gurgle emerged. His hands moved to my throat, earning him one last slash.

"Your boss's screams of pain will make me come harder than you ever will," I taunted as he slumped to the ground.

I stepped over his corpse and grabbed the black bag hidden behind the building's ventilation unit. Tossing my heels aside, I returned to the balcony, crouched down, and assembled my sniper rifle. A quick scan of the area through the scope revealed no guards or others around the building that held my interest. Perfect.

A single-storied red brick building around the corner housed a small restaurant. The most noticeable trait was it was how completely plain it looked. No neon lights, no doormen. My target preferred flashier settings to show off his power, but the quieter locale had its advantages. A lick to the back of my hand directed me to a slightly different angle. Once in position, I kept a watch to make sure my now dead companion's men didn't come to check on us.

A ghostly white SUV turned the corner and stopped. Two large men came out of the building and headed to the back driver's side door. Moments later, the tall form of Gio Sardi appeared. My finger moved to the trigger, and I sat, waiting for the time to strike.

Time didn't slow, but a feeling of calm swept through me. In my twenty-nine years of life, I'd never felt more alive than that moment, crouched behind a sniper rifle on a rooftop in a dress riding up my ass. The breeze shifted and I with it one last time. Deep breath. Hold. Squeeze.

"The Donovan family sends their regards," I murmured in Italian.

Through my scope, I watched the bullet strike him in the throat and then the wall, triggering the hidden detonator connected to the bomb inside the wall. The explosion tore apart the building, drowning out the music and illuminating the sky. Silence, followed by screams, told me it was time to go.

I tore apart the rifle and threw the pieces toward the surrounding buildings as I ran for the door. One of my dance partner's guards came bounding up the stairs. I lunged feet first, knocking him to the bottom in a heap. Jumping on his shoulders, I twisted his neck grotesquely to the side until his body went limp. After tossing my wig in the corner and freeing my natural dark brown hair underneath, I bolted back to the dance floor and ran out with the remaining bewildered and terrified patrons. A bouncer directed everyone to gather around the corner, but I ducked into an alley and caught a cab the next block over as the police sirens wailed on their way to the crime scene.

My taxi driver watched me closely, asking several times if I was all right. Nodding silently, I pretended to be too upset from the incident at the club to speak. Aside from a few strange looks from people in the hotel lobby at my dingy clothes and bare feet, I made it to my room without any issues. After a shower, I slid into bed just as the evening news started. Based on what the *Polizia* shared with the press, the reporter announced fourteen men died in the blast, including a shipping entrepreneur from Bari named Giovino Sardi.

After turning off the TV, I finally allowed my body to relax. "I finally got him, Dad," I whispered. "I promise I'll celebrate it properly when I get back home."

The tip about Gio came so quickly that I accidentally left a few items on my bed back at home, including my dad's cigarette. I'd been upset at first, but promised myself smoking it when I got home a couple days later would be just as sweet. I pulled the covers over my head and snuggled into the pillow with a smile. Victory at last.

· · · ● · ● · ● · · ·

Belfast, Northern Ireland
John

The pimple faced kid who couldn't be older than fourteen shoved me into the room and grunted at me to wait before slamming the door behind him. I dropped my bag on the narrow bench and looked around before sitting down. My stomach churned for the fourth time in as many hours, and my head dropped to my hands.

Seeking him out was the nuclear option; I had to be out of my fucking mind or beyond desperate to set foot in his territory. Actually, both were true. I was out of answers, and it was only a matter of time before her luck ran out.

The door opened with a bang, revealing Pimple Face returning with towels and medical tape. He threw it all on the ground. "He said he'll talk to you after the match."

"What match?"

"The one in ten minutes that you'd better win if you want to talk to him." He spun on his heels and made another loud exit. The little asshole was an absolute fucking delight.

I blew out a long breath and picked the shit up off the floor. I should have known when the fucker agreed to Lucas's request to meet. He knew damn well what was up and planned to make me go through hell. Not that I blamed him. Had the shoe been on the other foot, I would've done the same.

Quickly changing out of my suit, I opened my bag and put on a thick pair of black jeans and steel-toed boots. After taping my hands, I spent the remaining time pacing the room. I gripped the back of my head to calm my nerves, reminding myself what was at stake.

She'd evaded everyone for two years. I got close to catching her a couple times, only to have missed her by days or less. Three months earlier, I'd missed her by less than an hour in Greece. The cup of tea next to her bed was still warm.

The search was far from easy. Lucas didn't find a single shred of information for nearly a year, and what he found was deeply troubling. Less than a month after she escaped Portland, she was hospitalized in Rome, followed by a six-month stay in a psychiatric facility. About a month after her release, all hell broke loose. She forged a bloody trail across Italy and all the way into Greece. Twenty-seven men connected to the Sardi family, including allies and important associates, were dead. Last week she'd slaughtered three of my uncle's best collectors as they played pool in a Sardi hangout near the port. Their heads were discovered on the pool table, but their bodies were still unaccounted for.

My uncle was enraged, but too afraid to send Marco after her and leave himself unprotected. Instead, he hired mercenaries for the job. Two were found dead not far from where they were hired. The latest one quit after he woke up in a hotel outside Naples, missing six of his fingers and any memory of the previous two days. The last thing he remembered was approaching a woman with stunning blue eyes at the bar, offering to buy her a drink.

I whipped around at the loud bang on the door. "Yeah?"

"Get your ass out here!"

With one last whispered prayer, I found the little shit waiting for me in the hall. He eyed me with a bored look before motioning for me to follow. The yells of the crowd grew louder with each step down the corridor, as did my heart rate. I exhaled slowly. Failure wasn't an option.

We turned the corner and entered a large room full of people gathered around a square in the center. The spectators grudgingly cleared a path for me, yelling insults and jeers as I passed. The referee, a man in black slacks and a black polo shirt stood at the center of the square. To his right, a behemoth several inches taller than me and twice as wide paced. Our eyes met and his narrowed to green slits. He ran a hand through his spiky light brown hair and spat at the ground. I followed the ref's direction to the line on the floor. Behemoth clenched his jaw and bounced his head side to side before moving to his line. The referee's hand rose, silencing the crowd.

"A reminder that there is to be no interference from the audience," he bellowed before turning to us both. "The rules are simple. There are none. You fight until someone loses consciousness. Best of luck to you both. Begin when you hear the horn."

Best of luck. Right. I swallowed down the bile in my throat. Lasting longer than the beast in front of me was all that mattered. My stomach wrenched and threatened to rebel. Would puking count as a defensive move?

A loud horn buzzed, and Behemoth's arms snatched toward my face less than a second later. I spun to the right and successfully dodged, only to receive a quick punch to the ribs. Gasping, my legs buckled for a second and the shithead smiled.

Despite his size, he didn't have a clear advantage. Unfortunately, neither did I, so we fought back and forth for what felt like hours. The crowd buzzed like a hive of angry bees. When he got too annoyed, Behemoth took wild swings. Now and then, one of his blows connected and it hurt like a bitch. Catching him off guard, I whipped around and pounded my fist into his face several times. I felt eyes on me, and when Behemoth stumbled backward after another blow I looked around and found my goal.

He stood at the back, smoking a cigarette and looking like the arrogant fuck he was. His eyes caught mine, as my opponent lunged for me. I dodged and counterpunched, colliding with his head and knocking him on his ass. With one last glare at the asshole in the crowd, I jumped on the beast's body and reigned blow after blow.

I didn't stop when the first tooth fell from his mouth, nor when the third broke off and cut my hand. It was only when the horn blared, and four hands seized me from behind that I stopped. Three men rushed past to tend to what was left of the bastard on the ground. My mind flashed to her face, and I lunged forward. I was yanked backward and led to the center of the ring, where the ref lifted my arm and declared me the winner. The crowd booed, but I didn't give a fuck.

My eyes searched the crowd for the prick. He tossed his cigarette on the ground and left. I laughed until my swollen cheek throbbed. Two additional men brought a stretcher to the group around Behemoth, while two more cleared a path for me to leave. Someone tapped my shoulder just before I reached the corridor.

"Get yourself cleaned up," Pimple Face ordered. "He'll be in to talk to you in half an hour.

I showered and changed back into my suit. An ice pack covered the worst of the bruising on my face, but it did little to calm the throbbing in either my cheek or my chest. I paced the room, willing time to speed up, when the door slowly opened and he strolled into the room as if he owned the place, which, of course he fucking did.

The earlier smirk remained on his pale, weathered face and his blue eyes danced with something that made me uneasy. His thick, wavy hair, a mixture of light brown and gray, was slicked back. If I hadn't known for a fact he was a few years older than Seamus, I would've suspected they were twins based on the pictures I'd seen.

"Titus Donovan," I greeted, extending my hand.

"Gianni Martinetti," he sneered before lighting the cigarette dangling from his mouth. "You've some damn nerve showing your face around here. I'm amazed she didn't shoot you when she had the chance."

"I am too, sir. And it would have been well deserved. But that's in the past."

He quirked a brow as he blew a cloud of smoke in my face. "Is it now? You're her past and yet here you are. What in the bloody hell do you want?"

"I need to know where she is. It's absolutely vital."

"The fuck it is!" His tall, skinny frame vibrated as he moved his face within inches of my own. "Thanks to you and your family's messing about, she's almost fucking died twice now."

"And I take full responsibility. For all of it. Had I known, I would've been there for her. That probably sounds like a load of shit to you, but she means a lot to me. I care for her. That's why I'm here."

"You're here to do what?" His voice sounded like gravel. "To do her damn head in again? Absolutely not. She's been through enough. Leave her be and find another toy to break."

"Let's make one thing clear right now," I countered, pointing a finger at his chest. "You have every right to be pissed about what happened to her, but you don't get to sit there and tell me what she means to me. You have no fucking idea."

His nostrils flared. "Get the fuck out of here before I shoot you myself. I'll be goddamned if I'll let you within a hundred kilometers of her." Shoving his shoulder against mine, he stalked toward the door.

Swallowing down the lump in my throat, I knew it was time to beg. To hell with how it made me look. "He's about to send Marco to look for her," I called after him. Titus froze. "He was too afraid to be left unprotected, but she's making him look weak. You've heard of Marco, haven't you? What he's capable of? I have no intention of turning her over to him. I swear on the life of my grandmother that she won't come to any further harm from me."

"How can I trust you, huh? She trusted you and look what happened to her."

"Because I'm her only hope. My uncle is out for blood. He's determined to find her by any means necessary. The only reason I took part in that shit was because he kept my grandmother hostage and threatened to kill her if I didn't."

He raised his face to the ceiling and closed his eyes. "My brother and I hadn't seen each other for a very long time when he died. He left for New York, and nobody heard from him until he sent a letter to our grandmother announcing he'd married some Italian woman and they had a kid. His wife wrote every now and then, but then we got news he and Sera were dead and Lissi was missing and believed to be dead. Before my grandmother died, I swore to her I'd find her only great-granddaughter and keep her away from this shit."

"And I swore to my grandmother, just as I swear to you, that I will keep her safe. I'd rather die than see her in pain ever again."

The internal war in his head was obvious as he stared at me. He paced back and forth, rubbing his eyes, and then stopped. "She's living in a small cottage on the outskirts of the village of Doolin. Several hours to the southwest from here in the middle of absolutely nowhere."

I let out a slow breath. "Thank you. I swear to you that I'll guard her with my life."

"Then get the fuck out of here and find her. And remember you aren't the only well connected prick in this room. You hurt her again and the last thing you'll see is your blood dripping from my face."

He threw the door open and stepped back as I grabbed my bag and headed for the exit. I'd just crossed the threshold when his voice broke through the din in the hall. "Be careful, son. She'll see you long before you see her. Rest assured she won't offer you as warm a welcome as I."

I nodded and murmured my gratitude before hauling ass to the exit. My phone was in my hand, but it wasn't until I was outside and almost to my rental car that I dialed. He answered on the second ring.

"John, thank god. I—"

"Lucas, I got it. He told me where she is."

"John!" His tone meant business. "Listen to me."

I leaned against the car and gripped the phone. "What happened?"

"Gio is dead."

"What? How?"

"Happened last night. The police are still trying to figure out how it happened, but the restaurant where Gio meets his crew when he's in Rome was blown to shit with everyone inside. I've got to hand it to her, she's good."

"Explosives were never Liss's thing. She wouldn't just blow him up."

"That's what I thought, too," he replied. "But then they found pieces of a sniper rifle on the rooftops and the ground surrounding Avvilire. They also found Luciano with his throat slashed on the roof."

"Jesus fucking Christ."

"Not bad for a crazy bitch, eh?"

"I have to go. We'll talk when I get home."

My fingers were almost numb when I gripped the steering wheel. I leaned my head against the seat's back and tried to calm my racing heart. She'd done it. A chill shot through me as fear and panic took over. She had absolutely no idea what she just unleashed on herself.

"Larissa, baby, what did you just do?"

Chapter Two

Doolin

Two Weeks Later
Larissa

The morning air was bitter cold and thick with fog, making each breath a chore as I turned left from my cottage. It was a day for thermal underwear under my sweats and even then, my body protested. I'd stoked the fire in the living room before heading out, but a six-mile run still separated me from a warm room and a hot breakfast. The Madden family rooster crowing as he strutted around the yard was my only companion so far, but several chimneys in the distance told me I wasn't the only one awake at such an early hour. After finishing my stretches, I shoved my hair inside a gray slouchy beanie and set out on my morning run.

I followed my usual route up the hill leading away from the village, around the farms and cottages dotting the countryside, and ended at the top of a steep cliff near the shell of an old castle. My face and lungs ached from the icy air as I slowed my pace and headed left at the fork in the road. The pale sun shimmered through the fog, but didn't diminish the morning's beauty and silence. Sadly, none of it did anything to quiet the chaos in my head. Even as I strained to watch the waves from the top of the cliff, my mind still raced. After running through a maze of fallen castle ruins, I headed home.

After a hot shower, I changed into a thick black wool sweater, faded jeans, and wool socks. My hair, now several inches past my shoulders, swung in rows of damp waves as I moved to the front of the house. I stared out the windows in the kitchen until the whistle of the kettle alerted me that breakfast was ready. Sitting at the nook with my porridge and honey, I watched the flames dance in the fireplace. The occasional snap and pop broke the silence. Having eaten and warmed up, it was time to plan the day ahead.

I grabbed my coffee mug and wandered to the large bulletin board that hung in my makeshift home office down the hall. Several news clippings about the bombing in Rome were taped to the side, but the smile they brought to my lips was fleeting. I had no doubt the police were still cleaning up pieces of Gio and his crew, but my father's cigarette remained in its case untouched. I'd grabbed a lighter more than once, but the words *he* spoke still haunted me.

You don't know the whole story.

Fucking Gianni. Was his statement the one truth spoken in a sea of lies between us? Closure remained impossible as long as there was a chance it was true. The mess in Portland lifted enough of the veil to question everything I believed, but I had no way forward. Instead, I remained stuck in an emotional purgatory and unsure of my next steps. I didn't know if he was right, and there was no way in hell I'd get answers from the bastard who put the thoughts in my head to begin with. No, the healthiest thing for me would be to refuse to give him any more headspace and try to figure out the mystery on my own.

At the realization I'd been staring at his picture, I made a disgusted noise and turned away. Way to move on, Lissa. Determined to get out of my funk, I set the empty mug in the kitchen sink and grabbed my wool jacket. Once outside, I climbed onto my bicycle and headed for the village. The temperature had warmed enough to thaw the frozen puddles along the side of the road, but the air still felt cold and heavy. The black clouds in the distance sent a shiver down my spine. It looked like Mr. Madden's prediction of a nasty storm was correct.

My first stop was Mrs. Duffy's yarn shop, owned by the kindest woman I was fortunate enough to meet on my first day in Doolin. After watching me struggle in the market and finally have a small emotional breakdown in the tea section, she calmly guided me and my basket through the aisles. She stopped by the cottage every few days afterward for tea.

A few weeks later, she brought a skein of yarn and taught me to knit, patiently adapting her lessons once she realized I was left-handed. I needed a hobby to get my mind off my troubles, she'd said. At my terrible first attempt at a sock, she smiled, praised the yellow lump of fluff, and encouraged me to keep trying. Eighteen months later, the gloves, hat and scarf I wore that day were my creations. I'd joined the local group who met monthly for tea, gossip and needlecraft, donating most of our wares to the church at the edge of town. I also worked the occasional afternoon in her store when her husband's arthritis flared up.

Her eyes lit up when they met mine, and she beamed when she heard about the throw I planned to knit for my couch. I grabbed several bright colors, determined to add some cheer to the drab interior of my house. We talked as she rang me up, catching up on the past few weeks since my last visit. I told her about my trip to Rome to attend an acquaintance's funeral, and she shared the news that Mr. Murphy agreed to sell her the wool from the first sheering of his sheep in the spring. After agreeing to cover the store the following Tuesday, I gave her a warm hug and headed for the market.

Mrs. Flannery, the shopkeeper and a close friend of Mrs. Duffy's, looked up when the entry bell rang and smiled. "Ah, Aileen. I was thinking of you this morning. Siobhan said you were back. How was Rome?"

After five years in the intelligence community, I had over twenty aliases known to various people and agencies throughout the world. To the eight people who knew my true name, I was Larissa Donovan. In the village of Doolin, nestled on the western coast of Ireland and away from the rest of the world, I was Aileen McKillop.

I shrugged. "Rome was all right. I didn't get to see much since I was only there for the funeral. I would've come into town sooner, but I caught a damn cold and stayed home to keep my germs to myself. How have you been?"

"Aye, it's been fairly quiet here. I hope you're here to stock up for the storm?"

"I didn't see the clouds until I was on the road, or I would've put a bigger basket on the bike. I'll just grab a few essentials, and those should get me through."

"Nonsense! You get what you need, and Thomas can give you a ride home. More than enough room in the back of his truck."

My gaze went to the floor to hide my smile. She'd been trying to fix me up with her son for over a year. Anyone patient enough to put up with his sweet but sometimes overbearing mother was practically a saint in my book. His dark, curly red hair and deep green eyes were a bonus, as was his tall, athletic build. I'd never been opposed to the idea; I'd simply avoided her attempts because I just hadn't been ready for a relationship with anyone.

"Only if it's not too much trouble."

As if on cue, he appeared sand stood near the counter. A slight blush colored his cheeks when he smiled. "It's never any trouble for you. I promise."

"Thomas, grab a trolley and help her!" she barked. "The storm will be here before we know it!"

My stomach fluttered when he patted my shoulder and grabbed a small metal cart. His mother beamed as we walked each aisle, occasionally calling out "reminders" and pointing out both our favorite foods. He smiled and took it all in stride, which eased my nerves. Later, we laughed about her antics as his truck bumped along the narrow road leading to my house. I stole glances at him throughout the ride, smiling nervously when he caught me. For the first time in a long while, a conversation with another person didn't make me eager to find an exit.

After stowing my bike next to the shed, he insisted on carrying my groceries into the house and helped put everything away. We chatted the entire time, laughing easily and lightening my mood. After he closed the pantry door, he asked if I needed any firewood brought in until he saw the full stack near the back door.

"Thomas, thank you so much for all your help. I appreciate it."

"Like I said, it's never any trouble."

"Yes, but I'm sure you weren't planning on being volunteered by your mum."

He chuckled and shook his head. "She can be a lot to handle sometimes."

"She's a sweetie. I love her and Siobhan so much."

With a slow nod, he stepped closer. "I appreciate that. Listen, I've been meaning to ask you something." He paused. "Would you ever want to get together one of these nights with me? Maybe grab a bite or a drink?"

"That would be lovely."

His face split into a wide grin. "That's great! All right, well, after this storm my mother is sure will bring about devastation and an uncertain doom to us all, let's make it happen."

"I'd like that." I pulled a stray curl behind my ear. "Very much."

"Aye, me too. I should head back before she sends out a search party. I'm sure the temperature has dropped a degree or a couple drops of rain are falling by now."

"Drive safe. It could be treacherous out there."

He laughed and gave me a hug. His arms lingered for a long moment before falling to his sides. Our eyes met, and the butterflies in my stomach took flight again when he moved his face closer to mine. After a beat, he stepped back.

"Until next time," he whispered.

Dazed, I followed him to the door and waved goodbye as he left, leaving me alone in the silent house. My smile was genuine. He was attractive, attracted to me, and I liked how I felt around him. It wasn't a love match, not yet, but the possibilities were a step in the right direction. I stepped into the living room, and the emotional landmine detonated out of nowhere. Feelings locked away escaped, ones I hadn't felt since...

God dammit.

"No," I bit out, collapsing onto the couch. "Get out of my fucking head, you lying bastard."

I drew my legs up and rested my head on my knees. After holding it in for several minutes, a sob erupted and the tears came with it. God, I was a mess. I was ready, excited, to open myself up to someone new, and less than five minutes later it all felt wrong. It felt like I was cheating on the son of a bitch. I knew it was absurd. There was nothing left between us, but my heart refused to fully let go.

I didn't know I'd find myself on such a dark path after leaving everything behind. After my confrontation with Barton and Felton, I made it to Belfast and found my uncle Titus, whom I'd only heard my dad mention a few times when I was younger. Our first meeting was awkward, but it didn't take long for us to bond over our shared love of whiskey and hatred of English football teams. He let me stay in the city with him as he attended several business meetings. I'd been there only a few days when everything went sideways.

A lead too tempting to ignore led me to Rome. Titus, worried about my broken arm and emotional state, begged me not to go, but I insisted. The trip was an epic disaster. It turned out Gio had never even left his castle in Bari, and after a series of mishaps, I woke up in a psychiatric facility and stayed there for six months.

After my release, Titus brought me to Doolin, not far from where he and my dad lived before coming to the States. He stayed with me at the cottage, sleeping on the couch and conducting his business with daily loud rants while pacing around the living room or smoking in the backyard. Evening was family time, as he called it. One of us made dinner while the other told stories about our life. He remembered Felton from their school days, and even though they hadn't spoken since then he was glad I was raised by someone with ties to the family and their country.

Despite my new knitting hobby, my uncle recognized my restlessness after a few weeks. He used his connections to gain intel and turned the small storage room near the back door into a command center to track the Sardi family and their movements. Gio couldn't be tracked for long, but the lower-level soldiers and associates could.

When Titus headed back to Belfast, I set out for Italy. My first victims fell three days later, and it was nothing but a blur of death and carnage after that. Every person associated with the family throughout Italy and as far away as Greece that I found died at my hands. Gio continued to hide in his fortress, but not before hiring mercenaries to come after me. The flaw in that plan was I knew most of his hired guns, so finding and killing them was easy. After several sabotaged shipments and fires at the two largest ports in Sardi territory, the empire was battle scarred, weary, and slowly going broke.

I avoided Gianni. Part of my recovery included accepting sometimes harsh realities, and the bitter truth was I knew he was looking for me to turn over to his uncle or finish the job himself. I wanted to look him in the eye and pull the trigger the next time our paths crossed. Despite my hatred for the lying sack of shit, he was a charmer, and I wasn't yet strong enough to avoid falling under his spell a second time. Unfortunately, he was damn good at his job and got close to catching me more than once. After a narrow escape in Greece, I kept a closer eye on his movements.

If time indeed healed all wounds, it needed to hurry the hell up. He was a frequent star of both my dreams and nightmares, one moment my savior and my damnation the next. Groaning, I flopped face down on the couch. Staring at the tablet on my coffee table, I decided to put my energy to better use on some good old-fashioned research.

For dinner I ate a small bowl of leftover stew in front of the kitchen sink. The pale blue sky quickly disappeared and sunset came and went as I cleaned up. One of my favorite things about my house was the view, and I wanted to catch a glimpse of the sea and the sky before the storm. Thick clouds hid the moon, but with no immediate threat of rain I grabbed two blankets from the closet and headed to the backyard. I wrapped one blanket around my shoulders before plopping down on the other spread out on the grass. Leaning back, I inhaled the salt air. I shivered when a gust of wind blew past and pulled the blanket tighter around me.

Staring at the sky, I pushed the anger and anguish aside and thought of happier times. Sundays spent on the couch watching football and eating too many snacks. Long talks about everything from the worst album we ever bought to the chemistry of beer. Waking up wrapped around each other and starting the day with a kiss. I decided to give myself a break, and when my chest felt lighter, I knew I'd made the right choice. Until I woke up the next morning, he was just a guy I met at a party that I could've easily fallen for.

Did he miss me? Did our time together matter to him at all? Or was I just a loose end that he now hunted to finish off for his family?

I shivered in the yellow glow cast by the security lights behind me. My thoughts strayed into dangerous territory. Closing my eyes, I focused on the sound of the water below. I'd always found beauty in the chaos created when the waves crashed against the cliffs. Maybe that was me, enduring despite the endless violence and madness all around.

My body sensed a presence before the shadow approached. I tilted my head to get a better view and the faint sound of his footsteps left me completely frozen. My body sat as if made of stone for what felt like an eternity before my mind re-fired.

"I knew you'd find me."

• • ● ●• ● ● ● •• •

John

My heart fucking stopped upon hearing her voice. It held no emotion, nor did her face. She turned back to the darkness in front of her and stared ahead as the wind whipped her long, dark hair around.

I'd made it to the village earlier in the day and did my best to stay out of sight. My plan was to wait until dark to find her house, but those plans went out the window the moment I recognized a young woman in a bright green knit cap riding down the hill on a bicycle. She parked right across from a cluster of buildings and her eyes swept the street in front of her.

She was thin and nearly ashen, but her eyes were the same unmistakable pale blue. I watched her walk into the yarn shop several feet away and talk to the old woman behind the counter. The temptation to run inside and pull her into my arms was almost too much, but I resisted. Instead, I decided it was the perfect time to find her house and see what I was up against. After that, I'd figure out how to proceed. She wouldn't be happy to see me, not that I blamed her, but I needed to see how likely it was that she'd shoot me on sight.

The small cottage was set on a cliff overlooking the sea. It was locked up tight, so I peered through each window to get an idea of the layout. The interior was cozy, but drab. Her demeanor was always vibrant, full of life, and her surroundings echoed that. It could've just been the part she played, but I believed it was one of the few personal traits she allowed to shine through in a life steeped in mystery and deception. The bland environment inside the dark stone walls wasn't her, and that worried me.

To my relief, I was able to pick the old lock on the small shed in the back and slipped inside. The small windows faced the rear of the house. Not the best view, but better than nothing. The small crate in the corner wasn't a great seat, but at least I was hidden when an old pickup parked outside the house later. I froze as a man with dark red hair carried her bike toward the shed until she directed him to place it under the lean-to along the other wall. He took his sweet time covering the bike with a tarp on the ground, and I was just about to pull the pistol from my waistband when he finally ambled back to the front.

The smile on her face when he picked up several bags and followed her to the front door churned my insides. Who was he? A friend? More? They entered the kitchen and when he hugged her as they spoke, I fought another irrational urge to intervene. When I noticed they didn't kiss, some tension left my shoulders, but the bile in my stomach refused to settle.

Could I blame her for moving on? Absolutely not. After everything she'd been through, part of me hoped she'd finally found happiness.

It would've been painful, but the chances she'd ever see me that way again were slim to none.

She led him to the front of the house, and the ache in my chest evaporated moments later when the truck drove away. My vantage point was limited, but I watched her head toward the center of the house. The smile on her face was small, but it was there. She was happy. My heart sank a couple of seconds later when her face crumpled, and she disappeared from sight. Moving the crate, I settled into a corner near the windows and waited for the perfect opportunity to present itself.

I felt like a fucking stalker watching her lean against her counter as she ate from a small bowl, obsessing over how much her appearance changed. The light inside her was dull and barely shining. Gone was the woman who loved to cook and ate with gusto. Instead, she merely consumed the food in order to sustain her body.

While she scrubbed down her kitchen, I took advantage of the darkness and crept out of the shed. I moved to the front of the house, looking for points of entry. It was finally time to end the chase and get her to safety. Gio was dead, but a worse threat loomed. I pulled my phone from my pocket and sent a text to my team to remain on standby and wait for further instructions. Once she went to bed, I'd move in.

My pulse quickened when the back door opened, but calmed when she moved past the shed and got comfortable on the grass. She looked so peaceful I almost felt bad for confronting her. Almost. God only knew the weapons or traps inside the house, so this was my best shot. I made my way closer until her voice acknowledged me.

I froze, waiting for her to act. When her gaze remained fixed on the nothingness, I tested fate and moved to sit behind her. Stretching my legs out, my hands rested on her sides. Not a word, a flinch or any sign of objection. Nothing.

My chin rested on her shoulder. "You're a hard woman to find."

She removed the blanket from her shoulders and passed it to me. "You'll need this. The wind is chilly."

I spread it over my shoulders and, after pulling her tight against my chest, wrapped it around both of us. "Like I said, you're a hard woman to find. After a while, I thought I was chasing a ghost. All I found in Turin was your lifeguard hoodie."

"Didn't feel right to keep it. And give yourself some credit. You almost caught me in Greece."

"Considering how close I got, I thought you were toying with me."

A ghost of a smile crossed her lips. "Wish I could say I was smart enough to do that. But I learned a couple of years ago that I'm pretty stupid."

"Liss."

"Are you here to kill me?"

Shutting my eyes, I buried my nose in her hair, relishing her familiar scent. She had no idea of the vow I made back in Prague a lifetime ago. Would she even believe me if I told her? I pushed the thought aside and wrapped an arm around her waist. Her head leaned against my chest, and I closed my eyes. Fuck, holding her again felt good.

A quick buzz from my phone ended the euphoria. "It's time to go."

A simple nod was her only response. Alarmed, I looked at her face, but her eyes simply met mine for a moment before they closed. Her icy hand moved to the arm pressing her to my body. I freed the syringe from my pocket and gently injected her neck. She remained mute for what felt like forever until a single warm drop of liquid fell on my hand.

"Larissa?"

She sighed softly. "Thank you."

The small hitch in her voice cracked my heart wide open. Despite her soft sobs, she leaned into my chest and the lump in my throat threatened to choke the life out of me. I opened my mouth to tell her of my promise, but the words were lost when her body went limp. The waves roared, and in that moment, I felt just as battered as the rocks below. Gently, I moved her to my lap and kissed the top of her head.

I watched her sleep for a few minutes before sending a text to the team instructing them to pick us up. My guys would pat me on the back for a successful mission, but it hardly felt victorious. Finding and capturing her was the easy part. It was only a matter of time before she woke up.

Chapter Three

Weak

John

I propped my legs up on the coffee table and cradled the phone to my ear as the fourth voicemail from an associate droned on. We were still in the air when one of my guys sent word to the family that Liss was spotted near Monte Carlo and we were looking into it. It wouldn't buy me a lot of time to figure out a better solution, but she was safe for now.

"Is this your office now?" a voice sarcastically remarked.

Lucas, my cousin and second in command, strolled into the room and plopped down on the couch next to me. He stared over my shoulder at the screen of my laptop and smirked. The lieutenant who lost his best enforcers at the hands of our guest demanded proof of her death within three days or he'd send his own men after her. Idiot. I closed the lid and set it on the floor.

I narrowed my eyes. "I assume you're here because you have something to tell me and not just to nitpick my work location?"

"You've been in here since you got back. Go outside or something. A change of scenery aside from this damn room, anything."

Crossing both arms behind my head, I sighed. "I have to be here when she wakes up. She's gonna be pissed and I'd rather she take it out on me than anyone else."

He glanced at the bed and arched a brow. "She hardly looks like the holy terror everyone's made her out to be, but the trail of dead bodies she's left says otherwise."

"Forty-one, including our not so dearly departed uncle."

"She's going to rip you apart."

I wadded a piece of paper on the table and threw it at his head. "Appreciate the vote of confidence."

The door opened and Santino, the estate doctor entered. We had a small infirmary, but I wanted to keep her closer to me and away from his equipment. The last thing anyone needed was her waking up in a room with scalpels and unknown potential weapons. He nodded to us before walking toward the bed.

We both stood and Lucas clapped me on the shoulder. "I'm sure you want to talk to him. Let me know if you need anything."

Briefly looking up, Santino shifted his gaze back to his watch. "Her pulse is stronger today and her eyes aren't as sunken. Overall, I'd say she's improving."

"Is there a reason she's still asleep? The sedative I gave her wasn't supposed to last this long."

"She was in terrible shape when you brought her in. Dehydrated, anemic, malnourished, no doubt severely exhausted. She's getting some much needed rest and her body is taking this time to recover. My best guess is she'll wake in the next eight to twelve hours."

I blew out a long breath. "Thanks."

"Once that happens, there are other issues that need to be addressed." His eyes went to her left side. "Long-term effects are my main concern."

"Me too."

He stood next to the bed for several minutes and typed his notes into a tablet. I watched her sleep as the pit of anxiety in my stomach deepened. Her rage when she woke up worried me, but not nearly as much as her emotional state. Santino reviewed her medical records from Rome, and though the discharge notes showed no remaining cause for concern, he shared my view that only time would tell. With a small nod, he left.

I sat in the plush armchair next to the bed. "I'd ask how you're doing, but that's a dumb question, right?"

Brushing a lock of the now dark brown hair from her face, I stared at the circles under her eyes. I kissed the back of her hand before turning it over and forcing myself to face what I'd been avoiding.

The scars were a mess, a series of deep cuts and slashes that showed how hard she'd tried to cut through the cast on her broken right arm before giving up. Her left arm bore one perfectly straight line that showed she hadn't hesitated before slicing through the skin less than a month after we last spoke. By some stroke of luck, she hadn't cut through any tendons or caused permanent damage. No permanent *physical* damage. The fact she thought I was in Ireland to kill her and fucking thanked me after injecting her was all I needed to know about her state of mind.

I'd read about the cuts plenty of times, but nothing prepared me for the glimpse under her sleeves back in Doolin. Like a coward, I avoided looking at them on the plane back to Verona. Instead, I kept her covered in a blanket so I wouldn't see how she'd become so broken that she tried to take her life in the bathroom of some shitty hotel outside Rome on New Year's Eve.

Lies. Betrayal. Abandonment. I was guilty of all three and more. Forcing myself to stare at the scars, I cursed myself to hell. Instead of laying on the ground and bitching that she'd escaped that day, I should've run after her. I could make all the excuses in the world, but the bottom line was I failed her.

Looking through her house was excruciating. The only pictures on the walls were those of my uncle and his minions. Most of them crossed out for obvious reasons. No bright colors to break up the dull gray monotony in each room. Even the food in her fridge was dull and lacked vibrance. The cherry on top was the worn rucksack in her closet containing one change of black clothing, a few toiletries, her pistol, and an old cigarette case. A "go bag" packed and ready for her to leave at a moment's notice, whether it was to take care of another target or make a quick escape. It was no life. She existed to dole out her revenge. I'd brought it with us since it was clear the items inside were important to her.

"I am so, so sorry, baby. I'm going to spend the rest of my life making it up to you. Whether you want me to or not. I promise I'll be there for you. Always."

Her blanket, the one we shared in Doolin, covered her legs. I pulled it over her shoulders and couldn't help smiling when a small sigh escaped her lips. She hated being cold, especially in bed. The thought of crawling under the covers and holding her was tempting, but not worth the loss of life or limbs if she woke up and found me.

Lucas knocked before strolling in with a stack of papers. "Sorry to interrupt," he began with a nod to Santino next to him. "I need to talk to you about something in private, and Doc wanted to adjust her IV."

Confused about what couldn't be said in front of the doctor on our payroll, I followed him down the hall. I turned my ear toward the bedroom every few steps until we stopped by the balcony. He stared at me for a few seconds until I couldn't handle the silence anymore.

I tried to control my impatience. "What's going on?"

He rolled his eyes and pointed out the window. "Do you see that? That's the outside world. Remember it? You need to spend some time away from that room. There are more than a dozen people here who can handle her when she wakes up."

"Look, I know you mean well. But you have to trust me on this. She had a broken arm and still beat the shit out of me."

"And according to the doctor, her body is so worn down she's needed the past couple of days to recover. Even when she does wake up—"

A crash, followed by panicked shouting, interrupted his rant. The papers in his hand fell to the floor when I shot him a glare and raced down the hall. I tore through the door and froze. Santino was on his knees on the bed, one hand flailing in front of him while the other grabbed at his throat. Larissa stood directly behind him with the tubing from her IV wrapped around his neck. Blood seeped down her arm from where she'd ripped out the needle, but she paid it no mind. Her eyes met mine and narrowed. In that moment, I saw the face of the killing machine I'd only seen a brief glimpse before.

Lucas entered and cursed. I motioned him to the right of the bed while I went to the left. She watched his movement for a second before turning back to me and pulling the tubing tighter. The only sounds in the room came from the man gasping for air at her feet.

I held up my hands. "Liss, he's a doctor. He's not going to hurt you. None of us are."

I took a step closer. She jerked violently toward Lucas and released the tubing, throwing the doctor forward. They both hit the table next to the bed and crashed to the floor in a pile. The few seconds I paused were enough for her to strike.

We both fell to the floor. Somehow, I was lucky enough to get one arm around her. She struggled against me like a feral animal. Screaming in my ear, she aimed her kicks at my knees and crotch. Lucas tried to grab her legs, receiving a kick to the face before he pinned them to the floor.

"Listen to me," I murmured as she tried to elbow my side. "I know you're pissed off and probably scared, but I promise we aren't going to hurt you. If that was going to happen, I would've done it back in Ireland."

"Knock her the fuck out!" Lucas bellowed when she tried to knee him.

She let out a screech and butted her head backwards toward mine. Instead, she hit my shoulder, twisted her body sideways and shook Lucas off her legs for a moment before I tightened my arms around her in a bear hug and rested my chin on her shoulder. Her body stilled.

"Doc, she doesn't want to be knocked out," I said, and her body relaxed a fraction. "Liss, I promise he won't give you any medicine without your consent, but you need to stop hurting yourself. Your arm is bleeding pretty badly. Can you let him see it, please?"

She looked up at Santino and stopped struggling. When he held out a hand to help her up, I raised my arms and kept still until she'd moved a few feet away from me. He led her to the bed and examined her arm. She kept her focus on him as they spoke, ignoring everyone else in the room.

Lucas stood near the door as he tried to catch his breath. I gripped my throbbing ribs and limped over to him. She allowed her arm to be bandaged, and we watched for any signs of another attack. Leaning against the wall, I watched their every move.

"Jesus Christ," he whispered.

"Still think you can handle her?"

He clutched his jaw. "Point taken."

Santino joined us several minutes later. "The injuries to her arm were not that bad. She's resting." His voice was low and scratchy. "Her blood tests from yesterday show she's still very malnourished, so you need to have some food sent up. Quickly."

Lucas's eyes widened at the bruises forming on his neck. "You okay?"

"I'll live. I guess it's a good thing I'm not the source of her anger or I wouldn't be standing here."

Their voices faded into the background as I watched her. She curled into a ball on the bed but watched our every move with laser focused eyes. Eventually, her lids grew heavy and closed. A few seconds later they snapped open, only to close once again. The process repeated several times before Lucas poked me in the arm.

"John? Are you even listening?"

I shook my head. "Let's pick this up later. Lucas, can you please have some noodles sent up?"

He made a snide comment under his breath about me being whipped before he followed Santino down the hall. I rolled my eyes. Of course, he wouldn't understand. Lucas never stuck around a woman long enough to remember her name, let alone worry about her feelings. I had a similar casual attitude in the past, but it had already lost its appeal before that fateful night in Prague. She was stubborn, maddening, and being around her made me feel complete. If that made me whipped, so be it.

The kitchen staff brought two trays while I worked on my laptop. I'd just finished eating when she stirred; she peeked from inside her gray cocoon and glared as soon as she saw me.

"Are you hungry?" I grabbed a forkful of pasta and ate it in the hopes she'd see she could trust me. "The doctor said you need to eat, so the kitchen brought up some noodles with butter, along with garlic and potato soup."

Without a word, she sat up. She was so thin my black t-shirt slid off her shoulders, earning an annoyed grunt when she pulled it back into place and failed. I couldn't resist the alarm bells in the back of my mind when she stabbed her noodles and dug in without another word. She was way too agreeable for someone who tried to strangle someone with her IV only a few hours earlier.

"Soup needs more cream," she mumbled.

"You can make your own once you're feeling better."

The scowl she gave me over the bowl was a clear enough message. I moved to the opposite end of the room and stood facing the floor to ceiling windows. Night had fallen and the moonlit view of the estate was breathtaking; one of the reasons I picked the room for her was her love of watching the night sky. Something, anything, to bring her some peace.

At the sound of breaking glass, I looked up to see her rushing toward me with a shard clutched in her hand. Her feet were unsteady, but that didn't stop her from almost hitting my arm with several wild swings. She shrieked and lunged again, slashing at the top of my hand. Just before she struck again, I grabbed her wrist and squeezed hard enough to cause her to cry out and drop the weapon. I yanked her back against my chest and held her firmly in place.

"I get it," I said in a low voice. "You fucking hate me. I accept that. But if you're going to keep attacking people, I'm going to have to have you drugged and restrained. We both know you don't want that."

Her arms dropped and her body went slack. I looked down and she merely nodded her head. As soon as my grip eased, she walked away. When I tried to hold her hand, she shook it off and sat on the bed with her legs crossed.

I approached the side of the bed but kept my distance. "Are you ready to talk?"

She stared at me for a moment before turning her gaze to a spot on the wall directly in front of her. "Lance Corporal Larissa Donovan. Serial number 14955813. Date of birth twenty-five December—"

"Larissa."

"Lance Corporal Larissa Donovan. Serial number 14955813. Date of birth…"

I raised my head to the ceiling and exhaled slowly. Part of every standard military training included how to respond in case of capture. As she recited that response for the fifth fucking time, I knew there wouldn't be a conversation. Not yet. "All right, I'll let you have some space. There are people who are going to come in from time to time to make sure you're okay and bring you anything you need. If you attack them, you know what will happen. Understand?"

The door opened and Lucas's eyes widened as she recited her info yet again. Shaking my head, I yelled at her to have a good night and brushed past him. Paolo, a man not known for his warmth or charm, stood outside the door. I'd briefed my guys on how difficult guarding her would be, and to expect the unexpected. After giving them a few last instructions, I walked to my room and securely locked the door. I had slept little during my vigil and couldn't fight the exhaustion any longer. My bed felt like heaven, and I fell asleep almost before my head fully sank into the pillow.

It was torture, but I stayed away from her room to keep the peace in the house. That didn't mean she behaved peacefully. According to her file, Slovenian wasn't one of the twelve languages she spoke, so we decided Maja would be the safest choice to clean her room. To everyone's surprise and horror, Liss told the maid in her native tongue about Lucas's sexcapades with the cook's assistant. One screaming catfight later, it was decided Lucas would always accompany visitors to her room and monitor all interactions. To say I was his least favorite person after that assignment would have been kind.

Things settled into an uneasy quiet. The new clothes I ordered were delivered to her room with no trouble, and aside from the occasional glare or muttered curse word, she didn't harass or attack anyone else. Santino examined her on the third day and reported that she'd improved and was getting stronger. We all expected that sooner or later she would lash out, and I reminded everyone to stay vigilant.

The fourth day started just like the previous three. I woke up and went about my usual routine. I'd just finished brushing my teeth when

I heard a loud commotion in the hallway. Opening the door, I found a group of people arguing over who would tell me.

"Tell me what?"

Lucas's jaw clenched and he glared at Paolo. "Whomever had four days in the betting pool won. She fucking escaped."

Chapter Four

Siege

John

I walked the perimeter of the storage building in a daze. Well, what was left of it. The explosion destroyed the door and most of the north wall. A crate smoldered next to the window, while several loose electrical wires snapped and popped in the background. The combination of gunpowder and melted plastic stung my nose and eyes. Christ, what a mess.

Lucas's shoulders slumped, and he hung his head. "Okay, I'll say it. You were right and I was wrong."

I brushed past him. "Asshole."

We knew were in trouble when she escaped, but didn't realize just how much until I found she'd raided the safe in my closet. Not only did she grab her rucksack, but she also stole my primary sniper bag. The dog tags I kept in a side pocket were left hanging from a hook on the wall of the safe. Based on the boot prints in the carpet, she'd kept herself hidden for several hours before the theft.

She wasn't done. Somehow, she disarmed the motion sensors in Lucas's room and stole his cell phone right off the table next to his bed as he slept. His phone had several apps that controlled the security system and utilities for the entire estate. When he tried to change the access codes, he was pissed to find out she'd locked him out of everything. To rub salt in the wound, she remotely erased my phone while I was in the middle of a call with our IT guy.

We were totally fucked.

The estate was built like a fortress, but we still locked down every building and the guys patrolled the grounds in shifts. They found nothing, which led to loud grumblings about wasted time. She already left, they predicted. Why would she stick around? After the first day, even Lucas expressed doubts she remained hidden to get revenge.

I knew better. My uncle toyed with her, and she killed him and forty other people connected to him. I'd been on her shit list long before I landed on Irish soil, and made it worse when I kidnapped her. There was no fucking way she'd just leave without making me pay.

Very early on, I realized a serious problem. She was pissed off, loose on the grounds, and armed. If it were any other person, I wouldn't have hesitated to give the order to kill on sight. Instead, I declared she was to be captured but not harmed. It went over as best as anyone could imagine. By the second night, the tension was almost unbearable.

"Wake up, shitheads!" the house intercom screeched on the third morning.

After maybe three hours of sleep, the words barely penetrated my mental fog. I groaned and buried my head in the pillow. At that point, I didn't care if the house was going to blow up.

"I've been running around for the last two days, and you idiots haven't even come close to finding me. Everyone has five minutes to be in the foyer of the main house, or I'm going to put you all out of your misery."

Fuck. I fell out of bed and stumbled to the intercom on the wall. "Larissa, I know you're pissed, but there are better ways to handle this."

"Good morning, Mr. Martinetti." Her voice was way too cheerful. "I disagree. Let's just hope you and your band of morons move quick enough before everything falls down around you."

I dressed in jeans and a t-shirt. By the time I ran into the hallway, she announced we had two minutes. Lucas rounded the corner from his room and narrowed his eyes.

"Why couldn't she just shoot you in the ass or something?" he grumbled as we ran downstairs. "Thanks to you, we all have to suffer. Way to think with your dick, asshole."

"That's rich coming from the guy who's banging half the maids in this house."

"Only two! And your girlfriend had to fuck that up by telling them."

"If she was my girlfriend, I'm pretty sure she wouldn't be doing all this," I retorted once we got to the bottom of the stairs. The guys rushed in from their sleeping quarters, either half dressed or still in their pajamas.

"Well, it's good to know you guys can hustle when your lives depend on it," she mused over the intercom.

I stepped in front of the nearest security camera. "Liss, can we please have a calm, rational discussion about this?"

Her laughter filled the room and stopped as suddenly as it started. "I don't think so. We're beyond conversations. The last time we talked, you drugged me, and I woke up here. In fucking Italy. Here's how it's going to work. There are currently fifty traps spread throughout the estate."

Angry voices drowned out her next comment. My head dropped to my hands to quell the dull pain that erupted. Everyone demanded answers, but I didn't have a single fucking clue. A loud rumble shook the house, throwing everyone into silence.

"Correction," she interrupted. "There are now forty traps. We can't have any of you escaping or calling in reinforcements. That would spoil all the fun, so I took the liberty of blocking the road. You have twenty-four hours to find and disarm the remaining traps or I'll detonate any that are left. And the house."

The power flickered and went out, causing another swell of curses and threats. Lucas and I exchanged looks before I rolled my head skyward. The walkie talkie in his hand beeped, signaling another device was trying to connect. His eyebrows pinched as he pressed the button.

"Hey guys, it's me again. I forgot to mention that I have one of the walkies. All the other channels are jammed except this one, so you can use these, but I'll hear everything."

"Fucking hell," Lucas groaned.

"One last thing before I go," she paused. "I'm sure Mr. Martinetti is going to tell you to find me at all costs. He thinks it's a good idea, and he may be right. But I'd advise each of you to ask yourself which makes more sense: saving your home or finding your boss's 'crazy bitch ex' as Mr. Luccetti calls me. I'll let you guys decide. Good luck and Godspeed!"

Everyone stared at the damn thing and then at me. Lucas's jaw clenched a few seconds before he placed the device in my hand and avoided my glare. I tightened my grip and fought the urge to throw it against the wall. "I want everyone suited up and in front of the house in ten minutes."

Paolo stepped forward. "What about weapons?"

"Pistols only. Ten minutes," I bit out when he scowled and several others protested.

The guys ran toward their rooms while I raced upstairs to the large linen cabinet at the end of the hallway opposite my room. A few moments later, I pulled my secondary sniper bag from the back and headed to my bedroom. I changed into my tactical outfit: black cargo pants, t-shirt, and combat boots. After tossing my bulletproof vest over my shoulder, I grabbed the bag and headed outside. The temperature was chilly, but the bigger problem was the light fog making everything hazy. With the weather on her side, we had our work cut out for us.

We met in the driveway, away from the buildings in case she was listening. Several trees were missing from my line of sight over the gate, confirming she'd blocked the road. Lucas looked up from the burner phone in his hand and shook his head; he was still cut off from any access.

I motioned everyone into a circle and spoke in a low voice. "We're going to separate into groups of three. Two teams will sweep traps, while the other two search for our guest. The house-guest teams will use extreme caution. Not only do we have shit visibility, but we're trying to find someone who's armed and extremely dangerous. She's angry and for now she's running the show, which makes her even more willing to do crazy shit if she's cornered. If you see her, you are not to engage. I repeat. Do. Not. Engage. I guarantee she'll return fire and kill you without a second thought. If you're pinned down, use your pistol only to get to safety. Note the time and her location and text it to my phone. Since she has a walkie, we'll use that strictly for trap chatter. Any questions?"

Minutes later, everyone left. I threw my bag over my shoulder and headed toward the back of the estate. My eyes narrowed as I scanned the lush forest surrounding the estate. A walk along the perimeter trail would have been welcome on any other day. At the feeling of a hand on my arm, I palmed my pistol and looked up.

Lucas held up his hands. "It's just me. If we aren't supposed to engage, why are you walking around with a sniper rifle?"

"I'm going to use the scope to search the area. I don't plan on shooting unless I absolutely have to."

We moved past the pool until the ground changed from manicured grass to the rough dirt and leaves of the forest. He drew his gun as I headed for the large tree to my left. A light drizzle dissolved some of the fog, but it still made for a miserable environment. He bitched under his breath on the ground as I made the slow climb to the first sturdy branch. Once the rifle was set up, I brought my eye to the scope and scanned the area.

After finding five traps and relaying them to the guys, my focus turned to scanning the area for clues to her location. I saw nothing at first, but soon a group came through and removed the trip wire hooked up to several pepper bombs. Moving my scope, I focused on another area when something whizzed past me. I looked up and found a bullet lodged in the tree several inches above my head. Lucas let out a yelp and hit the deck, which I would've laughed at if another bullet hadn't flown by an inch lower than the first.

"Cute, Liss," I said into the walkie. "Now may I climb down?"

Another bullet sped by before her voice crackled back. "Oh, sorry. I'm just over here reminiscing about Prague. You can climb down whenever you want. I probably won't shoot you."

"That doesn't give me much confidence."

"Bummer."

I slid the rifle to Lucas and climbed down. Not more than a second after my feet hit the ground, I heard a small click and an ear-splitting screech filled the air. We both collapsed and scrambled to find the source. After a few moments, I uncovered a sound grenade from the brush and turned it off. I buried my face in a pile of leaves and caught my breath.

"Jesus fucking Christ," he panted, lying on his back.

"Only thirty-four to go."

Three additional sound grenades and four stun grenades were found, though some of the other traps were more dangerous. A pipe bomb destroyed an observation tower overlooking the road leading to the property. We found four more that could've done extensive damage to the perimeter fence and anyone unlucky enough to be nearby. Two men fell into leg snares hidden in the ground and one suffered a sprained ankle when he slipped in the mud while running through the forest.

After nineteen hours, everyone neared their breaking point. Five traps remained, but seven men were injured and in the infirmary. It was just past four in the morning and Lucas and I huddled in my office looking over a map of the estate. The desk was a mess of portable lights and bits of paper with scribbled info about traps. Exhausted, I stared at it to get some idea of how to continue.

"Why haven't we secured the bunker in the northeast corner?" he groused. "She got all the shit she needed for the traps from there, so it's obvious that's where she's holed up."

Our last shipment of weapons included a crate full of goodies, an assortment of explosives and other shit we were probably never going to use. We shoved the box into a corner of the storage shed along the back perimeter of the property. Little did we know we'd left a perfect assortment of toys for the woman now loose on the grounds.

"That just means she's had plenty of time to get everything she needed and move on."

"If you don't think she's there, why not secure it?"

"And risk anyone who might corner her?" At his eye roll, I slammed my fist on the desk. "Did you read her file? She's a genius who kills anyone and anything you set in her path."

He narrowed his eyes. "Don't treat me like I'm fucking stupid. I read the file."

"She could have killed us all a hundred times over, but hasn't. Why?" The office phone rang, ending our debate. "Yeah?"

"We have a situation," Joey, one of my men, replied. "A trap detonated and breached the eastern wall."

Fuck. "Any sign of her?"

"None."

My cell phone buzzed. I put Joey on hold. "Paolo, what's up?"

"Southeast corner. I think we found her."

"Perfect. Stay there. Don't move and don't engage. We're on the way."

Sick of the sight of everyone, I swiveled my chair away from the desk and stared at the darkness outside. I took another long drink of coffee and leaned my head back as I considered our next steps. We still had a few hours to find the last four traps, and all I wanted to do was sleep for a week. Maybe two.

"John?"

"They spotted her and one of her traps blew a hole in the wall."

"How do you want to handle this?"

I tried to rub the exhaustion from my eyes. "Joey is guarding the wall. Jay and Max are coming back to the house. Since you're so sure she's in the storage bunker, you and Max go check it out. *If* you find her, or even think you've found her, call us."

"Okay. But I thought they saw her on the opposite end of the property?"

"It's too easy. She's been a ghost this whole time. You think she's going to get sloppy and let herself be seen? Fuck no."

"Then why are we doing this?"

"I can't take the risk that I'm wrong."

Lucas and Max headed for the shed shortly after the guys arrived back at the house. Jay and I set out to the southeast. The weather had changed little since the previous morning, but the exhaustion made my body slow in the cold, damp air. We found and disarmed another trap, this time a stun grenade and several pepper bombs. Three more to go. We inched forward with caution, unsure of what we'd find. We finally found the two men hunched down behind a group of thick bushes.

Gino pointed to the left when we joined them. "We saw something sitting in the tree over there. Second branch up."

A mound leaned against the trunk of the tree, but in the dark it was near impossible to tell if it was her. I pulled my pistol and inched forward. The air was silent, but my nerves felt electrified. My stomach lurched when I saw something flutter at the top of the object. Even from less than ten feet away, I still couldn't tell. Holding my gun aloft, I crept closer.

A loud explosion shattered the silence. It was barely visible in the dark, but a small gray puff of smoke floated upward from the north. I moved closer and felt like a complete fucking idiot seconds later when the shockwave loosened the object in the tree and it fell to the ground, revealing it to be a decoy.

"Fuck!" I kicked the ground and rejoined the group behind me.

The four of us moved quickly. Gino got Jay on the walkie, who reported he and Lucas were okay. They were about ten feet away when the building exploded. He assured us they didn't cross any trip wires or find any traps.

"Fucking proximity triggers. She's watching them," Paolo said, moving faster.

Lucas and Max appeared from their hiding spot in the brush once we got there. I raced past everyone to round the corner and stopped at the sight of the concrete slab flooring. Lucas swore when he came up behind me, but stayed back. Gino kept his gun out as he swept the opposite end of the building. He yelled out he'd found another trap, which he cleared a moment later.

I clenched my jaw and looked around. "Do you guys notice any-thing?"

"Percussion grenade," Max grunted.

"After that last delivery, this place was full of crates and boxes," Gino stated. "Where did it all go?"

Lucas closed his eyes. "Fuck. She played us."

"Yes. It would appear that she did." I bit out.

"Okay, I'll say it. You were right and I was wrong."

"Asshole."

I threw my walkie at him and headed back to the house. Whispered voices and rustling followed, which did nothing to help the pounding in my head. Not only was she still missing, but she also stole a ton of weapons and ammo. Just. Fucking. Perfect.

Stomping upstairs, I unfastened my bulletproof vest. What the hell did she want with it? There was no way she'd be able to move that much crap off the estate undetected. What was her end game? My head throbbed. Fuck it. I needed a nap. The rest could wait.

Entering my room, I thought about the traps. Thank god we'd at least found and disarmed all of them. I'd tossed the vest on a chair and was halfway to the bathroom when a flash of panic ignited. Five traps left. The one that blew out the wall. A stun grenade with a cluster of pepper bombs. Behind the storage shed. Inside the storage shed. Four traps found.

Fuck.

Movement in my peripheral vision stopped me from turning to the door. Our eyes met, and it was then that I realized I was facing the final and most dangerous trap of all. She stood next to the window near my bed, dressed in black. Her exhausted face mirrored my own weariness. I opened my mouth and her hands moved.

In the blink of an eye, a blast rang out from the shotgun that magically appeared in her hands. The force sent my body backward to the floor, where I crashed down hard. My side throbbed and burned as my hands moved to assess the wound. To my shock, I pulled my hand away and found it clean and dry. What the hell?

My gaze went to the fabric on the ground. A fucking bean bag round. My relief was short-lived upon hearing her footsteps. A few seconds later, she stood above me with the shotgun still in her hand.

"Miss me?"

Chapter Five

Surrender

John

My lungs were on fire and my side throbbed. I opened my eyes to the barrel of a shotgun inches from my nose and her stony face behind it. As soon as she heard the rapid footsteps, she tossed the gun into the hallway behind me. She then pulled the pistol from her waist and aimed it at the door. Too afraid to move, I remained on the floor facing her while the entrance to my room filled with people.

"Drop it, bitch!" Lucas snarled behind me.

"Leave." Her voice was icy.

"You're outnumbered. All it takes is one bullet."

"Indeed." She lowered her hands, aiming at my head. "Go ahead. It'll only take one bullet for him, too."

At my cough, bodies shifted behind me. "John, are you okay?" Lucas called.

She glared at the door for a second before lowering her gaze to mine. With a small nod, I rolled onto my back, wincing. Paolo looked ready to storm inside, but Max wedged himself against the frame to hold him back. Lucas stood in the center with Gino to his right, his gun aimed at her chest.

"He's just fucking dandy, but you're interrupting our conversation," she replied. "Leave. *Now.*"

"Larissa, you need to lower your weapon, and then we can have whatever conversation you'd like." Lucas's attempt to calm her was useless, but he didn't know that.

"I have no idea what you're talking about with this 'we' shit. I'm going to talk to your boss and unless the rest of you back the hell off, he's going to have a really shitty day."

"I get that you're a crazy bitch, but don't be a stupid bitch," Paolo taunted.

Everyone's control hung by one rapidly fraying thread. My heart plummeted when her finger made the smallest twitch, and I knew there was only one way to keep everyone alive. Holding up both hands, I slid closer to her feet. Lucas's eyes widened, but hers never left the throng of men she saw as a threat.

"Guys," my side protested with each breath. "I want you to stand down and leave."

"No fucking way," Lucas snapped. "We're not leaving you alone with her."

"If she wanted to kill me, she could've done it at least twelve times since she escaped."

"Fifteen, but who's counting?"

I placed my hand on her ankle. "Liss, stop. You're here to talk, aren't you?"

Lucas narrowed his eyes. "I really think that's a bad idea."

"If she promises not to tie me up and I call in regular updates, would you leave then?" I shot him a look all but begging him to calm down.

"She hasn't agreed."

Her jaw tensed for a second before she stepped back. "Fine. I won't tie him up and he can let you know he's okay. Happy now?"

"Not really. You're still a crazy bitch."

"And you're still a whiny little—"

"Enough!" I bellowed. "Everyone, lower your fucking weapons and settle down."

She exchanged glares with everyone as Lucas helped me stand. He saw the spent bean bag round on the floor and turned toward her with a snarl until I pulled him away. Everyone lowered their guns but watched her every move.

After a few tense seconds, she smirked. "While I have you all here, I'd like to make a recommendation. The guy who hides his weed in the storage bunker needs to talk to the guy who has black sheets on his bed and find out where he gets his stuff." Seeing Max and Joey's reactions, she crossed her arms over her chest and grinned. "Black sheets guy's is much better quality. I haven't seen shit that good since I was in Ibiza a few years ago. Honestly, I think I did you a favor by blowing it up."

Lucas's eyes widened as Jay shoved Max and Joey into the hall. Paolo stepped just past the door and held out his hand with an expectant look. Rolling her eyes, she slid the magazine from her gun and handed it to him. At his arched brow, she tossed the pistol onto the chair in the corner and turned in a circle to show she was unarmed.

Lucas gestured toward her. "Do you know what you're doing?"

"If she wanted me dead, I would be."

He didn't look convinced. "All right. Call the office phone every fifteen minutes."

"He can text you," she announced. "Here."

She pulled his phone from her pocket but whispered in his ear before placing it in his hand. His face hardened into a glare until she spoke again. They nodded to each other, and she stepped away. With one last look over his shoulder, he stepped into the hall and closed the door behind him.

"What did you tell him?"

"The access codes for all the systems and where to find the crates from the shed." She freed her hair from the tight braid. I watched as she tried to run her fingers through the messy curls until she opened her eyes and caught me. Turning abruptly, she moved toward the fireplace and stared at the framed pictures on the mantle.

I moved closer until the look in her eyes made it clear to stop. "So, is that your natural hair color?"

"Is that what you really want to talk about?"

My eyes rolled skyward, but I wasn't sure who frustrated me more in that moment. Her penchant for being direct sometimes rubbed me the wrong way, but she had a point. A mountain of issues lay between us, and it was time I grew a spine and addressed them. "Fair enough. There are half a million things I want to say and a million questions I want to ask, but the first thing I have to do is apologize. For everything."

"What do you have to be sorry for, John?" her voice was strained. "Killing a CIA officer to infiltrate my op and shooting the civilian I was sent to rescue? Helping your uncle with his sick little game? Pretending to give two shits about me and almost getting me killed?"

"Yes. I'm sorry for almost all of that and more."

"*Almost* all of it?"

"I never pretended how much I care for you."

"You expect me to believe that?"

"Not at all."

"Then why?" she clenched her hand into a fist, but it stayed on the mantle. "If you supposedly care so much about me, why did you do it?"

After the silence turned into awkward tension, her hands relaxed, and she soon fidgeted with her thumbnail. She clenched her jaw, but I caught the smallest flash of doubt and pain in her eyes. Of course, her first question was the hardest to answer, one I still struggled with.

She deserved the truth, no matter how complicated. Would she believe me? I sure as fuck wouldn't. After all she'd been through thanks to my family, she wouldn't believe me if I told her the sun rose in the east.

"Telling you it's complicated is the last thing you want to hear, but it's the truth. If you'll let me, I'll do the best I can to give you the explanation you deserve." At her nod, I continued. "The story about my gambling debt wasn't bullshit. When I left the CIA, I owed over two million. My uncle agreed to cover it in exchange for my services."

"And those services are, what, exactly? Spying?"

"I'm the family's hitman. He has his enforcers, but he basically uses them as his own personal security. This house belonged to my dad's family, so I stay here in the north away from all the Sardi bullshit. It allows me freedom, but not much. In between assignments, I got my teaching degree."

Her eyebrow quirked upward. "And here I thought that was also fake."

"Nope. I'm one hundred percent the Professor Hypocritical Shit-stain you called me. It pissed my uncle off until he realized he could use it to his advantage. Then he introduced me to the right people in the education field. I was the history teacher who taught a mob class that fascinated everyone. Nobody knew it was a front."

"Our intel said you found local contacts to boost the family's drug or gun trades. For a while, at least."

A chill shot up my spine at the memory. "A student overdosed at a party supplied with drugs from my uncle. Her name was Michelle Baylor, and she was only twenty years old. Died on the back porch of some shitty house in South Jersey and wasn't found until the next morning." I cleared my throat to free the gravel in my voice. "After that, I refused to do it anymore. He left me alone for a while until the day he invited himself into my home with his plan to drag you out into the open."

"Why would he want to do that? Until then, I hadn't gone any-where near your damn family."

"All he said was the time had come to get rid of the traitorous Donovan family once and for all. I tried to refuse, pointed out it was an old debt we hardly needed to trouble ourselves with. He threatened to kill my grandmother."

"Surely not."

"Yes. His own mother, the same woman who raised me after my parents died when I was nine. The same woman he almost beat to death a few years later. Please trust me when I say I had no desire to take part in his shit at all.

She cursed under her breath and focused her attention on the mantle. I moved closer and found her gaze on the framed picture of Lucas and me with a small elderly woman with her arms wrapped around our waists. Her mouth formed a wry smile before glancing over her shoulder and noticing me.

The urge to touch her was almost too much, so I shoved my hands into my pockets. "I had no intention of hurting you in Prague. I only shot at you so you'd take cover. And I shot at the guards so you could finish the job and get the hell out of there."

"You shot the professor in the arm! And strangled an officer in the alley."

"I grazed the professor, and it's not like I meant to. As for the shithead in the alley," I paused when her eyes narrowed. "If I hadn't killed him, they would've figured out you were the target and pulled you from duty."

Her eyes were ablaze when they widened. "What the fuck—"

"Prague was a shit show. Your guy got shot, and I had to deal with the consequences of not killing you when I got home. Well, Lucas had to deal with it." Her eyebrows pinched. "He's my cousin. Gio sent several of his guys here to keep him and my grandmother hostage while I was away. When I got back, he forced me to choose who would receive the beating for my failure. Lucas volunteered himself."

"Jesus," she whispered. "I'm sorry."

I shrugged and tried to calm my churning stomach. The story was headed into dangerous territory, and I had to tread lightly. As if she knew our next topic, she brushed past me and started pacing. When she shivered and wrapped her arms around her waist, I turned on the gas fireplace. She gazed at the flames briefly, and then looked up at me.

"Do we have to talk about Portland?" her voice was barely audible.

"Yes. There are things you need to know. The most important is that my position hadn't changed by the time our paths crossed at the party that night. I was never going to hurt you."

Her fingers flexed and she moved to the other side of the room, her posture rigid. "No, it was just a coincidence that we both came to Portland at the same time."

"And it's a damn good thing I did. I made it my mission to fuck up Gio's plans as much as I could. You were supposed to be kidnapped and taken to him the night you were attacked in my office. Given to his head enforcer to be tortured and eventually killed. When I got there, you were already unconscious, and Trevor was—" I broke off, not wanting to tell her how I'd found him fumbling with her clothes that night.

"Trevor was in on it?"

"They all were. Karl, Rachele, Trevor. They were all spies or mercs who owed favors to the family. Just like the FBI told you."

The hand over her heart moved upward and rested on her collarbone. "Nicole?"

"She's the only one who wasn't a spy."

Her gaze stayed glued to the floor, but she gave a small nod before pacing again. The sound of her booted footsteps was soft on the carpet, but the inner turmoil on her face spoke volumes. Testing my luck, I moved closer. Her back was to me when she froze.

"Liss?"

"After all the lies," she got out in a brittle voice. "How am I supposed to believe you now?"

The knot in my throat threatened to choke me. "I wish I could give you the magic answer to that. Because I want nothing more than for you to believe I care about you. That's why I spent the last two years chasing after you. I knew you'd go after him, and that it was a suicide mission."

"Hardly a suicide mission if the sick fuck is dead."

"Yes, but now there are bigger issues to worry about. Which we'll get to once we have everything between us resolved."

"As if that will ever happen, John." She moved to the windows and leaned against the wall. Her arms crossed in front of her chest and she stared at the setting sun outside. Her eyes met mine as she scanned my face. I forced the groan down my throat; the conversation was over if she caught a hint of my frustration. There was still one more major issue, the million-megaton elephant in the room, which needed to be addressed.

Steeling myself for the explosion, I kept my steps slow. She turned back to the window but tensed when she felt me near. I was well within her personal space, but she refused to turn around. Resisting the urge to touch her, I closed my eyes and said a silent prayer. Now or never.

"I know about the miscarriage."

I dodged her elbow when it flew back, but stumbled when she shoved me. Her eyes were wide and red. "You don't get to talk about that!"

"Given the circumstances, I'd say I have every right to talk about it."

Her laugh was hollow. "Well, at least your first question wasn't asking if the baby was yours."

"I know what we had. There wasn't anyone else."

"We had nothing. What *you* had were shitty condoms." At my glare, she shook her head. "I threw up the morning I left D.C.. Thought nothing of it until I got to Ireland and kept getting sick. Titus brought his doctor around, and that's when I found out."

Memories of her beating in Portland turned my stomach. Forcing the bile down, I opened my mouth with no clue what to say. "I...what—"

"It was a very emotional and confusing time. I hadn't made up my mind about keeping it. I was leaning toward it, but I was stupid and never got to make that choice."

"What happened?"

She blinked rapidly and wiped her eyes. "I got a lead on Gio, that little restaurant of his in Rome."

"The one that exploded?"

"Yep. Titus didn't want me to go, but I was too stubborn to listen. He'd been right; I felt horrible. I was climbing around a fire escape, trying to get a closer look when I got lightheaded and fell." Her bottom lip shook, and she covered her mouth. "It was a miracle the few guys patrolling didn't find me, but thankfully someone who didn't recognize me did. I woke up two days later in a hospital and I...wasn't pregnant anymore."

No longer able to stand the distance, I wrapped my arms around her and held her close. She threw her elbow backwards and cursed loudly until I caught her wrists and held them in front of us. My lips hovered near her neck, and the faintest hint of her scent was a temptation I didn't need in that moment. Finally able to focus, I held up her wrists in front of her face. She fell against me and froze.

"I have to know," I choked out, barely able to breathe. "How did you wind up in that hotel on New Year's Eve? What happened to your wrists?"

I released my grip. She placed a shaky hand on her collarbone, a show of anxiety. "I was a mess. I got out of the hospital just before Christmas. Titus sent one of his men to bring me home, but I refused to go and gave him the slip. No matter how many times he swore he wasn't mad at me, I just couldn't face him. I checked into the hotel, started drinking, and never stopped." She drew in a shuddering breath. "Found a lot of demons in those bottles, ones that told me over and over again how stupid I was for falling for you and how selfish I was. After a while, the razor in the bathroom started making sense."

The pain in her voice was like a punch to my already bruised gut. "I am so, so sorry," I whispered before pressing a soft kiss to the top of her head. "I didn't find out until a few months after you left Rome, and by then you were in the wind."

She was kind enough to not hit my injured side when she struggled out of my grip. I followed her but stopped when she moved toward the chair that held her gun. Relief flooded me when she backed away, only to feel helpless as her agitation grew. Gripping the back of her head with both hands, she paced in a circle and then closed her eyes. Without warning, a low wail erupted from her body and she crumpled to the floor.

I scooped her up and sat on the couch, placing her sideways in my lap. "I've got you," I whispered. "I should've had you from the very beginning."

She curled into herself and cried. I cradled her head in my hand and raised her face to mine. Her weary eyes hid none of the anguish, exhaustion and pain she'd endured since our last meeting. She jerked free and stood. I reached for her, but she slapped my hand away.

"You don't have me," she snarled, swiping at her face. "You sit there and talk about what we had like it was anything special. Our relationship was built on lies, no more and no less. You've got nothing, the same as me." Her face twisted, and she slapped a hand on her chest. "I thought I could navigate those lies, but I was stupid and selfish. Now I have nothing."

"Liss—"

"I killed our baby!" she screamed, and fresh tears fell from her eyes. "I should have stayed home, but I was so goddamned arrogant. That was my fault, and I'm sorry."

I took her hands in mine and held her in place when she tried to escape. "Please hear me. You have nothing to apologize for. *Nothing.* I was the one who left you in that shitty situation." My voice sounded as if I'd swallowed a ton of sand.

She collapsed against me. Her sobs grew louder. At the words whispered in her ear, she buried her face in my chest and wailed. Her anguish tore through me until I felt pressure behind my own eyes. Unsure what else to do, I enveloped her body with mine, praying the gesture absorbed even the tiniest part of her pain. Over her shoulder, the bedroom door opened a crack and Lucas peered inside. His eyes softened as her cries continued and with a small nod, he disappeared.

We stayed locked in our awkward, watery embrace. After a while, she quieted, and her body relaxed. I kept my arms around her, refusing to break contact until she forced me. Soon her arms tightened around my waist and the weight in my chest eased.

"What do we do now?" Her muffled voice was still shaky.

"I honestly don't know. But I'm sure we can figure it out after we get some sleep."

"You're right. I've kind of kept everyone up for over twenty-four hours. Can I crash in my old room?"

My arms tightened. She was fucking crazy if she thought I'd let her go so easily. "You could stay in here."

"Not sure that's such a good idea since I shot you less than four hours ago. I'm sure your cousin is probably lurking somewhere nearby so he can kill me. Either that or get one of your guys to do it for him."

"All the more reason for you to hide out in here. Besides, he's just as tired as the rest of us. His text messages are getting whiny at this point. Let's put him out of his misery or it's only going to get worse."

She pursed her lips. "All right. Tell Mr. Cranky he can go to bed."

Lucas's responding text was snarky and inappropriate, as expected. After telling him to go fuck himself, I tossed the phone on my night table. She stared out the window, watching as the wind whipped through the trees. The gray sky looked like rain was imminent. She wrapped her arms around herself as I closed the curtains.

She looked exhausted. "What are we going to do? Where do we go from here?"

"We're too tired to have answers at the moment. Let's get some rest and we'll go from there."

"I'll take the couch. I'm smaller." She spun around and gave a wide berth as she walked past.

"We can share the bed. I promise to behave. I just—," I paused. "It feels good to be close to you. To know that you're safe. I don't want that to end. Can we please just pretend everything is okay between us for a few hours?"

She hesitated before nodding. "Not gonna lie, I probably smell," she admitted with a laugh as she climbed into bed. "There weren't many opportunities to shower when I was hiding out. That's the price you pay for wanting to sleep with me."

"I can live with it if you can. It's not like I smell much better." I kicked off my boots and slid under the covers fully clothed next to her.

"John?" Her voice was muffled from under the blankets.

"Yeah?"

"I'm sorry I shot you."

I chuckled. "Don't worry about it. I would've shot me, too. Good night."

"Night."

To my surprise, she didn't protest when I wrapped my arm around her waist. Feeling bold, I buried my face in her hair. Her body relaxed against me not long after, and I bit back my laugh when the soft snores she swore didn't exist broke the silence. I moved my hand to her stomach, a sad ache settling into my heart.

"I failed you both and I'm sorry," I whispered and kissed the back of her head. "I promise I'll never put you in that position again."

Hearing no response, I closed my eyes and finally allowed myself to relax. I wasn't sure how she'd react the next day when she realized we'd only crossed the eye of the storm and an even bigger battle loomed ahead. That night, I decided to just enjoy the feeling of having the woman I love in my arms and allowed myself to feel complete.

Chapter Six

Into the Fire

Larissa

Except for a handful of eastern European countries, a bed was always several hundred times better than trying to sleep in a kitchen pantry (don't ask) or even a storage bunker. A soft mattress in a quiet room was nothing short of paradise. Thoughts tried to form in my head, but I resisted the need to think and nestled my body further under the blankets. A familiar scent teased my senses, but I refused to pay any attention to it. Not until I pressed my face against the pillow beside me and realized it wasn't made of cotton and had a light dusting of hair.

My eyes snapped open, but the room was too dark to see. On instinct, I pushed against the non-pillow until an arm tightened around me and caressed the skin between my shoulders. A familiar scent fully invaded my nostrils, causing my body to relax. Cursing myself, I gently patted the arm holding me in place.

"Good morning." His voice was low and gruff.

He released me and propped himself up on an elbow. A soft click sounded, and the lamp on his bedside table filled the room with a soft glow. For the first time since he'd burst back into my life, my eyes trailed the length of his body. His hair looked casually mussed, nothing like the rat's nest on top of my head. Feeling self-conscious,

I tried to push down my tangles but gave up after several seconds. My skin heated as I took in his broad shoulders and thicker arms. At the sight of his lazy smirk, I fidgeted with the dark blue duvet in my hand.

Ignoring his soft laugh, I narrowed my eyes. "Where did your shirt go?"

"Took it off. I forgot how warm your body is."

I snorted. "You could've just turned over." I tried to decipher the bird-like tattoo just above his heart. "When did you get that?"

"That is a story for another day. And I would have rolled over, but someone grabbed my arm every time I moved."

I groaned loudly. My traitorous body and I needed to have a talk. The conversation the night before lifted a tremendous weight and gave me the small bit of closure I needed. However, I didn't want him, or my overactive hormones, to think that meant anything remained between us.

"John."

"Shh." He placed a finger to my lips. "We're pretending every-thing is okay, remember? And if everything were okay, you'd wake up in my arms because I'd held you all night."

"All right, I'll play along. I wouldn't have a problem with that. It always felt good to sleep in your arms."

"I know."

I rolled my eyes. "Always so humble."

He chuckled and rested his hand on my hip. "I'd make pancakes for breakfast every morning. And on Sundays we'd spend the day snuggled on the couch watching football."

"I'd totally steal your hoodies," I giggled.

"And I'd enjoy taking them off you."

My face flushed and I dropped my gaze to my fidgeting hands. I watched the slow and steady rise of his chest, but refused to acknowledge him. My fingers twisted around the duvet again as I tried to figure out how to escape his scrutiny.

"Relax. This is all just hypothetical. I know everything isn't okay. It might never be okay ever again. But I can hope, right?"

Keeping my face blank took every ounce of strength. Hope was a dangerous emotion, one that led me down paths I had no business treading. It led to trust, a slippery slope that was even more dangerous. After surviving the dark times in Rome, the only thing I allowed myself to hope for was that my mind someday made sense.

His voice broke through my thoughts. "You okay?"

"I need a shower." And space to think clearly.

"Wait." I raised my face to his. "When you left my place that morning, I didn't know it was the last time I'd get to kiss you. Had I known, I would've demanded something more than that pathetic peck on the cheek as you raced out the door. May I please get one small kiss before we get out of this bed and stop pretending?"

I knew what he was up to, but my body didn't care. The warmth of his hands on my skin ended the battle between my heart and head before it began. I moved closer to give him a small, gentle kiss. Our lips came together, and memories of breathless moments flooded through me. My arms flew around his neck and a small moan escaped. He lowered me onto the bed, never breaking contact, and I ran my fingers over the stubble on his cheek. He nestled between my legs and the kiss deepened. My tongue teased his and my hands moved to his side. A second later, he released a loud hiss.

I broke away. "Shit, I'm sorry! Are you okay?"

"Yeah. It's just the bruise—"

"From yesterday." Tears filled my eyes. I covered my mouth and turned away.

"Liss."

Shaking my head, I nudged his shoulder. "I can't do this." My voice cracked. "Please let me up."

At once, he moved away and put his pillow between us, creating a buffer. "I'm sorry. Are you okay?"

"If anyone needs to apologize, it's me. I'm the one who let that go off the rails." I gestured to the large, dark purple bruise over his left rib. "And I should definitely apologize for that."

"You already did."

I stared at his injury, burning it into my mind as a reminder of the crater full of problems between us. The pewter carriage clock on his night table ticked softly, as if counting out the horrible things we'd both done and said to each other. After a dozen, I cursed myself. Kissing him was a trap, one I'd barely survived the first time.

He opened his mouth to speak, but my feet had already hit the plush carpet and were carrying me away. "Really need a shower."

"Liss?" The gentle timbre of his voice stopped me at the door. "Promise me you'll eat something. The doctor said you still need to build your strength back up, and I'm fairly sure you didn't eat worth a damn while you were outside."

I shrugged a shoulder and scurried to the next room without another word. Once the lock clicked, I leaned against the door and banged my head on the wood. Jesus fucking Christ, my hormones were out of control. My breaths steadied my racing heart but did nothing for my jangled nerves. It was only when I ran my hands through my hair that I refocused my energy. Yes, I was filthy and needed to bathe. Pronto.

My ensuite was nothing short of luxurious. Deep blue wall tiles surrounded the room and a large white bathtub sat to the right of the room under windows that overlooked the back of the property. To my left was a shower stall that easily fit four people. Locking the door, I found the pale green bathrobe still hanging on the back as if he knew

I'd return. The new toiletries stacked in a neat pile on the counter confirmed my suspicion.

The shower felt divine. Sleeping in the wilderness sucked, even when it was on a sprawling Italian estate. No matter how much training you'd had, nothing lessened the toll climbing trees and avoiding detection took on the body. I'd long since scrubbed and shampooed the muck away, but stayed under the spray to avoid facing what awaited me outside the room.

I was convinced John would kill me when he appeared in Doolin. His gentle words and touch were disarming until the asshole knocked me out. Laying siege to his house was an overreaction, one he could've easily killed me for. Hell, I would've shot me for half the shit I'd put them all through.

Groaning, I laid my head against the tile. Hating him after I'd found out he was Gio's nephew and a lying shitstain was easier than the current situation. He said he cared about me, and most of his actions led me to think maybe he did. I wanted to believe it, but I couldn't. For all I knew, it was just another ruse and a bullet to the head still awaited me.

That settled it. I'd get dressed, eat, and then get the hell out of there. I dressed warmly in dark blue jeans, a black long-sleeved shirt, and a gray and white infinity scarf. Returning to the bedroom, I took in the bright, warm colors for several minutes before moving to the windows. Pulling back the deep red velvet curtains, I opened the balcony door and stepped through. Ignoring the guards below, I gazed at the olive grove to the right. The trees were still bare thanks to the cold. In several weeks, however, their limbs would come alive and be filled with leaves.

If only I could stay.

Shivering, I headed back inside and headed to the closet for my knapsack. Not finding it, I cursed his name several times and grabbed a pair of boots. He and I were going to have words, but first I needed food.

To my relief, the kitchen was empty. After the comments I'd overheard while hiding, I concluded I was surrounded by pigs who spent way too much time obsessing over the size of my ass. John's men could finish their debate about it after I was long gone. I sank into a plush dining chair and enjoyed a full plate of food. After grabbing a few protein bars from the pantry, I headed down the hall. The door to the office was partially open, and I was just about to knock on the door when two raised voices gave me pause.

"I get it, okay? It was a huge risk bringing her here." John's voice was full of malice.

"Was it worth it? After your big talk yesterday, did you fall back into each other's arms?" Lucas sounded like a smug…

"You really are an asshole sometimes. Bringing her here wasn't about getting back together. It was about making sure nobody else found her first."

Lucas scoffed. "I may be an asshole, but you're a liar. You and I both know that's bullshit."

"I never said I didn't still want to be with her, but there are more important matters than our relationship status. Like keeping her off his radar."

Hearing enough, I rapped on the dark wood before entering. John leaned against the desk with his arms crossed while Lucas sat in the black leather chair in front of him. His eyes narrowed once they met mine until John cleared his throat. Right. The task at hand.

I stood in the doorway. "So, I just wanted to say thanks for the hospitality and for the field training exercise, but I really need to get going. If you'll just give me my knapsack and guns, I'll be on my way."

John stood. "You're not going anywhere."

"You say that like it was a request."

"And that's my cue," Lucas said.

I stalked into the room as Lucas rushed by, ignoring the warning under his breath. When the door closed, John's focus returned to me. "It's too dangerous to let you leave."

"Um, you aren't 'letting' me do jack shit. Who the fuck do you think you are?"

His body vibrated as he approached. "I'm the one who found you in your little hiding spot. It could've just as easily been one of the fucking goons hired to find you, but I've kept them off your trail."

"You had to beg my uncle for help, and that was after two years of searching. Don't act like you actually found me on your own."

"If I can find Titus, so can others."

"By the time you left the warehouse, he had already vanished. That man has spent his entire life off the grid."

The asshole blocked my path. "We could fight about this all day, but the fact remains you have no idea what you set in motion when you killed Gio. Your victory will be short-lived if you aren't careful."

"Look, you've been in my head long enough with this shit." At his pinched brows, I blew out a breath. "When my dad was shot, the cigarette in his mouth hit the ground next to his body. I took it and swore to myself I'd smoke it after I killed Gio. He's dead, but I can't bring myself to make good on that promise because all I hear is your voice telling me I don't know the entire story."

I cursed my loose lips at the revelation, but he stayed mute. Stepping backward, I felt his gaze follow my movement to the deep brown leather couch. My body relaxed when it sank into the cushions, and the exhaustion from the past two years tried to convince me to stay. I pushed those thoughts aside as he sat on the coffee table facing me, resting his arms on his thighs.

"No, you don't know the whole story. If it was as simple as your dad being a rat, Gio would've made a spectacle of killing him as a warning to others. Gio was just an underboss and wouldn't have the authority to call a hit squad to wipe out your entire family. It would've come directly from Massimo."

My stomach dropped to my knees. Massimo Sardi, Gio's twin brother, was the official boss of the family. The man was a recluse who never left his secret estate in coastal Bari. "No one has seen or heard from Massimo in years. Some people in intel doubt he even exists."

"I'm here to tell you he's very real. The *public* doesn't see him or hear much about him, but the family sure does. He's more unstable than Gio, and you just killed the only family member he gave a fuck about. He will stop at nothing until your head is brought to him on a gold platter."

That meant Portland wasn't one of Gio's crazy whims. It came from the top. Was the whole family involved? Did the brothers plan it all out while swilling bourbon and smoking cigars? Most importantly, why? What the hell created such a vendetta?

Closing my eyes, I leaned my head against the back of the couch. "Which is why I need to get the hell out of here and figure out a plan to take him down."

He steepled his fingers in front of his face and stared at me for a long moment. "It's not that simple. Now, I want you to fully listen to what I'm about to tell you before flying off the handle." At my slight nod, he exhaled slowly. "Right after I returned from Portland, he called and ordered me to kill you. Which I was *never* going to do. Every few months, when he felt I hadn't been searching hard enough, he'd hire a couple of mercenaries. You efficiently killed all of them, but it only made him dig in deeper. I've been doing everything in my power to either delay or send fake intel to his guys, anything to keep him off your trail. What worries me is that he's been quiet since Gio died. I would've expected him to triple his efforts and be on my ass to find you ASAP."

Every alarm bell ignited in my brain. I was either right where he wanted me, or he had something worse up his sleeve. Staying put wasn't an option. I stood and deflected John's hand when he reached for me. I paused before the antique map on the wall. He followed, but stopped when I glanced over my shoulder.

I gazed at the islands in the Indian Ocean. "I need to get out of here, John. You can tell him whatever the hell you want once I leave."

"I'm not taking that chance. If you go after him, you're as good as dead.."

"I don't care!"

"Well, I fucking do!" he roared back. "I just got you back and I'll be damned if I lose you again!"

"Do *not* romanticize this. You kidnapped me. I was doing fine until some asshole showed up and stuck a needle in my neck."

He closed the distance between us, looming over me. "Bullshit. You said yourself that you haven't felt any closure. Explain to me how you were doing fine."

"Last time I checked, I don't have to explain anything to you."

Brushing past, I crossed the room and stood in front of a bookshelf. My eyes focused on a worn chess piece, the queen, inside a broken decanter as I tried to calm my racing pulse. Damn my body and its reaction to him and his words. No, he didn't have me back. He never would, and both he and my heart needed to understand that and move on. *I* needed to move on.

His presence loomed behind me, and his warm hands touched my shoulders. "You were waiting for the family to come after you."

My fingers twitched and I walked to the center of the room. His refusal to let me leave, to give me the space to think, made my skin tingle. Unable to stand still, I paced the length of the rug in front of his desk, trying to oust his voice from inside my head. He demanded to talk about things I refused to acknowledge; subjects I didn't want to admit to myself or anyone else.

He moved closer and I held up my hands. "You need to back off and let me go. Just let me leave and I won't be your problem anymore."

"Not happening. End of story."

"Fine, have it your way. Are there any other buildings you'd like me to blow up when I escape? Again?"

"Oh, I'd love to see you try." He strolled to his desk and picked up the phone. The house intercom beeped. "Guys, this is John with an important safety alert. As everyone knows, we have a special guest on the premises. Effective immediately, Larissa Donovan is *not* to leave the grounds unless she's accompanied by Lucas or myself. If you find her trying to leave or escape, put her in a holding cell. I'll remind everyone to use caution as she's extremely dangerous. Thank you."

The system speakers clicked when he hung up. His eyes burned into mine as he walked around the desk and leaned against the front, crossing his arms. "Just so you know, Lucas called for reinforcements. They cleared the driveway and now they're patrolling the grounds. So, I'll say it again. I'd love to see you try."

"You asshole!"

"You can call me all the names you want. I'm the motherfucker trying to keep you alive. I suggest you make yourself at home. You're staying here until I figure out how to keep your head attached to your body."

I mentally ran through all the ways to kill the bastard. Shooting him was too quick and easy, unless I shot him in the gut. The down side was I'd have to listen to him bitch as he bled to death. Strangulation. He wasn't wearing a belt or a tie. Sliced femoral artery. Fuck, my scalpels were in my knapsack.

"Liss?"

Before he could react, I balled up my fist and punched him. His head jolted back as he grabbed the nearest chair to keep from falling on his ass. Ignoring the throb in my hand and enjoying the small groan as he regained his footing, I backed away toward the door.

"That's Miss Donovan to you." Turning, I left the room and slammed the door so hard the sound echoed down the hallway.

Chapter Seven

Gilded Cage

Larissa

"Good morning, Miss Donovan. Can I expect another day of silence from you?"

John sank onto the stone bench next to me. We sat in a small clearing surrounded by white and yellow flowers, which was the halfway point of my daily jog around the property. The air was still chilly, but no fog obstructed my view of the blossoming magnolia tree in the distance. A small puff of air out of my right eye told me he was still staring, willing me to acknowledge him.

The chime from the watch/fitness monitor/fucking tracking device the jackass made me wear broke the silence. Break time was over. He watched as I stretched and zipped up my pale blue workout jacket. After tying my shoes, I took off down the trail.

"Great talk, Liss!" he called after me. "Let's do it again tomorrow."

His appearance at the bench started the previous week. Every morning he appeared and tried to engage in conversation, and every morning I said nothing. The ten-minute argument over the watch three weeks earlier was one of our few conversations. Throwing up my hands, I agreed to wear the damn thing just so he'd leave me alone. I'd given him the cold shoulder for damn near a month, but I wasn't sure how much longer I'd last.

I made the most of my time in captivity. My workouts in Doolin were nothing more than jogs through the countryside and using castle ruins as an obstacle course. Despite the sour looks from most of the guys, I had free access to the gym. The first week kicked my ass, but it felt good. I could only visit the shooting range for an hour and only when John or Lucas escorted me. It was annoying as shit, but not surprising. Though every fiber of my being told me to do the opposite, I toed the line and behaved myself since my mother always said more flies were caught with honey. Or some damn thing.

When I wasn't training, I snuck by his office and tried to eavesdrop every chance I got. Unfortunately, the walls were sound-proofed and nobody spoke once the doors opened. I had no idea how he planned to keep me alive. He'd probably share the information with me if I asked, but my pride refused to waver. Did that make me irrational? Immature? Absolutely.

My one surrender in our battle of wills happened every morning when I woke up in his arms. The anger and confusion I felt the first time caused me to push his arm away and run to the bathroom. We never spoke of it, and while the look in his eyes suggested his want for more, he remained respectful and never even tried to kiss me. After a while, I couldn't ignore or deny how peaceful and safe he made me feel.

I finished my run and followed the pebbled trail back to the house, slowing when I rounded the corner and found him standing by the pool. He looked delicious in his black suit, but it was the black and burgundy paisley tie that almost made me blush. Back in Portland, a favorite ritual when I got to his apartment every night was to remove his tie, undo the top two buttons of his shirt, and kiss his neck. The last time I saw that garment was when it was tied around my wrists as he fucked me silly on his couch, a night I still dreamed about.

As if sensing me, he turned, and we stared at each other long enough for me to hate the fact I was a red faced, sweaty mess. Smiling, he held up one of my sports drinks. "Thought you might like this."

"Thank you," I mumbled after a pause, long enough to ensure the seal was still intact.

He narrowed his eyes but said nothing. Shaking my head, I bit back the urge to pick a fight and stared back at the trees. I guzzled the drink in record time before sitting on the ground. After another moment of scrutiny, I turned my back to him and stretched my legs.

His expensive oxfords came into view. "Can I tell you a secret?" I shrugged and he crouched down. "I've always known you to be a restless sleeper, but it seems like it's gotten worse. Kicking the covers, arms flailing. That's all normal. But now you yell out or cry."

My cheeks flushed. "Oh." I kept my gaze on the ground and hoped he didn't notice my shaky hands. "Sorry. I can move to another room if I keep waking you up."

"It's nothing to apologize for. Luckily, I have experience with that sort of issue, and I've found the same solution still works." My eyes met his and he gave me a warm smile. "You've slept peacefully every night since I started going into your room and holding you."

I froze, almost unable to breathe thanks to the lump in my throat. "John."

"I'm not the enemy here, Miss Donovan. I know it was a shock to find me there that first morning, and I appreciate you not breaking my neck for it. But know this, I'm not going to sit around and do nothing when you're in distress." His eyes bored into mine. "So, you can expect that I'm going to be there when you wake up for as long as it's needed."

"Okay." My voice was barely a whisper.

He stood and helped me to my feet. "I have a meeting to get to, so I'll leave you to your shower. This meeting isn't about anything related to you or Massimo, so there's no need to linger in the halls or harass Max. Talk more later?"

I glared at his retreating back. "Jackass."

My head dropped into my hands the moment I closed the door to my ensuite. He'd been around me at my weakest for almost a month and I'd come to no harm. I wanted to trust him, but memories of being chained and hanging from a pipe chilled my skin. In the early days of my recovery, I'd lost count of the number of times I thought it would've been easier if he'd killed me that day. Trusting him again was a level of vulnerability that terrified me, one I'd never take lightly again.

I showered and changed into a pair of black jeans and a gray thermal shirt before heading downstairs. It was pure coincidence that my path to the kitchen took me past his office, something that didn't stop Max's nasty glare when I rounded the corner into the hallway. He clenched his jaw as I approached.

"Honestly, I don't get why you're still so pissy," I said. "Personally, I'd take it as a compliment that you had the better weed. Was it because of the black sheets?" In response to his scowl, I made a dismissive gesture. "Looks like someone could use another smoke break."

Breakfast at the estate was served buffet style so everyone could come and go as they wished. With John and his crew locked away down the hall, the room was blissfully quiet. At least it was until Lucas sauntered in just after I sat down. He strode to the coffee station and busied himself with preparing a cup that looked like it had way too much creamer. Biting back a catty comment, I focused on my plate and hoped for his quick exit.

He sat in a chair and pointed at the pastry I held. "Do you have enough jam on that?"

"I'm sure I could probably scoop some more on there. Can you please pass me the pot?"

"Knock yourself out." His voice was curt as he slid the glass bowl across the table.

"You sound just as uptight as Max."

"And you just love to stir things up."

Lucas and I still lived to annoy each other, but with a lot less hostility. About a week after the "incident" on the grounds, he approached me one night as I lounged by the pool. He looked uncomfortable and out of place when he slumped in the chaise next to mine. Unsure of his intent, I remained alert.

After several awkward minutes of staring at me and the sky, he took a deep breath. "Would you have shot him if we'd pushed you too far?"

I stared at him for a moment. "If I'd wanted to kill him, I wouldn't have shot him with a bean bag round."

He nodded and left without another word. His demeanor softened after that night. We'd probably never be the best of friends, but at least he stopped calling me a crazy bitch and I stopped trying to kill him and make it look like an accident.

"I'm sure you have better things to do than criticize my food choices," I said as I rinsed my dishes. "Why are you here?"

"He's in a mood, so you're my problem today. If you want, we can go to the range."

It was no surprise that John didn't allow me to wander the house unsupervised for extended periods of time. Since Lucas and I reached our détente, he was lax about my restrictions. He was also the least annoying of my babysitters. Target practice took as long as I wanted, he didn't follow me as closely as the rest, nor did he ignore or treat me like a leper. We spent most afternoons in the library playing chess, which was often competitive since we both hated to lose.

The day progressed like any other. I spent several hours at the range while Lucas's thumbs were constantly typing out messages on his phone. Afterward, we got into a cutthroat game of chess until John yanked the library door open and grumbled that dinner was ready. Lucas's bravado vanished at the look on his cousin's face, and he shot out of his chair as if the room were on fire. Now alone, John held out his arm for me to follow.

"You look nice," he murmured as we headed downstairs.

"Thanks. So do you." The sleeves of his burgundy dress shirt were rolled to his elbows and the top two buttons were undone.

Shaking off my impure thoughts, I said nothing else as we continued down the hall. We reached the dining room, and I felt his hand on my lower back as we entered. His touch was gone just as quickly, and I tried to hide my disappointment. My seating options were limited since most of John's men refused to sit next to me. That night I wound up between Lucas and Paolo, who'd become fractionally less hostile. The sneers and glares between John and Lucas made the atmosphere around the table quiet and tense. Desperately uncomfortable, I looked at Paolo, who shrugged and turned back to his plate.

Evenings at the estate were casual. The men's sleeping quarters were in the north and south wings of the estate, connected to the main house via breezeways. Aside from whomever was my assigned escort, they were free to unwind for the rest of the night. A couple of guys who had wives or girlfriends went to their permanent homes. John spent most of his nights locked away in his office while Lucas sought his nightly companions down the hill in the city. I kept to myself in the library thanks to its decent collection of books.

That night I felt restless and wanted to be alone, so I stretched out on a chaise lounge by the pool and watched the sky. Jay was engrossed in a game on his phone and agreed to watch me from inside the house. The slight chill in the air was a welcome change from the stuffiness inside. I reclined and observed the sky, completely carefree. My eyes felt heavy after a while, and it was only when Lucas's loud voice announcing my location that I hopped up and came inside. John's watched me as I passed, but I kept my gaze straight ahead.

I closed the bedroom door and my hand hovered over the lock, hesitating now that I knew the reason for his visits. Maybe it was the right moment to take that first step. I withdrew my hand, deciding to leave it unlocked before changing into my pajamas. After pulling the dark red comforter over me, it didn't take long to fall asleep.

My face was pressed against his chest the next morning, his body enveloping me like a favorite warm blanket. His hands caressed my back as he pressed a kiss to the top of my head. My eyes met his and widened at the small scratch on his cheek.

"Don't," he ordered in a soft voice. "Whatever you fought in your sleep didn't win. That's all that matters."

"Yes, but you don't deserve to be on the receiving end of it."

"I'll let you in on a little secret," he whispered. "Your ability to beat me up is part of your charm."

"Oh, really?"

"Absolutely."

Neither of us moved. His deep brown eyes stared at me with an intensity I hadn't seen in a long time. Closing my eyes, I released a slow breath but remained pressed against his body. Every morning brought the temptation to let him back in, something I couldn't allow.

"I'll let you get up so you can go for your run."

Regret was heavy in his voice, but he released me and got up. I emerged from the bathroom a few minutes later and stopped short when I found Lucas. He stood a few inches shorter than John, with paler skin, black hair and light blue eyes. The black sweatpants and light green hoodie he wore looked strange for someone who was usually so polished in his appearance.

"Mind if I join you?"

I wasn't quick enough to hide my shock and confusion. In the month I'd been there, the most physical activity I'd seen from him was when he ran his mouth. Now he wanted to come with me. Jogging. For at least two miles around the estate. Not suspicious at all. Smirking, I crossed my arms in front of me. "Think you can keep up?"

"Is that a challenge?"

I proceeded through my normal route at top speed to move the charade along. He tried to keep up for maybe ten minutes. When he arrived at the garden bench, he held his side and begged for mercy. He exhaled dramatically as he sat down.

"Jesus Christ, you two are insane with this exercise shit." His accent was light, making me wonder if he'd spent any time outside Italy. Lucas was a mystery. His loyalty to John and the other guys was undeniable, but that didn't assure my safety.

"Out of shape spies quickly become dead spies."

He carried on for a little longer, telling me to go on without him and he'd catch up. No longer able to keep quiet, my laughter broke free and I sat next to him.

"Wanna tell me the real reason you're out here? We both know this isn't your thing."

With a rueful nod, his face turned serious. "What's up with you and John?"

"Who's asking?"

"The guy who saw him nearly lose his shit when Massimo threatened to send his enforcer, easily the sickest son of a bitch this side of hell, after you. I've watched him spend the last two years tearing this fucking planet apart looking for you. I helped him follow every lead and then weathered his emotions every time he came back empty-handed." He paused and his voice softened. "And I'm the guy who had to destroy his world and tell him what happened in Rome."

"Lucas, I—"

"He moved into that room and barely slept for three days when he brought you here. Wouldn't let anyone shoot you when you had that little tantrum on the grounds. Did you know he makes it a goal to run into you at least twice a day in the hopes you'll talk to him? So, I'll ask you again. What's up with you and John?"

"I wish I had the answer to that. I really do. All I can tell you is that while we weren't together for very long, our relationship left an impact. And a lot of scars."

Nodding, he looked at his feet. "I won't get into too many details because it's not my story to tell, but he wasn't okay for a while after he found out what happened. To make matters worse, we didn't find out until three months after you were discharged." His lips turned upward with a small smile as he bumped his shoulder against mine. "You're quite good at covering your tracks."

"Thanks, I guess. It's a blessing and a curse. I can stay off the radar, but it's damn near impossible to trust people. That's what makes everything so damn complicated with him."

"You still don't trust him." Not a question, I'd noticed. He was a perceptive one.

"I want to, but it's hard when you're trained to suspect everyone you meet. It also doesn't help that trusting him nearly got me killed. Add up all the shit between us…him kidnapping me and now forcing me to stay here. It's hard to get past all of it."

He shook his head. "Miss Donovan—"

"Lissa, please. Though apparently Liss is a new nickname, too."

"Yeah, I'm not making that mistake again. That's his name for you, and he's made it clear to everyone that only he gets to call you that."

I shrugged. "Whatever works I guess. But I digress. You were saying?"

"Go easy on him. He wouldn't be forcing you to stay without a damn good reason. Based on what I know, you're in a fuckton of trouble."

"Which everyone knows but me," I bit out.

"If you'd just talk to me, I'd tell you everything," a deep and familiar voice interrupted.

Leaning against a tree in jeans and an old blue hoodie, John looked casual at first. His crossed arms and the edge to his voice were anything but. He shot a glare at Lucas, and I didn't envy the argument they'd have later. When he moved toward the bench, Lucas jumped to his feet.

"I just remembered I need to...get the hell out of here." Within seconds, Lucas retreated out of sight.

John sat next to me, but I moved to put some distance between us. "So, was that interrogation for your benefit or his?"

"That was all him. The fucker duped me into a phony phone call before I realized what he was up to. I'm sorry if he was out of line.

"He's not so bad. Glad I didn't shoot him."

"Liss, we both know you were never going to shoot him."

"Yeah, but he doesn't know that. And what's up with this nick-name of mine?"

He shrugged. "Everyone else calls you 'Lissa.' I'm not everyone else. And when you hear that name, you know I'm the one saying it."

"Always so humble. So, what news do you have?"

"Massimo has been in seclusion since Gio's funeral, but things are too quiet. He's up to something."

"Any ideas?"

"None yet, but that's why Lucas called for so many reinforcements after your escape. If he knew you were here, he'd waste no time storming this place and killing us all."

"You're his nephew. Aren't you supposed to take over for him?"

"Family means nothing to those two," he replied. "Only Massimo and Gio trusted each other, while the rest of us were mere pawns. He gives me a lot of latitude because I'm next in line, but I know the minute he has proof that I'm not loyal, he'll make me watch as he kills everyone I care about before he finishes me off."

"That's fucked up."

He shrugged. "That's the Sardi way. Those two are the definition of ruthless. Gio threatened his own mother countless times over the years. Massimo killed their father to take over the family, and I know he had something to do with the car accident that killed my parents. He'd been arguing with my mom about my role in the family and the next thing you know, they're both dead. I'm not a genius like you or Lucas, but even I know that's no coincidence."

"Jesus."

"It doesn't matter where you go or how long you hide, he'll find you. And then he'll make sure you die the slowest, most painful death possible. That. Will not. Happen. Not if I have anything to say about it."

The steel in his voice caused a shiver low in my spine. His hand edged closer to mine on the bench until I traced the faint scars on his knuckles with my fingers. He blew out a long breath and moved closer. "Yes, I have other reasons for wanting to keep you here. I'll never deny that. But even if we're never together again, I can't just let you go until I know you'll be safe."

Damn his ability to always say the right thing. And damn my heart and brain for wanting to believe him. The warmth in his eyes, always there when I needed it from him the most, made my heart stutter. The sound of a car horn in the house's direction mercifully broke the spell.

He stood and held out his hand. "How about some breakfast? Lucas mentioned how much you love our assortment of jams."

"Your cousin needs to get a life," I huffed, walking past.

"Lucas has a life. It just usually means choosing between a blond, brunette or a redhead."

My faster pace was no match for his long strides, and he caught up in no time. His hand closed around mine as he led us through the woods. He told me about each of his men during our journey. Several of the guys he'd known from childhood as their fathers worked at his dad's law firm. He saved the best stories for last, telling me about Lucas as an awkward teenager and some of his dumber exploits through the years.

I was still laughing when we walked into the kitchen and nearly ran into him when he stopped at the doorway. Lucas sat at the nook shoveling food into his mouth, which was no surprise. My guess was John wasn't expecting to see the small elderly woman stirring a large pot on the stove. Her curly hair was tied into a small ponytail at the nape of her neck and was the color of fresh snow, except for a small circle that was a mixture of black and dark grey on the crown of her head. She muttered something and then tossed a sprig of thyme inside before moving clockwise to check the three other pans. John gently pulled me closer and led us down the small steps.

"Nonna! I didn't know you were coming today," he greeted in Italian

She glanced over her shoulder and smiled, her brown eyes sparkling from behind a pair of eyeglasses. "I had to come and make sure my grandsons were eating properly."

He laughed and bowed his head. She scooped another dollop of food onto Lucas's plate and removed her apron. My posture straightened as soon as she walked around the island toward us. John opened his mouth to speak, but froze when the smile on her face widened.

"My goodness, child, you look just like Serafina," she murmured. "It is so nice to finally meet you, Larissa."

Chapter Eight

The Chronicles of Nonna

Larissa

John's arm closed around my shoulder as I tried to control my breathing. "Nonna, how do you know Larissa?"

"Gianni," she barked. "Where are your manners? Introduce me to this lovely young lady!"

"So sorry. And here I didn't think she needed any introduction since you already know her name. Liss, this is my nonna, Luciana Sardi."

"Use that tone again, young man, and I'll grab my spoon."

"Someone's in trouble," Lucas taunted from his seat, earning a glare from John.

"And you'll see the end of my spoon, too, Lucas."

"It's very nice to meet you, Senora Sardi," I greeted, extending my hand.

"At least the girl has manners," she said. "But stop with this *senora'* business. You call me Nonna. And I don't shake hands."

Her body muffled my apology as she pulled me into a bone-crushing hug. She had amazing strength for such a small woman, but that was nothing compared to the warmth I felt in our embrace. Her small hands rubbed my back, and even though she was at least six inches shorter, I felt cocooned. I closed my eyes to keep the tears at bay and never wanting the feeling of someone treating me like family to end.

Over her shoulder, I watched Lucas's eyes widen before John placed his hand on her shoulder. She released me and then wrapped her arms around his waist. He laughed at the words she whispered in his ear in rapid Italian. Lucas studied me as I held the counter for support, looking away when I wiped the moisture from my eyes.

"So, Nonna. How do you know Larissa?" John repeated, following her to the stove after a long moment.

"As I said, she looks just like Serafina," she answered, grabbing her wooden spoon and checking each pot. "Except her eyes. She definitely has Soren's eyes."

I froze, while Lucas looked like he was going to be sick. My stomach churned, and I took a cleansing breath to keep from doing the same. John's hand enclosed mine. My eyes met his and he shook his head; he was just as clueless as me.

"Seamus Donovan is my father," I said in a shaky voice. "I don't know anyone named Soren."

She whispered something I couldn't hear as she signed the cross over her chest. "No, my dear. Your father is Soren Luccetti."

I flinched at the sound of a loud clang to my right. Lucas dropped his fork and wiped his mouth. His jaw clenched and the look he gave John was raw, pained. An unspoken conversation passed between the pair, one that left me with more questions than answers. What the hell was going on?

"How do she and Lucas have the same father?"

"Because my father is a fucking manwhore." Lucas struggled to keep his voice even as he clenched and unclenched his hands.

"Lucas Emilio, you watch your mouth!" Nonna yelled before turning toward John and me. "You two come and sit down. I'll explain."

John rubbed my back as he led me toward the vacant chairs next to Lucas. I braced myself for a story I knew wouldn't end well. Lucas picked up his fork and resumed eating, but his body was stiff. The sound of a plate being set on the counter brought my attention back to Nonna.

"As you know, most marriages in this life are arranged and have nothing to do with love. My daughter Elena's marriage to Soren was no different. What I don't understand is why his father made the match, since everyone knew Soren's heart belonged to 'Sera' as most people called your mother. But he was insistent that his son marry into the family, and Massimo agreed."

Lucas pursed his lips but said nothing. As she tended to the stove, I caught the glances in his and John's eyes. An almost unbearable tension radiated from them, and the subtle shake of John's head added another layer of mystery. What the hell?

"Lucas was about a year old when Soren left for the States," she continued after finishing her circuit of the stove. When he placed his fork down and tossed his napkin onto the plate, she frowned. "Lucas?"

"Nonna, I'm sorry. I know you don't like to talk about it. I sure as hell don't enjoy hearing about it either, but Lissa deserves to hear some details you left out. Please."

Her eyes dropped to the counter as she signed the cross again and said a blessing. She stared at both her grandsons for a moment before nodding. "I'm sorry, *tesoro*, you are right. My daughter did not give birth to her son. Soren did not love my daughter and had many affairs. Lucas was the product of one of them."

"Good thing he has a thing for dark haired girls," Lucas mumbled.

Nonna narrowed her eyes and hissed several swear words at him. "The truth is known by only a few outside the family. Massimo told everyone Elena went to a medical center for care because of pregnancy complications. She came home with a baby several months later."

"What happened to Lucas's real mother?" I had an idea, but needed confirmation.

"Dead," Lucas answered. "Leaving my mom with a baby to raise and my dad free to go back to fucking anything with tits and a heartbeat."

"Lucas!" she exploded before reaching across the counter and slapping the back of his hand with her wooden spoon. He lowered his head as she alternated between swinging the spoon and cursing.

"Nonna," John interjected after she swatted him several more times. "The story. Please?"

She nodded and folded her hands in front of her. "The Genovese asked Massimo to send a couple of family members to New York. It wasn't until later that we realized Soren had left with Sera. Once they were there, they had nothing to keep them apart. That is, until she caught him cheating. The problem was she'd been working at one of the Irish bars to gather info on one of the gangs that had been giving the Genovese trouble. I'm not sure exactly how it happened, but shortly after she and Soren broke up, the Irish caught her spying. She should have been killed, but Seamus wouldn't allow it. My guess is he knew she was pregnant. They got married and he passed the baby, you, off as his."

John rubbed my back as I drank several gulps of water. It was a story, a fairy tale. Pure fiction. None of it was true. It couldn't be. Seamus, my real father, loved my mother with every breath he took. He never would've forced her into marriage.

"My parents loved each other very much," I argued. "It didn't seem like she was there against her will."

She smiled. "I think the reason he wouldn't allow her to be killed was because he had already fallen for her. And I do know that in one of the last letters she sent to her grandparents before she died, Sera talked about how much she loved him and how happy she was. It may not have started off as the most romantic story, but their love for each other grew immensely."

John leaned forward. "How do you know all this?"

"Elena. Serafina called her when she caught Soren cheating and told her everything. Elena forgave her and agreed to keep her secret."

"What secret?" My voice was barely a whisper.

"You, my dear. Your mother was adamant that Soren could never know about you. Her parents didn't even know the truth, not that they would've believed her. They were less than thrilled when they found out she had taken up with some Irishman and had his baby. She never set them straight because she was afraid it would alert Soren to your existence."

John grabbed a seltzer bottle from the fridge and rejoined us. "Why would she want to keep her hidden?"

She shook her head. "Nobody knows. All she told Elena was that he was a heartless bastard and could never know she'd had his child. As I understand it, my daughter is one of the few people who knows the truth."

I stared at the plate before me. Food, no matter how delicious it looked, was the furthest thing from my mind. John rubbed my shoulder, his eyes asking if I was okay. Looking down, I shook my head.

"Whatever happened to Soren?" I choked out.

"No idea," Lucas replied. "Mom never heard from him again. And good fucking riddance, I say."

"Lucas!"

"Nonna, you really can't blame him for that one."

I tuned out their bickering and picked at the plate, willing myself to force a mouthful of food down. John whispered in my ear that he had to talk to his grandmother for a few minutes and would be back soon. Dazed, I nodded and then more emphatically when he asked again if I was okay. He looked over his shoulder twice before disappearing from sight.

I stared at a grain of salt on the counter as my mind reeled. In under an hour, I'd gained a brother and lost a father. In his place was a sick, cold-hearted bastard as described by my mother. No, just...no, I told myself. I was the child of Seamus and Serafina Donovan. He loved me too much for me not to be his daughter. Fuck Soren Luccetti. I gripped the island and took a deep breath, willing myself to focus.

"Lissa?" The voice was soft, cautious.

I bobbed my head, which did nothing to keep my tears at bay. The air was too thick to breathe, causing me to gasp. Two hands gently turned my chair.

"Lissa, look at me," Lucas's voice sounded like he was in a tube. "I think you're having a panic attack. Can I help you?"

My heart collided with my ribcage and I fought the urge to claw at my throat. The kitchen blurred in and out. I felt myself falling until something seized me around the middle. My fingers barely brushed the floor before my body was upright once again. A hand gripped my shoulder as I fought to catch my breath.

Lucas appeared in front of me. "Deep breath," he ordered. "Inhale. Exhale. I want you to name three objects you can see."

"Lemons, um...a plate. And pots."

His voice stayed even. "Very good. Can you name three sounds?"

"Birds...something boiling, and someone's annoying voice."

He smiled. "Okay, that's two for two. Now I want you to move three body parts."

My body relaxed slightly, but my legs still felt unsteady. Leaning against the counter, I raised my left foot, followed by my right. At his expression, I smiled and raised my middle finger.

"Smartass," he said, smiling. "But seriously. Are you okay?"

"He's not my dad," I blurted and immediately regretted.

"Okay."

"I'm sorry. That slipped out and probably sounded really shitty." I looked around the kitchen and noticed John and his grandmother had left. "I hope my being here didn't make things awkward for your nonna? With all the cooking she was doing, I thought that meant she was staying a while."

"She was visiting a friend of hers not far from here and decided to stop by on her way home. She lives outside of Venice with my mom. And she always takes over the kitchen and cooks a ton of food, even if she's only here for a few hours."

"She seems nice. I wouldn't want to piss her off, though."

He held up his hand, exposing the red welt on the back. "That wouldn't be wise."

We shared a smile before falling into an awkward silence. I felt his eyes on me several times, but my gaze stayed fixed on the coffeemaker. After several minutes of staring at the countertop, he gave my shoulder a gentle nudge.

"Do you want to talk about it?"

I shrugged. "I'm still trying to wrap my head around all this. When I woke up this morning, I knew who my father was, and you were just my ex's annoying cousin. Now that's all sideways."

"Tell me about it. I started the day as an only child and now apparently you're my sister."

His words weren't meant to hurt, but they cut through the last defenses holding me together. The shock of Nonna's story, my conflicted feelings about John, and even my fear of Massimo that had been safely locked away all broke free. Lucas swore under his breath when I crumpled into myself against the counter and let out a loud sob. He murmured something and placed a hand on my shoulder, but I shrugged away and retreated upstairs.

I ran to my closet and grabbed my knapsack, tossing items on the floor until I produced the metal case from the bottom. The small door let out a creak as I opened it, petrified the cigarette was gone since Seamus might not be my father. Part of me felt foolish at my relief that it was still there. My mind still numb, I closed the door and clenched the case in my hand before collapsing onto the bed. Placing it on the pillow, I stared at it, convinced it would disappear if I didn't keep it in sight. My eyes grew heavy after several blinks and just before I fell asleep, I grabbed it and held it to my chest.

I didn't care what anyone said. Seamus Donovan was my father.

• • • ● • ● • • •

John

The front door swung shut as I raced to the kitchen. "Fuck, fuck, fuck."

She'd tried to keep her mask in place, but the blank look in her eyes told the real story. Liss was strong, but she'd just absorbed one hell of an emotional blow. The sparkle in her eyes during our conversation on the trail showed a glimpse of the feisty hellcat I loved. Her fire smoldered but still burned, and I'd be damned if anything extinguished it.

I almost tripped down the steps when I saw Lucas alone in the kitchen. The cup of coffee in his hand was full, but untouched, as he stared out the window above the sink. He turned as I approached, but my pace slowed when the tension on his face had me on high alert.

"She had a panic attack," he began and looked down at his mug. "I got her calmed down, and she was okay. Until I opened my mouth and fucked it all up."

"What happened?"

"I made a joke. A bad one. She started crying and took off. I went to check on her. She's in her room. She's not okay, man."

I clapped him on the shoulder. "You don't look so okay yourself, either."

"Go. She needs you more right now. Tell her I'm sorry."

I found her curled up in bed, still in her workout clothes. Her body molded to mine the second my arm wrapped around her, and the knot in my stomach eased. I couldn't help the small smile when she pulled my hand closer and held it between both of hers. Taking offered comfort wasn't the same as trusting me, but it was a start. Baby steps.

It was a few nights after she'd punched me in my office that I heard her cries. Sobs followed, and when she wailed she was sorry, I couldn't take it anymore. I felt bad for using the master key and invading her space, but she'd been through enough, and I was willing to do anything to ease her pain.

Her thrashing and wailing stopped as soon as she felt my touch, and it didn't take long for her to be completely still and silent. I watched her sleep for a while, promising I'd stay only long enough to ensure she didn't wake up. Her deep breaths caused my body to relax and the next thing I knew, it was morning and I was face to face with my enraged blue-eyed hellion. I breathed a sigh of relief when she simply went into the bathroom without a word.

After a week, I didn't know who benefited more from our sleeping arrangement. Her presence calmed me, even if her hostility and silence were like a knife to the heart. She never demanded that I stop or even leave. It wasn't the approval I wanted, but it was enough.

My fingers skimmed over a metal object and I held up the small case against her chest. Inside had to be Seamus's last cigarette. If Nonna was right, the unconditional love this man had for her was admirable. Our world put way too much emphasis on blood. Lucas was treated like shit thanks to the literal sins of his father. That same father who she possibly shared the same blood with and was connected to the family she hated. God, what a fucking mess.

I tucked a lock of hair behind her ear and left a gentle kiss on her tear-stained cheek. "I'm sorry, baby. I promise we'll get this figured out."

Leaving her was the last thing I wanted to do, but Lucas was on equally shaky ground. I covered her shoulders with my hoodie, feeling a small amount of joy when she buried her face in the fabric before standing up. After one last glance over my shoulder, I headed downstairs. I found Lucas sitting on the couch in my office, holding a glass of scotch to his lips.

"She okay?"

"Asleep. I'll check on her soon. How are you?"

"Well, that was one hell of a mind fuck." He downed the drink and grimaced. "I'm fantastic. Nothing like finding out you have a sister completely out of the blue."

"Sorry. Stupid question."

"I know nothing should surprise me when it comes to my dad. He's a piece of shit. I feel bad for her, though. She's really shaken up."

I poured myself a drink and sat down next to him. "We'll see how bad when she wakes up. I won't even try to pretend I'm not worried."

"Do you think it's true? Nonna could be wrong."

"Is she ever wrong?"

"Fuck," he drawled. "What the hell does this even mean for her?"

"It won't mean shit to Massimo. She's still marked for death. What worries me is that her mom didn't want Soren to know she'd had his baby. Why?"

"No idea. Mom hasn't mentioned that shithead's name in fifteen years. I don't even know if he's still alive."

"Fuck, this is a nightmare."

He handed me a drink after refilling his own. His tense jaw told me the situation bothered him more than he let on. I knew a phone call to his mom and a bottle of vodka was in his future. Elena had long since made peace with Soren's absence. Lucas struggled with his parentage and the way the family treated him.

The quiet was broken when he let out a low chuckle. It grew louder and soon he nearly doubled over. Well, laughing was a welcome change to his other coping mechanisms. He shook his head. "I keep thinking of all the times you acted all jealous and shit whenever I was around her. I kept telling you I'd never see her as anything more than a sister. Bit ironic, really."

Fuck, I knew I would hear about this for a while. I'd acted like an asshole and deserved every bit of his shit, but he didn't need to know that. Flipping him off, I smiled. "Get out of here before I talk your sister into kicking your ass."

"Fine. I'll leave you to your brooding."

The hallway filled with his goofy laugh as he walked away. It seriously sounded like a drunken hyena. Rolling my eyes, I strolled to the window behind my desk and stared at the magnolia tree. This new chapter in the mystery of her life worried me. What I knew of her family was limited to my uncles' version of the story, the version that cast her father as a traitor and her mother a whore. What they never explained, however, was the reason that justified their grisly murders. Add to that the knowledge she had four birth certificates and a mother who was adamant that her biological father didn't know she existed and the mystery deepened.

Who the hell was Larissa Donovan?

Chapter Nine

The Call

John

An unease settled over the house in the days that followed my grandmother's revelation. Liss grew quiet and withdrawn. She spent a lot of time in the woods, perched on the bench in the clearing, usually staring straight ahead with her knees pressed to her chest. Lucas and I stayed watchful, holding her close when she cried and making her come inside to either warm up or eat.

She still allowed me to come into her room, and for that I was thankful because her night terrors got worse. My heart bled every time she cried out Seamus's name and begged him not to leave. Waking up every morning to her swollen and bloodshot eyes, I wanted to hold her close and shield her from the fucking pain slowly ripping her apart. The brave smile on her face never wavered as she kissed me on the cheek and headed downstairs to start the day.

Lucas met her in the kitchen every morning for breakfast. The first couple of days were quiet and strained, but he persisted. Their conversations improved and not long after they brunched by the pool, eating food and toasting mimosas. Her smile was bright, but her laughter guarded. The only forbidden topic was their possible shared genetics, he told me. Since he'd never wanted to talk about the man he referred to as his sperm donor, it was easy for him.

A week after the bombshell I found her seated in a lounge chair by the pool, where she went after dinner most nights. I strolled out, carrying two cups of coffee, and found her wearing the hoodie I tossed over her on the bed that fateful day. "Coffee?"

The lights from the pool cast a soft blue glow on her face. "Thanks."

I motioned to the chairs, and she nodded before turning her gaze skyward. Her head spun around when I pushed the chair closer to hers. We sat and watched the stars wink and twinkle for what felt like hours, neither of us making a sound.

"How are you doing?" I hated breaking the silence, but I had to know.

"I'm okay. Still figuring things out."

"Did you and the stars come up with anything?"

"Sadly, no. You'd think with all the time I've spent staring at inanimate objects or off into space, I'd come up with something. So far, nada. So tonight I'm letting the sky win."

"And that means?"

"Sitting outside under the stars helps me think. It's helped me figure out some really difficult situations. But there are plenty of times where I just don't want to think about anything, so I just look up and appreciate how small I am in relation to the universe. That's letting the sky win. It helps me keep things in perspective; it's bigger than all of us and our problems."

"That's a great way to look at it."

"When it works," she shrugged. "Hasn't helped at all with current events."

"How are you and Lucas getting along?"

"He's not so bad. Kind of grows on you after a while."

"Like a fungus."

Her face lit up when she laughed. "He's great. It's the other part that's so hard. Seamus Donovan is always going to be my dad. I don't care what biology says. This Soren guy, he's nothing more than a sperm donor."

"Seamus knew you weren't his biological daughter, and from the sounds of it, that didn't matter to him. Sounds like a great man to me."

"He was."

"Then it changes nothing."

She opened her mouth but paused a moment. "I know she didn't mean anything bad when she told us, but it was a jolt. Is there any way Nonna was mistaken?"

"That woman knows everything, so it's highly unlikely."

"Did you know? About him? I guess that makes him your uncle?"

"Not a clue. I would've been about two when he left, so I don't even remember him. He was never really my uncle."

"Well, he's not my father so I guess we're both lucky," she joked.

"This is probably the time to confess that I knew about your parents. That's why I gave you the info for those assignments. I didn't know how much you knew about their pasts, so I wanted to at least give you a chance to learn something about them. I'm sorry if any of that was hard for you."

"I knew about my mom. Dad used to joke about her being a mafia princess, so that wasn't a surprise. Learning about his past was a shock. I later found out from my FBI handler that he got himself out of the gang before the feds busted them. Apparently, he wanted to make sure he made it home to his family every night." She paused. "What does it even mean if Soren really *is* my father?"

I sighed. "I know I said Nonna knows everything, but we should probably confirm it. I can have someone come and give you both a DNA test as soon as tomorrow."

Her gaze lingered on the pool, lasting for quite some time. I was just about to apologize for my suggestion when she nodded. "Okay."

I wanted to say so much to her, but the timing wasn't right. I changed the subject and she relaxed back in the chair as we chatted. When she shivered, we realized it was almost midnight. I wrapped my arm around her shoulder as we headed inside.

She yawned and motioned upstairs. "Meet me in there when you're ready for bed."

My heart nearly stopped. "Seriously?"

"I think we're well past you sneaking in, don't you?" Sauntering away, she paused and looked over her shoulder. "But you're not sleeping in your undies."

Over the years, there'd been plenty of times I couldn't undress quickly enough. Never had I been in a situation where I hurried to put on sweatpants. Not until she came along, I mused. Five minutes later I knocked on her door. Once we were under the covers, I hugged her tightly to me and we both relaxed. Her fingers caressed my arm before moving to my side. With a small smile, she leaned her head against my chest and closed her eyes.

My thoughts went to our earlier conversation. "Can I ask you something?"

"Sure."

"You were staring at the sky that night when I found you in Ireland."

"That's not a question, but I was. I'd been struggling all day with trying to keep you out of my head. That night, I decided to stop fighting it and think about the good times we had. And then you appeared."

"Maybe it was a sign," I suggested, leaning down to kiss her forehead.

Her hand moved to my back, but she said nothing. I held her close until her breathing slowed. Frowning at the dark circles under her eyes, I watched her sleep, ready to respond if her dreams haunted her again. When her brows creased a short while later, I whispered in her ear and she pressed tighter against me. Feeling content for the first time in a long while, my eyes grew heavy and I fell asleep, hoping the light at the end of the tunnel was close.

A technician showed up early the next morning to perform the paternity test. With a large wad of cash to put a rush on the results and to keep them private, she was on her way. Lucas took Liss to the shooting range while I basically spun my wheels for several hours trying to gain intel. There was still no word from my uncle, and none of my spies had new information. His continued radio silence deepened my unease, especially since the twist about her parentage came to light. Lucas could be used as leverage against both her and me.

The lab called barely twenty-four hours later. The two of them paced on opposite ends of the room while I put the technician on speakerphone and she confirmed their shared paternal DNA. Several emotions crossed her face in the few seconds it took her brother to cross the room. Tears filled her eyes and her body tensed, as if bracing for an explosion. Fighting the temptation to intervene, I watched their whispered conversation for several minutes. When she wrapped her arms around his neck and he lifted her off the ground into a bear hug, the knot in my stomach eased. His eyes met mine and he smiled.

"I'm sure you two have a lot to talk about." My voice sounded like I'd swallowed sand. "I need her for a few minutes."

After several murmured words, he patted her shoulder and left. The warning in his eyes was clear as he brushed past, and I knew he'd accepted her as family without a second thought. He closed the door behind him and I motioned to the couch.

"He's still not my father."

"No, he's not," I agreed, sitting next to her. "Seamus is your dad, and I'm hoping you'll see Lucas as your brother in time. The glare I got just now tells me he's already taking on the overprotective brother role."

She smiled. "Like I said, he grows on you after a while. And I can't exactly call him your asshole cousin anymore. It poses an interesting question now: how the hell do I introduce you? My brother's cousin who I'm not related to? Or my ex, who's kidnapped me and forcing me to live with him?"

"I figured you'd eventually introduce me as your husband, so I wasn't too worried about it."

She rolled her eyes. "Humble as ever, Gianni."

"Uh oh, the use of my birth name means I'm in trouble."

"You know what I mean. I guess I'll just keep introducing you as my asshole ex."

My eyes narrowed, but her laughter broke the tension. Her walls lowered and the brief look at the woman whose heart drew me to her like no other shone through. Our laughter died out, and we both leaned back against the couch in a comfortable silence.

She stared at the ceiling and sighed. "What does this mean for the shit with your uncle?"

"If he ever finds out the truth, Lucas will have an even bigger target on his back. It's not safe for either of you now."

"I figured as much," she sighed. "When did anyone last hear from Soren? I'm at my limit on surprises. If he suddenly shows up, that's going to get ugly."

"He pretty much disappeared the moment his plane left for New York. Zia Elena claimed spousal abandonment and divorced him after he was gone for several years. We don't even know if he's alive. If he is, that's something else we'll need to worry about. The fact your mom didn't want him to know about you worries the fuck out of me."

"So, what's the plan?"

"One you're not going to like," I paused as she pursed her lips. "I need you to be patient and stay here a little longer while I try to chase down some intel on Soren and see if there's any angle we can find to keep both of you safe."

She glanced at me before shrugging. "This place isn't so terrible."

"Hey, it gives me more time to impress you. Nonna always wanted me to marry a nice Italian girl."

"I'm not nice."

"I said *she* wanted me to marry a nice girl. I've always had a thing for not so nice girls. And it's an added bonus if she can kick my ass and shoot better than me."

"All the subtlety of an atomic bomb, Mr. Martinetti."

I wrapped my arm around her. "Can't blame me for trying."

The fact she didn't push me away was a minor victory. I savored as we sat together for several moments. There had to be a solution. I refused to believe fate brought her back just to rip her away. No goddamned way.

She sat up and stretched. "I'm going to go annoy my brother. Maybe tell him you've been hitting on me and see what he does," she added with a laugh.

"I'd love to see him try." I grasped her hand. "Talk more later?"

"We'll see."

I chuckled as she scurried through the door. Once she was out of sight, I sat forward and dropped my head into my hands. Despite a month of brainstorming, Lucas and I were still far from a solution. Now, he was also targeted. Short of keeping them from ever leaving the estate, I needed a miracle.

The sound of my cell phone broke the silence. I grabbed it off my desk and my fingers numbed at the name on the display. A ball of lead dropped into my stomach as I stabbed the screen. "Uncle," I answered with a sneer.

"Gianni," the baritone voice of Massimo Sardi greeted. Something about his tone made the hair on the back of my neck stand up.

"To what do I owe the honor?"

"The family ball is next week and your presence is required."

Fanfuckingtastic. Just what I needed. "Oh, wow. I can't believe it's that time already. I'll be there."

"Splendid! Make sure you bring that cousin of yours and the Donovan girl."

Every drop of oxygen left my body, and my knees buckled. I gripped the desk and lowered myself into the chair. My mouth sucked in several gulps of air, but my voice was lost.

"I know you heard me, Gianni." His voice was deadly. "Produce the girl at my estate next week or I'll send Marco to collect her. I know he's quite eager to make her acquaintance."

The phone dropped from my hand and slid to the floor as I fought the urge to puke all over my desk. I tore open the top button of my shirt, freeing my neck from the collar threatening to strangle me. After several long moments, I stood and took several breaths to calm my racing heart. The one thing I'd tried to avoid, tried to keep buried, had all been for naught.

He'd found her.

Chapter Ten

Into the Lion's Den

Larissa

"Wow, Nonna looks so young here," I observed, studying the picture of the matriarch taken in the estate's garden.

"But just as intimidating," Lucas replied. He studied the photo. "I think Zia Giada took that one."

We sat on the couch in the library with a stack of photo albums on the coffee table in front of us. Most of the pictures showed two boys who grew up surrounded by love. The next page showed an eight-year-old Lucas at a piano recital, according to the handwritten caption. Elena held him to her chest as she hugged him, the pride clear on her face.

We shared a sad smile as we looked at pictures of John and his parents, Francisco and Giada Martinetti. Several pages showed what looked like a family camping trip. John sat on his grandmother's lap in front of a campfire while his dad made faces at him with his mouth full of marshmallows. My eyes grew watery when I saw the date, taken only a couple months before the car accident that killed them. Lucas handed me another album, and I laughed at the picture of two boys standing in a soccer field. Both wore the same light green uniform and clutched a soccer ball between them. John's face looked like he was about to spring something on his cousin at any second.

"How long after she took the picture did he steal the ball?"

"As soon as she looked away." He grinned. "I got it back and spiked him in the head with it."

Our laughter stopped when John stumbled through the door with a panicked look in his eyes. His words came out in a winded jumble as he tried to catch his breath. "Massimo knows you're here. I have to bring you to the estate or he's sending Marco to bring you back to Bari."

My stomach jolted. I closed my eyes and envisioned the magnolia tree, using one of the calming exercises I learned in therapy. The tree refused to materialize and my lips felt numb. After being forced to stay, supposedly for my safety, it was all for nothing. My mind racing, I stood and moved to the corner furthest away from him.

I stared at the wall in front of me. "How?"

"I don't know." His voice sounded like it was in a tunnel. "But I'm going to find out. Liss—"

My eyes burned. I vigorously shook my head, desperate to tune out his voice. Trapped. I was fucking trapped and possibly in even worse danger than when he found me in Ireland. And it was all my own goddamned fault for not trusting my instincts and demanding he let me go. Sensing his presence, I found him standing directly before me with his hands splayed in front of him.

Without a word, I shoved him away. "I told you I couldn't stay here! I asked you to let me go so I could hide and figure out how to take him down. But you wouldn't listen and now you're all in danger."

"I promise I'll figure it out."

"Bullshit! You've had over a month and you haven't done shit! For all I know, you told him!"

"Lissa, stop." Lucas's voice was gentle but firm. "I know he wouldn't do that, and you know it deep down. He cares about you too much."

A humorless laugh erupted. "I keep hearing that, and then I wind up running for my life."

John lowered his head. "You still don't trust me."

"What am I supposed to think when things keep happening?"

"That I'm doing the best I can, but can't control my crazy fucking family!" he bellowed.

"That's enough." Lucas stepped between us. "Instead of screaming at each other, we need to come up with a plan. I just thought of something. Can I trust that you two can stop freaking out until I come back?"

I shoved past both of them and bolted from the room, taking off in a run as soon as my feet rounded the hall. They yelled after me, but I didn't care. The walls were closing in and I needed air. I ran through the back door and didn't stop until I reached the olive grove.

Leaning against a tree, I watched the branches sway. My harsh words shrieked through my head and with them regret. The panic on his face should have made it clear he had nothing to do with it. Instead, I turned into a crazed, irrational bitch. Cursing myself mentally, I placed my head in my hands and ordered myself to calm the fuck down.

"Do you really think I'd sell you out to my uncle?" a voice thick with emotion rang out, causing me to jump.

"No," I replied without hesitation, facing him. "I freaked out and took it out on you. I'm sorry."

I took a step forward, but stopped when he unbuttoned his dress shirt. His gaze held mine as he stood before me and pulled it back, exposing his tattoo. "What do you see?"

He had a small bird drawn on his chest, colored red and black. The bird drank from a flower that looked like it was made of fire. I traced a finger over the image, and his warm hand covered mine. "It's beautiful," I murmured. "Is that a hummingbird?"

He nodded. "It's you. You're like a hummingbird the way you flit from place to place and feed from a fire that would kill anyone else." Gently squeezing my hand, he smiled. "It's over my heart because you've had it for so long that I barely remember what it felt like before you came into my life. And I sure as fuck don't want to try."

"I—"

His arms circled my waist and his face hovered over mine. Closing the distance between us, I kissed him. My heart raced as his soft lips moved against mine. When his hand fisted into my hair, I was lost, my tongue dancing with his. We broke apart and held each other close.

"I love you," he mumbled. "I always have and I always will. I don't expect you to say it back, but I'm hoping someday you will."

Hot tears streamed from my eyes. "I've spent two years trying to forget you, to move on, and failed. I've always felt so lost because there's always a part of me that just won't let you go."

"The part that can't let go is correct, Liss. I just need a chance to prove it to you." He pressed his forehead to mine. "Can we try? Please?"

"Um, there's the small matter of your crazed, homicidal uncle. We can't really try anything if we're dead."

"Hey, no talking like that," he scolded, standing back. "We will find a way through this."

"I'm scared," I whispered, finally vocalizing the real reason I lashed out. Even top-secret assassins had moments of fear and doubt.

"I'm scared too, but between the three of us, we'll figure out a way. And *when* we make it through all this," he paused, smiling.

"Yeah?"

"Can you let me try to earn your trust again?"

I heard hope in his voice, looked up, and saw sincerity in his eyes. Everything he had done and said since I'd been there showed he cared and meant me no harm. I decided to indulge that part that never gave up on him. "Yes."

His face lit up, and then he kissed me. It was gentle, but the promise of what the future held was certainly there. I leaned against his chest, listening to his heartbeat until he sighed. "As much as I'd love to stand here and make out, we should probably go talk to Lucas and start figuring this out."

"Yeah, we probably should," I agreed, though regretfully. "And maybe button up your shirt so he doesn't think you were defiling his sister."

"Not yet, anyway."

"Let's not get ahead of ourselves," I scolded before heading toward the house.

He caught up a moment later fully dressed and looking handsome, as always. His hand found mine and gripped it tightly. I smiled up at him as we went to his office to figure out how to stay alive and not derail what could be the world's shortest attempt at a reconciliation.

• • • ● • ● • ● • ● • •

John

"And now, I present Signore Sardi's nephew. Signore Lucas Luccetti," the marshal's voice boomed over the microphone.

Lucas looked over his shoulder and nodded before disappearing through the heavy black curtains. The sound of polite applause told me he was making his way downstairs to join the party. I rolled my eyes. My uncle loved to flaunt his wealth and power. Living in a stone fortress carved into the side of a cliff on the coast made it easy to do.

As the future heir, my attendance that night was required. I'd always hated it but complied without question or complaint to keep the peace. Every year I played the obedient nephew and talked a big game to the associates while ignoring the women who flocked to the estate by the dozen. This time, we arrived early and checked into a nearby hotel to delay our arrival until it couldn't be avoided. Lucas almost started a brawl at the front gate when our guards were turned away. The reason for all my extra precautions paced the floor until I caught hold of her hand and held it in mine.

Liss was so tightly wound she almost vibrated. It was bad enough I'd been forced to bring her, but now she was about to be paraded before the family and associates like some kind of fucking sacrificial lamb. I let out a deep breath and tried to control my rage. Losing my shit wouldn't help her at all, I reminded myself.

She looked absolutely breathtaking. My uncle's dress code required women to wear either white or black, but Liss defiantly thumbed her nose at that rule by wearing a blood red velvet dress that hugged her every curve. The ruffled top looked like black roses covered in blood and was a bold contrast to her pale skin. Her hair was a sea of soft curls that my hands craved to touch. She was a nervous mess, but a stunning one.

Hugging her to me, I kissed her temple. "I'm right here with you. I won't leave your side for a second. I promise."

She closed her eyes and nodded. "I'm okay. Well, okay-ish."

The marshal smiled and stepped forward. "You two are ready, *si*?"

I nodded and said a silent prayer that we all survived the night. "To the lion's den?"

"To the lion's den."

"And now I present to you Signore Sardi's oldest nephew and heir to the family legacy, Signore Gianni Martinetti and his guest,

Signorina Larissa Donovan," the announcement rang throughout the room.

"I love you," I stated firmly, gripping her hand tightly before leading her through the curtain and into battle.

The applause echoed off the walls as we appeared at the top of the stairs. I plastered a fake smile on my face to hide my disgust. Of course, the jackals were clapping. They believed I had delivered the enemy, at last defeated. Her posture was stiff as she moved, and her hand gripped mine to the point of pain. I gave it a small squeeze and the look in her eyes when she looked up told me everything.

"Breathe. I'm right here. Don't worry about these leeches."

She closed her eyes and nodded. We reached the bottom of the stairs and met Lucas as he stood on the edge of the dance floor. I watched him scan the room and did the same. My uncle and his closest men weren't there, but plenty of other eyes watched us.

The ballroom was beautiful. Ornate frieze moldings adorned the curved ceiling. The walls were painted eggshell white and the natural light in the room was stunning when the heavy green velvet curtains weren't covering the floor to ceiling windows that faced the Adriatic Sea. Such a beautiful space seemed wasted on someone like my uncle, who spent most of his time in his office or bedroom.

She clutched my arm while staring ahead. "Any sign of him?"

"No, but he's watching," Lucas whispered, nodding at some bleach blond in a white dress that left nothing to the imagination.

"Let's give them the spectacle they've all come to watch, shall we?" I slid her hand in mine.

The crowd parted as we strolled across the white marble floor. The dumbstruck look on some people's faces was almost too much and I had to bite my lip to keep from laughing. I led her to the middle of the room and wound my arm around her waist. The orchestra positioned in the corner by the windows played a slow song and every set of eyes in the room watched us slowly move to the music.

Her eyes sparkled. "This is a bit conspicuous, wouldn't you say, Mr. Martinetti?"

"Just the way I like it, Miss Donovan."

She put her hand on my shoulder, doing her best to hide the discomfort in her eyes. There was no doubt she felt vulnerable. She worked in secret, hiding in plain sight while her target was unaware until it was too late. I hated to admit that was what made her so lethal, even more than I ever was. Hell, she tricked me, all of my men and her own brother into what was basically a war game in our own home. The only reason we survived was because she *chose* not to kill us.

Out of the corner of my eye, I saw several of my uncle's men had entered the ballroom. Her eyes followed mine and her steps faltered. When I pulled her body against my chest, her trembling eased. When I lowered my face to her neck, she gasped and her grip tightened.

"Relax," I whispered. "We knew they'd engage eventually. Lucas is here. Just stick to the plan and wait until they make a move. Okay?"

I rested my hand just above her ass and spun her around. When I stared into her eyes, it was easy to blank out everyone and everything else until it was just me and her. Holding her felt like the most perfect and natural thing. Twirling her around again, I envisioned her in white dancing at our wedding. The image ignited several new emotions, but fear was the one that clawed at my gut. I wasn't afraid of marrying her. Never. I knew she was the one and I'd wait forever if I had to.

There were things I still had to confess, things that would be difficult for her to hear and move past. They weren't lies, more like factual omissions, but the damage would be severe. That didn't change the fact I needed to tell her before she found out from someone else. But not that night. Instead —

"Gianni, your uncle has requested your presence in his study," a deep, heavily accented voice said in my ear, interrupting my thoughts.

Her body shook against mine. I traced my fingers over the bare and prickled skin on her back before acknowledging Silvio, one of my uncle's top security guards. "All right. Let my cousin come over and escort my date to our table," I replied, motioning to Lucas.

"Actually, we've been asked to leave Miss Donovan in the care of one of the guards while you and Lucas speak to your uncle."

I clenched my jaw. We'd prepared for the possibility, but that didn't mean my compliance would be easy. I held her close and opened my mouth to protest when she stepped away from me and squared her shoulders.

"It's fine, John. We knew this would happen. No sense in making a scene," she said, glaring at Silvio.

I nodded. "I love you. Please be careful."

"Always," she replied softly. She faced the group of men surrounding us. "So which one of you dipshits has the honor of babysitting me?"

"That would be Tito." He nodded to the bulky man behind him, who stepped forward. He leered as he offered his hand to her. She balled hers into a fist and offered two of her fingers. He bowed his head to me and led her away. Over my shoulder, I watched Lucas's face contort.

"Lucas, let's go see what Zio wants so we can get back to the festivities," I announced loudly, hoping to snap him out of his thoughts.

He nodded, his eyes still on her as she left the ballroom. "Sure. Business first."

Our uncle stood in front of a wall of windows that overlooked the sea when we entered his ridiculously dark and opulent study. Heavy black velvet curtains nearly blended into the dark gray walls. The dark wood bookshelves lining the wall opposite the windows boasted expensive books and trinkets he'd surely never looked at once or cared about so long as they showed his wealth and power.

The brothers were identical twins, but there were a few differences in their physical appearance. His athletic build was thinner than Gio and he kept his hair closely cut, masking their naturally curly hair. He sipped what looked and smelled like amaretto, ignoring us for several moments before turning around.

"Ah, Gianni and Lucas! My favorite nephews," he greeted warmly, buttoning his black tuxedo jacket. He strolled around his large dark wooden desk and walked towards us with his arms extended.

Massimo Sardi, boss of the family, was a tall and imposing man. As a kid, he intimidated the shit out of me with both his size and the power that radiated from him. Tonight, nearly three months after the death of the only other human he cared about aside from himself, his skin was pale and he looked thinner. That didn't mean he wasn't still capable of savagery.

"You summoned us?" I retorted, refusing to deal with pleasantries.

He narrowed his brown eyes. "Tsk, tsk, my dear boy! One might think you don't want to be here to celebrate the downfall of that murderous whore you brought me tonight."

"Yes, I brought her here, just as you ordered. And I will be taking her back to Verona tonight."

He drained his glass and tossed it across the room. "Mind your tone! I was almost willing to overlook your lies. Continue this insolence with me and she will pay the price."

"We had her contained at the estate. She wasn't causing any harm to the family," Lucas interjected. "Why not allow us to take her back and keep her there?"

"Jesus Christ, Lucas! I know you're useless, but I didn't realize you were stupid! She killed my brother and she will pay. Did I mention this ball is being held in Gio's honor? I thought it fitting that she meet her end while attending the event honoring the man she killed."

"What are you going to do? Execute her in the middle of the fucking ballroom while waiters pass out hors d'oeuvres?" I shouted. "Maybe if you assholes hadn't killed her family, she wouldn't have sought vengeance and killed your sick fucking brother!"

"Don't act like you know anything about her family," he growled. "Your balls hadn't even dropped when I eliminated that fucking Irish rat and his whore of a wife. I wish I could take full credit for the hit, but that honor belongs to Giovino."

"Why?" I argued. "She was a child and as I understand it, saw nothing. You both got what you wanted. Seamus was the rat and Sera wronged your sister. What was the point of Gio playing games with Larissa all these years later? All it did was stir the shit back up again. What good did that serve?"

He chuckled. "You think I care about anything that happened to my sister? That freak? Don't pretend to know anything, boy! That little bitch killed my brother. She *will* pay for that!"

"Have you considered all the implications of killing her?" Lucas's voice was casual.

"Lucas, I realize you're daft, but that doesn't mean the rest of us are as well. Once she's dead, it will show our enemies and associates what happens when you cross me."

"That's just it. Have you considered how her death may affect the relationship with your associates?" I didn't know where my cousin was going with his argument, but I knew to play along.

Massimo's face turned red. "What the fuck is that supposed to mean?"

"Take us to her and he'll explain," I replied, crossing my arms.

"I should parade you both downstairs so you can watch her beg for mercy before Marco squeezes the life out of her and then shoot you both in the head for your treachery."

"What if he's right?" I challenged. "Are you absolutely sure there's something you didn't miss?"

The scowl on his face was almost comical as he glared at both of us. He'd rather shoot himself in the dick than admit a flaw in his plan, but he needed the alliances to keep his power. "Consider it your last goodbye to her," he snarled at me. "But don't think I've forgiven you for fucking that filthy Irish slut. We will discuss that punishment soon enough."

Ten minutes later, we emerged from a small elevator and walked past the boathouse under the estate. We continued down a narrow pathway, gripping the rough stone wall so we wouldn't fall into the Adriatic Sea to our right. An old pier was located at the end of the trail and what I saw in the distance turned my blood to ice.

A large, hulking man stood at the edge. In his right hand, he held her up by a fistful of hair. In the other, he held a pistol against her temple. He turned her toward me and my anger and fear collided when I saw the dead look in her eyes and watched her arms dangle lifelessly. She'd obviously been drugged, and the bruises all over her face and upper body told me that she'd put up one hell of a fight. She stared blankly at the water and slowly blinked. I doubted whether she even knew what was going on, which was probably for the best. The metal contraption attached to her waist and cuffed to her wrists replaced my anger with fear.

"Marco, it appears you have something that belongs to me," I greeted, trying to control my voice. In the year since I'd last seen him, his once wild black hair was shaved into a buzz cut and he looked as if he'd gained a few more rows of muscles in his arms. The evil glint in his silver eyes stayed the same.

"That's not what I hear," he replied with a hint of glee. "Boss told me I could have a bit of fun with her before we present her to the family. Well, whatever is left of her, anyway." He pulled her head back and trailed his mouth from her neck to behind her ear. The bile rose in my throat as his mouth moved toward her breasts. As if sensing my anger, he winked at me. "Later," he whispered to her.

"What the fuck is on her waist?" Lucas demanded.

"I'm so glad you asked," Massimo replied. "This estate is over a hundred years old, you see. We recently found a storage area full of clothing and accessories for the women of the house at the time. This item here is called a crinoline, and it was worn under a woman's skirts or dresses to give them that full look you've probably seen in those stupid history books of yours. Some were made of metal, as you can see. Unfortunately, this made them dangerous, especially when a lady walked near the water."

With a grin, Marco guided her closer to the edge of the pier. I saw the panic on Lucas's face. Before I could stop him, he stepped in front of our uncle. "You can't kill her," he said.

"And why is that? Hmm? What's so fucking special about her that keeps her immune to my justice?"

"Her mother is a direct descendant of Giuseppe Morello, who founded the original Genovese gang. Killing her or even harming her could endanger that alliance, especially if they find out."

"And how would they know? I doubt the family even knows of her existence," he snarled.

"They've known about her for the past six days. I made sure of it."

Massimo glared at us before shifting his gaze to his associate as he dangled her from his arm like a rag doll. I kept my face blank while praying he realized Lucas was right. My heart almost stopped when an evil grin spread across his lips.

"You know, Lucas, you're right. Killing her would certainly displease the Genovese," he seemed to concede, nodding at Marco. "But accidents do happen."

My head whipped around, and I watched him carelessly fling her body from his grasp. Time slowed to a crawl as she slid into the water. Her eyes widened as she sank, but the drugs in her system and the iron around her waist kept her from moving.

"No!" I ran to the edge of the pier until Marco grabbed my arm.

"If I don't get her, neither do you," he taunted in my ear.

I heard a crash behind us, and my body jerked sideways. Massimo was on the ground, blocking Lucas's blows to his face. Marco tried to move closer to help his boss, but I kicked my foot backwards, connecting with his knee. He bellowed and loosened his grip on my arms. I turned and punched the sick fuck in the jaw. A gun shot rang out, and I spun to find Lucas firing at our uncle's retreating back. Marco shoved past both of us and followed his boss. Lucas shot again and gasped as we watched Massimo fall to the ground. Marco rounded on us and returned fire.

"Go!" Lucas yelled, diving behind two metal barrels.

I scanned the water, thankful for the underwater lights along the seawall. After steeling myself up for what awaited me below the surface, I jumped into the frigid water and headed to where I saw her fall. Her body stood on the ocean floor, held up by the metal cage that weighed her down. Her eyes were closed and her long hair swirled eerily around her. The lights cast a glow against her skin that made her look like a ghost.

Reaching for my belt buckle, I tugged open a secret compartment, yet another one of Lucas's genius creations. The small area held several essential items that were tethered to the liner. I grabbed the handcuff key and unlocked the shackles on her wrists. The waist band on the crinoline was fabric and released her easily. I wrapped my arm around her and swam like mad toward the surface, doing my best to kick free of the velvet train of her dress that clung to her legs and weighed us down.

Lucas's face hovered over the water when we broke the surface. He grabbed her limp body and helped hoist her up to the pier while I climbed out. His facial expression when he checked her pulse told me time was a luxury we didn't have. I gave her chest compressions while he performed mouth to mouth resuscitation.

"Lissa, come on," he croaked. "We all know you're stronger than this."

"You're the most stubborn little shit I've ever met," I growled as I pumped her chest.

The longer we worked, the more frantic Lucas became and the angrier I got. This woman was a tough bitch. No way she was going to drown. I wouldn't allow it. Not after all the shit we had been through. I looked up and noticed he'd stopped and was staring at her in horror.

"What are you doing?" I demanded.

"John," he nearly sobbed, putting his hand on my arm.

"No! We are not giving up on her!"

"We can't do this forever."

"I know we can't. But," I paused when my voice broke. "Just please try a couple more times. I'm begging you."

He nodded and resumed the rescue breathing. I continued chest compressions, willing her to come back. After a couple of moments, my heart sank as I felt my hope fade. "Dammit, baby, no," I pleaded.

"John! I found a pulse!"

I sat back on my legs while he felt around her neck. Her head lurched sideways and a gush of water burst from her mouth. Lucas rolled her onto her side as she coughed and gasped for air. I caught my breath and smoothed my soaked hair back as I watched her do the same. After a few minutes, her eyes closed. I tried to control my rising panic as Lucas looked her over.

"She still has a pulse," he sighed with relief. "I think she's just out from the drugs."

After watching her chest rise and fall for several minutes, I gently rolled her into my arms and placed her on my lap. "You are going to be the death of me," I sighed before kissing her forehead. "But I can't think of a better way to go."

Chapter Eleven

The Curious Case of Larissa Donovan

Larissa

I didn't bother to hide the annoyance in my voice. "You know this is completely unnecessary, right?"

"And the last time you said that, you got dizzy and slipped," he answered stubbornly as he continued to gently lather shampoo through my hair. "Unless you want a matching bruise on the other leg?"

I gave an exasperated look and stood under the water to rinse my hair. The worried look on his face as he kept a gentle hold on my arms was heartwarming, if not also frustrating. It had been three days since the ball. Granted, I'd spent the first one unconscious, so he'd been an overprotective pain in my ass for two days. Despite the bedrest, I felt woozy. Maybe I shouldn't have insisted on showering alone. Not that I would ever admit that to him.

"The bruises are looking better," he murmured, slowly leading me closer to him. "How are your ribs?"

"Still sore, but better than the alternative."

Television shows made chest compressions look easy. All it took was pressing on someone's chest a few times and they magically came back to life. What isn't mentioned is the fact that you're pressing down on a ribcage made of bones. Since a substantial amount of pressure is required to move the chest and pump the blood, those bones often break. In my case, two of them.

"Yes, it is," he whispered, kissing the top of my head.

We stood under the water and just held each other for a while, neither of us saying a word. Despite all our planning, I'd fully expected to die that night. When Tito led me into a room full of Massimo's men, I knew my time was up. I fought like mad but was no match for the four regular sized men and Marco, who was the size of a tree. When I felt the needle in my arm, I had prayed for a quick death even though I knew their boss would never allow that.

My memories after that were hazy, almost as if they were parts of a bad dream. I was on a pier, unable to move, and the only thought in my head was how beautiful and serene the water looked. After that, things came in brief flashes. I was in the water, trapped one minute and then floating toward a light the next. The light changed colors, a calming white light at first, followed by a dim light blue, and then everything went black. I woke up in John's bed sore, disoriented, and in complete shock that I was still alive. The visible relief on his face when his eyes met mine was unforgettable.

"We made it," I whispered.

"We did."

As if he could tell I had a million questions, he brushed a lock of hair away from my face and shook his head. "I promise I'll answer all your questions and you'll know everything that happened later. Right now, I just want to lie here with you."

"Okay."

I grasped his hand in mine and felt his body relax. He leaned his head against my shoulder and a few minutes later I heard his slow, even breathing. I kissed his forehead and closed my eyes. He was right; everything there was to know could wait. I drifted off shortly after.

The next morning, I pressed him to tell me what I'd missed at the ball, but he stubbornly refused to discuss it until I was up for it. His words. I could tell he wanted to talk about us, judging by the way he looked at me, but apparently that conversation was also on hold.

He leaned against the wall as I finished drying my hair. "Hey, do you feel up for venturing downstairs?"

"You mean you're going to let me out of this room finally?"

"Smartass," he chuckled. "Which means you're feeling better."

He hovered like a mother hen, but I walked down the stairs under my own power. After breakfast, we met Lucas in John's office so they could bring me up to speed on everything I missed. I groaned inwardly as John led me to the couch and instructed me to lie down, only to have Lucas then toss a blanket over my legs. What was worse than one overprotective pain in the ass? Two of them.

"Guys, I'm not that fragile," I huffed. "There's no need to treat me like I'm made of glass."

"So the biggest news is nobody has seen Massimo since Marco carted him off when you dove into the water," Lucas announced, completely ignoring me.

John sat down next to me. "What about Marco?"

"He was spotted at the port yesterday. As of right now, he appears to be overseeing day-to-day activities."

"Which also tells me he's not dead," John said. "If he was, I would've been summoned back to Bari to either face consequences for his death or to be formally presented as head of the family."

"He's hiding while he plans his next move," I offered.

"Exactly," John agreed. "So that means we need to be extra vigilant until he reappears. As for how he knew you were here, I have my suspicions, but nothing concrete just yet. Once I know for certain, we can work on fixing the problem.

"So, another thing we need to discuss," Lucas began, looking nervous, "Is your identity. More to the point, we need to untangle your identity. I think it might be the key to why Gio was so hell bent on killing your family to begin with."

"I'm not sure how much help I can be, but I'll try to fill in the holes that I can."

He looked hesitant for a moment, but then handed me several sheets of paper from the folder in his lap. "When Gio told John you were his next target, I did my usual research on you. Well, I tried to. It took a lot of digging because of who you are. The first thing I discovered was that you have four birth certificates."

I nodded, thumbing through the copies he gave me. "How much of this did you share with your uncles?"

"None."

John's brows drew together. "Why is that important?"

"I can think of at least a dozen people who would pay millions for even one shred of this info." I placed a single sheet in Lucas's hand. "That's a copy of the Irish birth certificate Seamus used to register me for school. The only reason I know is because I heard him and his friend talk about it before he died."

He scanned the paper. "Why didn't he use your real one?"

"I'm not sure." I handed him a second sheet. "This is the American certificate Felton had forged so I could enlist in the Marines and for work."

"He did what?" John's eyes were like saucers.

"He came home one day in a panic and asked me about the original. When I told him I knew nothing about it, he got really quiet and shut himself in his office. Shortly after that, I had a new one that said I was born in Virginia."

Lucas dropped the certificate. "Wait. You mean to tell me—"

"That I served in the US Marine Corps and currently work for the government thanks to forged documents purchased by an officer of the CIA? That's exactly what I'm saying."

John shook his head. "Wow. The great Felton Lynch committed identity fraud."

I studied the third document. "I didn't even know I had an Italian birth certificate. It's possible my dad had it made at the same time as the Irish one. For what reason, I don't know."

Lucas looked thoughtful. "Did you ever travel to Italy with your parents?"

"I don't think so. As far as I know, we stayed in the US from the time I was born until they died." I held up the last sheet. "This is a copy of the real birth certificate. I think I was about five and it was the one time we went to New York. My dad took me to visit the hospital where I was born. He took me up to the nursery and showed me which crib I was in and told me all these stories. I don't think he made it up. The middle name is the other way I know, and it's the most intriguing part."

Lucas eyed the document over my shoulder for several seconds before pointing to my middle name, Aednat. "How the hell do you even pronounce that?"

"It's pronounced 'ay-nit'. And for some reason, Seamus was adamant that nobody else knew that name. It was important enough that he practically drilled that into my head starting around the same time. That's why I asked how much your uncles knew about all this."

"But why?" John asked. "Why keep it secret?"

"That name must mean something to Soren," Lucas replied.

I shrugged. "What were you able to dig up on him?"

"Soren Luccetti's existence stopped about three months after he arrived in New York," he answered bitterly.

"My middle name is an Irish name," I pointed out. "What did you find out about his family?"

"Italian dating back six generations."

"So that's something we need to figure out," John interjected. "The other curious thing about all this is how your family wound up the target of my uncles to begin with."

"Felton told me it was because Seamus had been informing on your family's Italian activities to the CIA. My FBI handler corroborated that. Apparently, he had made some sort of deal to avoid prosecution just before the feds came in and wiped out his gang."

He shook his head. "Like I told you, that was a hit squad that killed your parents. My uncles wouldn't bother with something as trivial as being a rat. They would've had just killed Seamus in a public area to make an example of him. What happened to your family was a personal vendetta of some kind."

"True," I conceded. "There's certainly no love lost between the rest of your family and my parents. I've lost count of the number of times they've been called a whore and a traitor. But why?"

"Soren," Lucas said. "It all comes back to him."

"Yes, but they've been dead for over twenty years. Why chase me after so long?" I turned to John. "I'm guessing Gio didn't tell you why I was his target?"

"No, but that's normal. He just tells me who he wants dead and sometimes gives me a deadline. What wasn't normal was his reaction afterward."

"What do you mean?"

"Prague was simple. You were the target, and he wanted it done while you were there on a job. He was pissed when it didn't go as planned, and I expected that he'd tell me to try again. Instead, he doled out his 'punishment', threatened to kill Nonna like he always does and then left. A few weeks later, we were summoned to Bari, and he laid out this whole elaborate plan in Portland. I thought he'd finally lost his fucking mind, but he was adamant it had to happen that way."

Something didn't add up. "How long after Prague?"

"Maybe two or three weeks. Why?"

"All that shit in Portland would've taken months, not weeks, to plan. I'd only been on my break for six weeks when I was called back to D.C. for that assignment."

"So he'd planned that all along," Lucas said.

"But why?" John's frustration was visible. "Why do any of it? And if he'd been planning this game all along, why was I on top of a building taking shots at you?"

"Really bad shots, I might add," I grumbled.

"Don't start," Lucas snickered.

"Sorry." I turned back to John. "To answer your question, the best reason I can think of for making it a game was because he knew I'd go after him if he failed."

"And then he'd be justified in killing you," Lucas added.

"Yep. As for Prague, my best guess is he was trying to teach someone a lesson. Had John succeeded that night, the intended lesson would have been clear: don't mess with him. When that didn't happen, Massimo knew he still had this other plan in place to draw me out."

Lucas blew out a breath. "It makes sense, as fucked up as it is."

"So, is there any way we could find Massimo and finish him off?" He couldn't kill me if I got to him first.

"Don't even think about it," John snapped.

"What? It's just a question!" I protested.

"Yes, and we all know your penchant for doing crazy shit," Lucas countered. "So, before you can even think about it, it's not happening."

"Oh, for fuck's sake," I groaned, rolling my eyes. "So, what are we going to do?"

"You have two broken ribs and nearly drowned less than a week ago. *You* are going to rest and continue to recover," John answered. "*We* are going to continue to figure out how he knew you were here and where he is. And if we find him, we're just going to keep an eye on him. We will not storm his secret location and kill him. Rest assured, wherever he is hiding is well guarded, even without Marco there."

"Yes, Warden," I sniped. "Do they even know I survived?"

Lucas sighed. "I don't know. We managed to sneak out of the estate that night, but that's not to say someone didn't spot us. And if we have a mole in this house, they know you're alive."

I stared at my hands, feeling completely overwhelmed. The conversation was exhausting, mentally and physically. What I needed was time and space to think.

"Liss?"

"I need…" I shook my head and slowly stood up. "I need a minute."

"Dude, let her be," Lucas said as I walked out.

I made my way to the sunroom near the back of the house. Tired of sitting, I leaned against the wall facing the windows. It was another beautiful spring day. The sun shone brightly and the flowers and trees were in full bloom. In that moment I wished I was steadier on my feet. A jog through the grounds would've helped clear my head.

Once upon a time, I was a secret agent who used aliases with my fellow team members. I worked like hell to keep my identity a secret, sharing it only with a select few. Now that identity was in danger of being torn apart. The man I knew as my father wasn't, and my very existence had to be hidden from the monster who was my real father.

Why? Who was Soren Luccetti and what made him such a bad person? Was he the reason I was a target so many years later? Who the hell was he? More importantly, who the hell was I?

"You okay?" Lucas stood in the doorway.

I shrugged and sat on the pale green loveseat. "I'm trying to understand the meaning of all this. And wondering just who the hell I am and where I fit into this world."

"We'll figure it out eventually." He sat next to me. "And who you are hasn't changed. You're still a stubborn pain in the ass."

"*I'm* the pain in the ass?" I laughed. "You two have been like my shadows for the past three days! I'm barely able to pee by myself."

"John pulled you from the bottom of the ocean, Lissa. I had to help him resuscitate you and we almost didn't get you back. That scared the shit out of me. As for John," he paused, shaking his head. "I never want to see that look on his face again."

"All right, all right! I get it."

"You have a real family now. If you want to know where you belong, it's right here."

I placed my head on his shoulder, and we sat in silence. After a few minutes, he pulled out his phone and started typing, most likely giving my other keeper an update. I stared out the windows, glancing over at him every few minutes and getting a simple nod. After a while, my eyes refused to stay open another minute. When I woke up later, I was lying next to John on the couch in his office. The room was quiet except for the sound of soft tapping above my head.

"That sound is really annoying." I mumbled, sitting up.

"That's funny, you've slept through it for the last two hours," he chuckled, closing the laptop. "But then again, you probably couldn't hear it over all your snoring."

"I don't snore!" I protested, playfully punching his arm.

"Were you this combative when you had your concussion?"

"Nicole never complained. Then again, she rarely stayed for more than a couple hours."

Nicole was one of the teaching assistants, probably the only real student, in the history program during my assignment in Portland where I met John. She'd also been my neighbor in the dorm and a really great friend. After I was attacked in the office, she brought food to my apartment and hung out with me while I recovered. I'd always felt bad that I never got the chance to say goodbye to her when everything went to shit.

"I wonder why that was," he said sarcastically.

"Probably because our fake history professor kept bugging her about how I was doing."

He took my hand in his and gently pulled me closer until I was leaning against his chest. "It was the only way to check on you without visiting every day. As it was, staying away for that week was torture."

"Well, to answer your question, she never said I was combative. So it must just be you."

"I see," he laughed. "How are you feeling? Hungry at all?"

"I could eat. Where is everyone?"

"The guys are either on patrol, in their quarters, or home. Lucas went into town. So that makes me your dinner date."

I giggled and took his hand. We headed toward what I thought was the kitchen until he led me into the dining room. I stopped short when I saw the soft glow of candlelight illuminating the entire room. My eyes were wide when I turned to him.

"We still have one more topic to discuss, and I wanted to have the perfect setting for it."

I blinked innocently. "And what would that be?"

"I think you know."

"I do," I replied, suddenly serious.

He took a deep breath. "Look, I know you said yes, but I don't want you to do it just because you were scared of my uncle. I only want this if you do."

My head flooded with all the words I wanted to say, but I knew they'd come out jumbled and still not even come close to what I felt.

Did I love him? I was pretty sure I did. Was I still nervous about what could happen? Absolutely. But after everything we'd been through, from all the betrayals in the past to his homicidal uncle in the present, we were both still standing.

I glanced up and noticed his worried gaze. Without another word, I wrapped my arms around his neck and pulled him closer to me. His hands moved to my hips as our lips crashed together. We kissed as if our lives depended on it. As tightly as he held me to him, I was sure he felt the same way.

He pressed his forehead against mine when the kiss ended and traced the back of his knuckle down my cheek. "I promise it will be different this time, baby," he whispered in a rush. "It will be better. We'll take things slow. I'll make sure that you don't regret this. I'll—"

"Shhh," I soothed, placing my finger over his lips. "We don't have to figure it all out right now."

He smiled. "I love you so much. We're really going to do this?"

"Yes, we're really going to do this," I confirmed. "After dinner, though. I'm hungry."

He laughed and led me to my seat. We said little during dinner, commenting on the food now and then and exchanging glances and smiles. A couple times, he seemed as lost in his thoughts as me. It didn't surprise me since it had been a day full of news and revelations.

After we finished, he led me to the sunroom and grabbed the blanket from the back of the love seat. "Wanna go outside and sit under the stars?"

"That depends. Do you have something on your mind that you need to think about?"

"I figured you'd want to get out of the house. Plus, I know you're looking for an excuse to snuggle up to me."

"Ever so humble," I giggled.

We cuddled on the double chaise lounge by the pool. Trying to find a comfortable position because of my sore ribs was a challenge until he sat me on his lap and spread the blanket over us. I laid my head on his chest and inhaled his scent, enjoying the calm it brought. He wrapped his arm around my waist and I closed my eyes.

"Liss?"

"Hmm?"

"Don't be mad, but I overheard part of your conversation with Lucas. I know all the news was a lot to take in today, but he was right about one thing."

"What's that?"

"You'll always have a place here. No matter what. And I know you're the only one who can figure out exactly who you are, but I hope that you'll at least let me help. Because I'm hoping I fit into that somewhere."

I smiled. "I'm hoping so, too. And all joking and cockiness aside, you mean a lot to me. I'm sorry that I'm not ready to say the words I know you want to hear, but I think I'll be able to say them someday. All I ask for is a bit of patience."

"I told you I'd wait forever if I had to, and I mean that. 'Someday' is a goal that works for me."

"A goal? I'm just a goal now?" I teased.

"No, you're much more than that." He lowered his mouth to hover over my lips. "You're mine," he breathed before pulling me into another kiss.

Chapter Twelve

Exposure

Larissa

The voices in the hallway were loud, angry and in rapid Italian. When Nonna stormed into the kitchen that morning and demanded to see Lucas, I knew it wasn't going to be pretty. They'd argued for over an hour with no end in sight. John tried to diffuse the situation, but not long after, he started yelling as well. I stayed in the kitchen where I could eavesdrop without being caught. After a while, I got bored and made lunch.

I was shaping gnocchi with a fork when John walked into the kitchen, his eyes wide. He held a finger to his lips to remind me to be quiet when I giggled. After stealing a glance toward the hallway, he leaned against the island and propped his head on his hands.

"Damn, it sounds like someone had fun when he went to visit his mom," I whispered.

"I told you he gets more ass than a toilet seat."

"I know, but sleeping with her secretary? Her *third* secretary? The number got a little lost between all the curse words."

"She was her third who actually made it to their first day. There were two she hired, but he slept with them before they even started. When they found out that he doesn't do relationships, they quit."

My eyebrows shot up. "Well, hopefully he learns to find a better place to have sex than the library in the future."

"What are you making?"

"The kitchen was the safest place to be when they started yelling and after a while, I got bored. Found a few spare potatoes in the pantry and it's been a while since I've had a decent gnocchi. We could have it for lunch if you'd like. But that also means I'm going to put you to work."

"I like the sound of that. What do I have to do?"

"You get to make the pesto."

"Not quite what I had in mind, but I think I can still impress you with my culinary prowess."

Lucas suddenly appeared. "And what, exactly, did you have in mind?"

"She castrate you yet?" John teased.

"Gianni!" Nonna yelled as she stomped into the kitchen. "I didn't raise you to be so crude. Mind your tongue!"

"Sorry, Nonna."

She glared at both her grandsons. Her entire demeanor changed when she saw me. Shoving John out of the way, she pulled me into a rough hug. "Larissa! It's good to see you again!" she exclaimed in Italian. "I trust my grandsons are treating you well?"

"Yes, they are treating me very well."

"I'm very glad to hear that, dear," she replied. She watched me shape the pieces with a fork and nodded. "I'd love to stay and try some of your gnocchi, but I must get home and post an advertisement for yet another secretary since your brother seems to think my staff is his personal dating pool."

"Nonna!" Lucas protested as John snickered.

"You! Silence!" she yelled before turning back to me. "If you make enough for Lucas, make him eat in the kitchen while you and Gianni dine outside. It's more romantic that way."

"Nonna!" John groaned. "I don't think I need advice on how to be romantic with my girlfriend."

"What? You're thirty-three years old. You're not getting any younger and I want great grandchildren before I'm eighty, Gianni."

He rolled his eyes. "Let me walk you out to your car."

"Big baby doesn't want me to embarrass him anymore," she said, wrapping her arms around my waist.

Lucas smirked, but suddenly coughed after John shot him a murderous glare. I pursed my lips and forced back the laugh that threatened to burst out. He narrowed his eyes at me until I mouthed the word "sorry" over her shoulder.

"So, I guess I don't need to ask how it's going with you two," Lucas said as soon as we were alone.

I smiled. In the six weeks since we agreed to try again, he'd kept his word that things would be different. Back in Portland, much of our relationship, if it could've ever been called that, was physical. The few conversations we'd had were hardly genuine since we were both using fake identities. Early on, we agreed that "trying again" really meant starting over.

So that's what we did. We went on "dates" around the estate, strolling through the garden, watching the stars at night, or spending time together at the shooting range. Hey, we were both snipers who needed to practice, and it was a way to spend time together.

My feelings for him blossomed. I loved that he was the last person I spoke to before I fell asleep and that he was the first person I saw in the morning. From the butterflies I got in my stomach every time he smiled at me to the warmth that spread throughout my body when we kissed, I was falling for him and falling hard.

"Do you really want to know about my love life?"

He wrinkled his nose. "Now that you put it that way, not really. Because then that makes me think about you having a sex life."

"And I've heard plenty about your sex life from all the damn noises coming from your room. You might want to slow down before you break that thing off. Or Nonna shoots it off."

"I know, I know," he sighed. "Relationships just aren't my thing I've learned. One person always winds up hating the other one. Or it's just a pairing to make other people happy."

Given his family's dysfunction, I understood his view. "That's not always the case, but I understand where you're coming from. It's okay to not want a relationship. But maybe you shouldn't bang someone on Nonna or John's staff. Mixing work and sex isn't a great idea."

"Yeah, but you guys might be the rare case where it works out. And I'm really happy for you. Both of you."

"Thanks."

"Hopefully that means you won't be leaving us for a job or something anytime soon. What's the story with your work, anyway?"

"The story is she and I are having lunch and you're going to not stick your dick in any females in this house for at least seven days," John grumbled as he returned to the kitchen. He stood next to me and rubbed my back as he turned to his cousin. "You and I will talk later."

My head turned quickly when Lucas exited. "That bad?"

He waved his hand. "Let's eat lunch."

It was another beautiful spring day, so we went outside even though Nonna had already suggested it. We ate in silence for a few minutes before I noticed him watching me. He seemed deep in thought. "You know, he brought up a good point. What exactly is your job status?"

"I'm on extended leave with both agencies," I answered, leaving out all the sordid details from the last meeting with my handlers. I was pretty sure a jury would consider that meeting kidnapping, as well as a few other serious charges. "And I told them both under no circumstance were they to call me."

His eyebrows shot up. "Felton agreed to that?"

"I disappeared, so it's not like I really gave him much of a choice. If I ever wanted to go back, I could call him and he'd reinstate me." After a brutal interrogation and lecture, I was sure.

"Have you thought about going back?"

"No. I haven't talked to either of them since I left the States. But I'll be honest. There were times I really enjoyed what I did. How could I not? I got to travel around, help solve cases, and there were a few people I enjoyed working with. I don't miss the politics and the crap between the two agencies, but I'd be lying if I said I didn't miss it sometimes."

"But?"

I sighed. "But I could also see myself setting down roots here and staying somewhere for a while. For once, I have a reason to stay put. I have a family now. Lucas is a pain in the ass, but he's a lovable pain in the ass. And, more importantly, I have you."

"You'll always be welcome here, you know that. And that means you can stay here however long you want," he declared, grasping my hand. "And when I say that, I mean I would be perfectly okay if you wanted to stay forever."

"I know, baby. And believe me, I've given it a lot of thought. The only thing that weighs on me is my parents' deaths. I killed Gio, but now I know his death wasn't the end of it."

"And suddenly I don't like where this conversation is going."

I squeezed his hand. "I'm not making any decisions right now, nor do I plan to anytime soon."

"I have no problem with that." He pulled me closer for a kiss.

"Hey, are you guys done? Can I snag the leftovers?" Lucas called from the back door.

"I'm going to kill him," John muttered.

"You wanted to talk to him anyway. Might as well let him eat while you lecture him."

"Are you sure? I'd rather hang out with you than him."

"I'm sure. I'll occupy myself in the meantime. To be continued?"

"Count on it," he said, his voice low and husky in my ear. "And just so you know, once you're all better, I fully intend to have my way with you."

He kissed the inside of my ear, causing me to shiver. "Promises, promises," I teased. "Now go lecture the tomcat. I'll clean this up."

"So, are you guys going to answer me, or do I have to starve while you two make out?"

I laughed when John stood and marched toward the door. "What's your hurry? Did I recently hire a maid that you have to bang right fucking now?"

Smiling, I brought the plates inside. If someone had told me three months ago that I would be at this beautiful estate with my brother and the man who captured my heart, I would've laughed. After I killed Gio, I figured my life was forfeit and his family would find me and avenge his death. I never expected John would show me another option. Instead of waiting to die, I was hopeful and looking forward to a different life. A life I didn't know I wanted until I found it.

I'd hid in the shadows and avoided getting too close to people for what felt like forever. Now I had a family who accepted and loved me unconditionally. I'd been lucky enough to fall for a man who understood my complicated life and loved me in spite of it. Love. Something I never thought I'd be able to experience again and now welcomed with open arms.

"Hey, are you going to stare out that window all day?" Lucas chided, interrupting my thoughts.

I glanced over my shoulder. "Well, you aren't walking funny, so I guess he didn't castrate you yet?"

"Nah. We talked about my scandalous ways, and I told him I'd try to tone it down. But we spent most of the time talking about Massimo. No sightings of him yet, but Marco has been traveling. I'm not sure what it means yet, so we'll just keep an eye on him."

I finished wiping down the counter. "So, do you feel like putting some of your pent-up energy to good use? It's been a while since we've had a sparring session."

Over the past few weeks, I'd started dragging him to the gym to get in shape and teach him some basic fighting skills. He'd protested at first, but once he knew there was no getting out of it we had settled into a routine until he visited his mom in Venice and found a different workout.

"Why not? I might as well get my ass physically kicked as well."

"Oh, stop! You just need to keep practicing. The only reason I'm any good is because I've been training since I was a kid."

We headed down to the gym, where we spent most of the afternoon. After I got sick of hearing him whine about his aches and pains, I threw in the towel, literally at his head, and went back upstairs. The three of us watched a movie in the living room until Lucas's constant commentary caused John to banish him to watching the security feeds.

I felt I was being watched the moment I woke up the next morning. Sure enough, I opened my eyes and John was staring at me. He kissed my temple. "Good morning."

"It's not polite to stare," I grumbled.

"Couldn't help it. It's all your fault, really."

"How so?"

"By just being you. Every morning when I wake up and see you here with me, it just makes me thankful that we found each other."

"Me too, baby," I whispered.

"I love you. So much."

My heart swelled as it always did when he told me he loved me, but there was a new feeling this time. It scared me, but after everything we'd been through, I knew he was worth the risk. "I love you too."

He blinked. "What?"

I cupped his face with both my hands and smiled. "I love you, John Martinetti."

He inhaled sharply and suddenly his lips were on mine in a hungry, desperate kiss. I pulled him to me and wrapped both my arms around his neck, our lips never breaking contact. His tongue met mine and I let out a small moan. My hand moved to his upper back and held him to me, never wanting the moment to end. His lips moved to my neck where he continued his carnal assault. He nuzzled behind my ear and trailed soft kisses and bites until his mouth arrived between my breasts. My skin tingled when he kissed the skin gently while he massaged one breast through the thin fabric of my tank top.

"John," I gasped. My body was on fire and suddenly it felt like we were both grossly overdressed.

His head shot up. "What's the matter? Too fast? Did I hurt your ribs?"

I shook my head. "In fact, just the opposite."

He looked at the clock next to his side of the bed and buried his face in the crook of my neck. "Shit. I have to get up. I need to call someone, and if I call any later the guy won't be there."

"No," I whined. "Ten more minutes?"

"No way," he growled, giving me a quick kiss. "What I have planned for you is going to take a lot longer than ten minutes."

"Oh, all right," I grumbled, rolling away.

"Hey," he began, grasping my hip with his warm hand. "I won't apologize for wanting it to be more special than a ten-minute quickie first thing in the morning."

"You're right. I'm sorry."

"Don't apologize for wanting me. I sure as hell won't apologize for wanting you. I promise tonight will be worth it."

"Okay," I whispered, giving him one last kiss before we got up.

Thanks to our earlier bedroom shenanigans, I had a lot of excess energy to burn off. By the time I returned to the house and walked through the front door, I was pretty sure I'd covered almost every square inch of the property. The running had its desired effect, as I felt less...anxious afterwards. I showered and changed into a pair of denim shorts and a plain black tank top. It was a simple outfit, but one that showed off enough of my body to tease him a bit.

John moved all my clothes and belongings to his room shortly after we got back together, but it looked like we'd shared the room for much longer than a few weeks. We compromised on the color scheme, settling on dark gray with blue and purple accents. After joking about how two trained assassins were domesticated, we had a pillow fight like the mature adults we were. I smiled at the memory before heading downstairs in search of my man and breakfast.

The kitchen was empty, so I headed toward his office. I walked through the door expecting to find him sitting at his desk with a bored look on his face or still on one of his many phone calls. What I didn't expect to find was him trying to push away some bleach blond bimbo who appeared to be trying to shove her tongue down his throat.

"You know, if you'd just asked, I could've told you my boyfriend doesn't have his tonsils," I said loudly, crossing my arms. "It wasn't really necessary to check for yourself."

He pushed her away and looked at me with a mixture of shock and fear. I narrowed my eyes but kept my cool. In our line of work, things often weren't what they seemed, so he was bound to have a good explanation. I looked at the blond who stood next to him with a smug look on her face and did my best to show no reaction when I realized who she was.

Nicole fucking Turner, who stared at me with a mixture of annoyance and scorn. I took a deep, controlled breath and let it out, knowing the conversation I was about to have wouldn't be a pleasant one. She'd been my neighbor, my friend, and was the one person I thought had no part of the ruse in Portland. In fact, I had asked John if she was a spy and he had told me she wasn't. That was when I realized he'd worded his answer very specifically. According to him, she wasn't a spy, but apparently that didn't mean she hadn't been involved.

"Well hello, Nicole!" I greeted sweetly. "I'm guessing that isn't your real name."

"Hi, Larissa. You're right. My real name is Cassandra Noble. I've known Gianni here for a while."

"I see. He certainly never mentioned that. All he told me was that you weren't a spy."

"No, I'm definitely not a spy," she laughed. "Though it doesn't surprise me he didn't tell you my role."

"Oh, so it was a role? Well, I would certainly love to hear all about it."

"Liss," he began but stopped when I shot him an icy look.

"Gio sent me to make sure he stayed on task. Apparently, he picked up on the fact Gianni didn't really want to follow through with the project, so my job was to help move things along."

"And how did you do that?"

The grin on her face made me want to claw her eyes out. "Did you really think it was fate or coincidence that caused your paths to cross at that party? It was my job to bring you there, so we all had an early visual. 'Bathroom Guy' as you so cutely called him, had been waiting for you to show up all along. After that, it was just a matter of time before he made his move."

It would've been less painful if she'd slapped me. So many times he'd talked about that party and how it was fate that we met there. The same stupid fucking party that had been a setup all along, yet another part of the greater, orchestrated lie. I inhaled deeply and willed myself to keep my face blank. I refused to let either of them see me react, even as the pain crashed through my soul like a tidal wave. His eyes were on me, willing me to look at him, but I stubbornly kept my attention focused on her.

"Well, I must say that you both played your parts well. I'm sure you contributed to this project in various ways. Bravo. I certainly hope Gio compensated you well before I turned him into Psycho Tartare," I noted with sickening sweetness.

"I did other things, but I'm sure you don't want all the details. And yes, Gio certainly paid me well. However, I will say that Gianni here provided plenty of, shall we say, added benefits."

"Cassandra, I'm fucking warning you," he bit out, his voice low and deadly.

The fake smile plastered on my face was making my cheeks hurt. "Oh, please! I want to hear what she has to say! Cassandra, please do tell me about these added benefits he provided!"

She smirked. "You mean to tell me you didn't tell your sweet little 'Liss' here about our...friendship?"

So many times we'd talked about her friend with benefits, never realizing she was talking about him. The night I was attacked, she left early for a booty call. He left a couple hours later, but he was distracted, smiling and typing on his phone as he strolled out the door. Hours later, he lied to the police and said he came back to the office to retrieve his phone and found me. Was she the reason he lied to the cops?

It only took seconds for me to decide I didn't care. It was just another lie to add to the list, along with everything else I'd learned in the past ten minutes. What stung the worst was hearing her describe the whole thing as a project. I was merely an assignment, a checklist to them. Make sure the lying assassin crossed paths with the unsuspecting agent? Check. Help bolster the illusion there was a legitimate case? Check. Seduce the agent and make her feel like a fucking idiot? Checkity check.

"Well, that's certainly interesting. What I find even more interesting is that I know for a fact he left one of those booty calls early to take me to the hospital after I was attacked. The sex must not have been that great. I wouldn't know. He stayed with me all night each time I fucked him," I said with a smug smile. "Anyway, I'll let you two catch up. I'm just going to go upstairs and change. And schedule an appointment to get screened for STI's since apparently my ex-boyfriend has a thing for two faced sluts."

I spun on my heel and left the room, smiling to myself when she called me a bitch. The sounds of their argument faded once I made it upstairs. He called after me just before I entered what used to be our bedroom. I grabbed my knapsack from the closet and found the black metal object hidden in the side pocket. It slipped onto my left ring finger as his voice got closer.

"Please open the safe and give me back my gun," I ordered the moment I felt him behind me.

"Baby, I'm sorry. I can explain."

"Save it. Give me my gun so I can go."

"No," he growled, grabbing my arm and spinning me around to face him. "Not until you let me explain."

I flexed my left finger, extending the hidden blade inside the ring that I used to kill the Sardi henchman in Rome. Holding his gaze, I brought my hand to rest along his inner thigh, just below his balls. He froze.

"Touch me again, asshole, and the only thing I'll let you explain will be your choice between me slicing your femoral artery or castrating you," I hissed. "Gun. Now."

His eyes widened, and he slowly stepped back with his hands in the air. He studied my face for a moment before opening the safe in the back of his closet. "Larissa, I am begging you not to leave here," he pleaded as the door opened. He handed me the small metal box. "Massimo is still out there. It's only a matter of time before he starts looking for you again."

"I'd rather take my chances with him than spend one more minute here with you."

Panic filled his eyes as he watched me lift the Colt out of the box and load a clip. "Hit me. Shoot me in the ass. Do something. I deserve it."

I dropped the case into my bag and tucked the pistol into my waistband. "You're not worth it. Neither of you are. Now get on the intercom and let security know I'm free to leave."

He went to the phone on his night table. His hands shook as he dialed. The intercom system beeped, and he closed his eyes. "This is Gianni. Larissa has permission to leave the estate unescorted. I repeat, she does not need to be accompanied by either Lucas or myself. Please allow her to leave if she approaches the gate. Thank you."

"Don't even try to find me this time," I warned before stalking out of the bedroom.

"Keys are in the left drawer of the table by the front door." He followed me to the stairs, but stayed several steps back. "You can take any car you want. Liss, I—"

I shot him a nasty glare and he stopped in his tracks before I ran downstairs. I rounded the corner and made my way to his office to say my goodbyes to Cassandra. She jumped when I threw open the doors and breezed into the room. "I wish we could catch up, but I have a million and a half better places I'd rather be than here, so I'm going to go. I hope you're doing well, Cassandra," I gushed, enjoying the look on her face when she saw I was armed. "Oh, and just so you know, he and I messed around a bit this morning, so I can't guarantee he won't be thinking of me for at least a bit if you get him to fuck you. Good luck!"

He sat at the bottom of the stairs of the foyer with his face buried in his hands. As I walked closer, he raised his head abruptly and his eyes met mine. I brushed past and stopped at the table by the door. After shuffling through the drawer, I grabbed a set of keys, along with a disposable cell phone.

"Liss, please."

I grabbed the doorknob and turned to him one last time. "Go fuck yourself," I replied before slamming the door behind me.

The two guards stationed by the front door nodded as I strolled past them to the garage. I entered the code into the keypad and walked directly to John's red Audi R8 with a smile. Him and his red Audis. Less than five minutes later I sped down the long, winding driveway and away from the estate that had been my home for nearly three months. With each passing mile, my heart felt heavier and my eyes stung more with the tears I held back. Shaking my head, I pushed myself to keep going. There was nothing for me back there, nothing he could have said or done that would have made me go back. However, there was one person who needed to know why I disappeared.

I pulled over and retrieved my phone. Lucas went into the city to meet one of his contacts, and I'd be long gone by the time he got home. It killed me not being able to say goodbye in person, so I did the next best thing. I typed quickly as the tears in my eyes threatened to fall.

John and I broke up. I won't go into detail about what happened, but I had to leave. I'm sorry you weren't there so I could properly say goodbye. I'm okay, but it's for the best that he and I stay away from each other. I'll try to get in touch once I get to where I'm going.

The tears finally fell, and moments later I was hunched over the steering wheel trying to calm my sobbing. He promised things would be different, and I fell for it again. I didn't know if I was more hurt about his repeated betrayal or angry with myself for allowing it to happen a second time. Exhaling slowly, I fought to get my emotions back under control. There was no way of knowing if he intended to honor my demand not to follow me. Wiping my eyes, I drove off. By the time I got to Venice, I had a clear plan. I parked near the seaport but left the car running. My heart hammered in my chest as I dialed the phone, watching the people make their way from the terminal toward the city as I waited for the other end of the line to answer.

"This is Felton Lynch. Who am I speaking to?" His voice was guarded.

"This is Field Operations Officer Larissa Donovan, requesting reactivation and extraction."

"Larissa? Is that really you?"

"There are only two people who have this phone number, Felton. I'm not in the most secure of areas. We can catch up once I'm stateside."

"Yes, of course. I'm reactivating you right now. Where and when do you need to be extracted?"

I'd studied the map on my phone and found a location across the Adriatic that nobody back in Verona would've considered. It was a pity since it was suggested to me by Maja, one of John's maids and also one of Lucas's many conquests. According to her, it was quite beautiful.

"Koper, near the port. Give me 24 hours. Text the coordinates to this phone ASAP. I'll keep it for another four hours and then it'll be tossed."

"Copy. We'll talk more once you're stateside. And the first thing I want to know is what the hell you're doing in Slovenia."

"I'm not. But I will be soon. Later."

I tossed the phone in my bag and put the car in gear. It took a few minutes to find a large, empty area but soon enough I found the perfect spot. Not long after, I watched the car gracefully plummet into the sea. Smiling as the roof disappeared below the water, I hitched my backpack over my shoulder and headed for the water taxis.

Chapter Thirteen

Fallout

John

Empty.

Lost.

I sat on the steps and watched through the glass panes in the front door as she took my car, sped out of the driveway and out of my life. My breathing increased as I fought the bile rising in my throat. I closed my eyes as the crater in my heart widened.

I lost her and it was my own fucking fault.

My brain nearly shattered from all the conflicting shit that ricocheted inside. I stood up and paced, desperate to focus, hoping to figure out what to do. Pausing briefly, I gazed out the door once more. It was all a dream, I told myself. A horrible nightmare that I'd wake up from any second. My eyes darted to the open garage door, to the empty spot where my Audi was parked, and the pain tore through me again. It wasn't a dream. The sound of Cassandra's high heels on the floor drew closer. I inhaled deeply and resisted the temptation to strangle her.

"Are you fucking happy?" I snarled, turning to face her.

She smirked. "Don't act like you're innocent. You're just as much to blame as me. And don't act like you weren't a willing participant. I seem to remember there were a couple of times you sought *me* out."

Glaring at her, it pained me to admit she was right. I should have told Liss the truth long ago. When we got back together, we agreed there would be no more lies or secrets between us. I'd meant to tell her so many times, but I was a coward and allowed my fears of losing her to convince me to keep quiet. In the end, that silence cost me what I'd tried so hard to keep.

"You were a drunken mistake, Cassandra."

"Sure," she scoffed. "The first time. But yet you kept coming back for more."

I laughed humorlessly. "You were the reason I stopped drinking! I was thankful for the hangover that morning because it gave me a reason to leave quickly. As far as 'coming back for more', don't flatter yourself. It was the easiest way to keep you away from Larissa. I imagined you were someone else. Every. Single. Time. Can you guess who?"

"You bastard!"

"Lucas can barely stand to even talk to you! And that's saying something!"

"I fucking hate you!" she screamed.

"Did you honestly expect me to overlook what you did to her? You disgusted me even more, you sick bitch!"

Her face contorted and her eyes showed her fury. She opened her mouth to respond, but her eyes widened at something behind me. The front door slammed, and I spun around.

"What in the fuck did you do?" Lucas yelled, holding up his cell phone.

Fuck. Fear crept into me as his eyes went from my face to Cassandra's. There was literally nothing to say to calm his rage, but I had to try. "Lucas, I don't know what she told you, but I can explain."

"You son of a bitch." He stalked toward me, pulled back his arm, and delivered a stiff uppercut to my jaw. Jesus fucking Christ on a crutch. She'd taught him well.

After the second punch, this time to my eye, I fell back on the steps. "Just let me explain," I wheezed.

"Get up, fucker!"

My head throbbed as I gripped the banister and slowly stood. I was barely upright when his fist connected with my jaw a second time. I clutched my face, which was a mistake. The distraction gave him the perfect opening to kick me in the balls. As I doubled over, he delivered one last punch that knocked me to the floor.

"Stop it!" Cassandra screamed at the top of her lungs.

"And you," he glowered, pointing a finger at her. "You're god-damned lucky I don't hit women, or your beating would be twice as bad as his for what you did. I knew you were a disgusting piece of shit, but to be an accomplice to that, knowing that would happen to another woman," his voice trailed off.

Her eyes widened as he marched toward her. She retreated back-ward, her eyes frantic and pleading when her back slammed against the wall. "I'm sorry," she got out in a shaky whisper.

"Lucas, stop," I ordered gently as I dragged myself off the floor. "Cassandra was just leaving. Weren't you?"

She nodded as she watched Lucas's every move. I should've known she was up to something when I read her message, but I'd been desperate to get even the tiniest shred of intel on my uncle. Cassandra still worked for him, even if she'd also failed in bringing Liss to him. Whoring herself out to half his men helped her gain intel, too.

"If I ever catch you in this house again, you'll leave in a fucking bag. That's a promise," he bit out. "Get the fuck out of here."

Her hands trembled as she tossed her purse over her shoulder. She took several steps around him and then sprinted to the door. The front door slammed for the third time in less than an hour, and I groaned loudly.

"What in the fuck was she doing here?" he demanded, clenching his fists.

"She said she had intel on Massimo. Turns out it was all bullshit and she's the one who's been passing info on to him."

"So for all your lecturing about me fucking around, it turns out you were screwing the leak in this house?"

"Actually, *you've* been screwing the leak in this house. Remember when Liss told Maja you were banging Valentina?"

He paled. "Oh god."

"That's right, asshole. Paolo has been keeping tabs on the staff. Val and Cassandra are friends, so much so that Cassandra is renting the room above Val's sister's cafe and they all hang out and 'catch up' whenever Val goes to visit. So yeah, I'm an idiot for fucking Cassandra. You share equal blame in this situation."

He sat on the bottom step and put his head in his hands. "What happened this morning? Lissa didn't tell me anything specific. All she said was it was best you guys stay away from each other."

I sighed and sat down next to him. "Cassandra said she had info on Massimo and that I'd want to hear it. I suspected she was full of shit, but we haven't heard a single peep, so I took a chance. She said she'd be here first thing this morning. While I was waiting for her to show up, Mauricio called and wanted to talk about security at your mom's house. While I was on the phone, Cassandra came in."

"Shit."

"I realized she had to know Liss was here when she started hitting on me as soon as she got here. I shot it down, but it didn't stop her from shoving her tongue down my throat. Of course, that's when Liss walked in and that's when Cassandra told her everything. And I do mean *everything*."

"I'm surprised she didn't shoot you."

"She told me I wasn't worth shooting."

"Why didn't you tell her?"

"I'm a fucking coward. I knew she wouldn't take it well. And I didn't want to hurt her. She considered Cassandra a friend and I was reluctant to be the one to tell her how badly that bitch was willing to betray her."

"John, she's a fucking assassin. I think she could've taken it. You're the one who lectured me about underestimating her. She would've been pissed and probably upset, but I think she would've understood. You asked her to let you earn back her trust, and she finds out you've been keeping things from her. How did you think *that* was going to go?"

"I'm an asshole," I said, running my hand through my hair.

"We're both assholes. I'm the one who gave Val a reason to spy on us."

"Liss will forgive you, man. You had no way of knowing this would happen. I fucked this up all on my own, knowing full well I could lose her."

"She could come around."

I shook my head, resigned to the truth. There was no way in hell she'd forgive me a second time, not now that she knew our first meeting was a setup. The fact she heard it from Cassandra only made it worse. "She held a knife to my balls. I'd say the chances of her forgiving me are gone."

"Fuck," he swore under his breath. After a few minutes of silence, he stood up. "Let's go."

"Where are we going?"

"To take your mind off this for a little while before you cry, jack-ass."

"You better not be taking me to a strip club."

"No, I'm not taking you to a strip club," he mocked, rolling his eyes. "Game room. Let's see how tough you are after a couple rounds of pool."

"Keep dreaming if you think you've got a chance at beating me."

He demolished me in two rounds of pool, but I redeemed myself by winning three rounds of darts. Despite all the shit talking and dirty jokes, it was as if we had an unspoken agreement not to mention Liss, Cassandra or any part of the mess we still needed to fix. It was late afternoon when we ate, and while I'd managed to take my mind off the shit for a while, it all crashed into me the minute we crossed the foyer.

Lucas pulled open the fridge. "Beer?"

I stood by the sink in a daze. His question didn't even penetrate until he repeated my name several times. "Sure," I answered, staring out the window.

"Here, you need to eat something," he ordered, placing a container of reheated food next to the bottle.

I nodded glumly before digging in. I tried my best to focus on eating. It was the only way I could keep all my emotions in check. Cassandra probably hadn't even driven her car more than ten feet past our driveway before she called Massimo to tell him that Liss was in the wind. My stomach dropped and the food I'd just eaten felt like lead. I pushed the container away.

"John, you need to see this." Lucas pointed at a folder on the island with a note attached. "Max found something."

I grabbed the folder and studied the few pages inside. The more I read, however, the deeper my anger grew. "Holy shit. Soren and Massimo are still in contact with each other."

"What the fuck? Where is he?"

I scanned the papers. "Max couldn't find a location, but it looks like he's still in the States. He found bank and phone records that show the two have been in contact and working together."

"How long?"

"Last communication was a few months ago. Soren opened an offshore account when he first arrived in New York and I have several wire transfers from several of Massimo's smaller accounts. There's a cluster of phone calls from his burner phones to what I can assume are other burner phones right around the time of each transfer."

His face contorted, and he opened his mouth to speak when his phone rang. Groaning, he answered. I turned back to the papers in my hand and read and reread them, trying to glean as much information as I could.

"Are you fucking kidding me? When?" he yelled. He listened to the caller, pinching the bridge of his nose. "What? Fuck! No. Just...fucking clean it up. No, I'll tell him. Yeah. Bye." He tossed the phone on the counter and took a long drink of his beer before shaking his head. After a couple of seconds, he threw the bottle against the wall.

"What is it?"

He ran his hand through his hair. "Which news would you like to hear first, our uncle or your girlfriend?"

"What happened to her?" My voice was barely audible.

"She drove your car into the water just outside of Venice and disappeared. That's the good news."

"And the bad?"

"Massimo arrived back in Bari last night, returning from Athens."

My blood ran cold. "Son of a bitch."

I gripped the back of my head and paced the kitchen. This was bad. His sole reason for going to Athens was to make his final move against her.

"John."

"I know."

Athens was the home of my cousins, Athena and Alexa Sardi, the product of a very short-lived affair between Massimo and a Greek heiress. Shortly after their birth, he had their mother killed, and the girls were raised by associates who were loyal to the family and willing to train two small girls to become vicious killers. Fighting one was a formidable task. Taking them on together was a sure death sentence. I wasn't even sure Liss could survive it.

"If they find her..."

I held up my hand. "They won't. We'll find her first."

"How?"

"Honestly? I don't know. She might shoot me, but we *will* find her. I promise you."

"I'll make sure she doesn't shoot you," he joked. "But we can't lose her."

"I've already lost her."

"No, you haven't," he said. "You two love each other and you've been through way too much for it to be over. I'll take the bullet if I have to."

Chapter Fourteen

Rebellion

Larissa

I stifled a yawn as four armed military police officers escorted me down the hall. It was five in the morning and the hallway, as well as this section of the building, was empty aside from our little group. It wasn't often that a CIA officer sought refuge at a military base and certain protocols had to be followed.

Three days after my phone call, I arrived at the Air Force Reserve base outside Miami. The trip was long and miserable, which was an unfortunate caveat of covert travel, quick arrivals and painfully slow departures. I couldn't complain too much since I was the one who selected an extraction point in Eastern Europe. Departures out of Western Europe were easier, but with ease came the risk of being seen and tracked. And when you might be wanted for kidnapping an FBI agent, it was best to stay off everyone's radar.

We arrived at the base commander's office and entered after a loud, booming voice granted us entry. One MP opened the door and led me inside while the other three remained. Commander Robert Paxton stood at his desk with his arms behind his back. He was tall and had an athletic build that was easily noticed through the gray t-shirt and black hoodie he wore. He appeared to be in his mid to late forties, judging by the light flecks of silver in his black hair and the wrinkles that surrounded his brown eyes. His complexion was tan, which could have been because of his natural skin tone or from the time spent in the sun. He nodded at both of us.

"Thank you, Private. Please remain in the reception area to escort her when we're done."

I stood a couple feet behind Paxton's desk after the MP saluted and left. "Good morning, Commander," I greeted politely.

"Good morning, Agent Yates."

"Members of the CIA prefer to be called 'officers'," a voice interjected from my left.

My head snapped toward the interruption and my eyes widened when I saw Felton seated in a chair. As always, he was dressed impeccably in a black suit and a crisp white shirt. He curtly nodded at me, though his eyes showed warmth.

"My apologies," Robert replied. "I wasn't aware."

I turned back to the commander. "It's not widely known. I see Mr. Lynch is here."

"Stephanie," Felton greeted.

I'd never worked using my own name, which kept my identity secret and therefore safe. However, after two years it felt odd, almost foreign. I had become accustomed to just being Larissa Donovan. Reminding myself I was no longer a civilian, I mentally shook myself. Officer Stephanie Yates nodded to her boss.

"Yes, it seems my base is being turned into some kind of hub for wayward CIA officers," Paxton retorted.

"And once again, you have my apologies, Robert," Felton countered. "I didn't know Marianna would need to base her operation in this area until I had already secured this location for Stephanie. It was last minute, and not my intent to disrupt your operations with two of my staff."

"We'll address Marianna and her operation later," he snapped. "Our chief concern at the moment is deciding how to handle Officer Yates. How long are you planning to be here?"

"A week, maximum. She will accompany me back to Langley after Marianna leaves for her assignment," Felton answered before I spoke.

My anger flared at his intrusion. A week as a guest at an air force base that didn't want me there wasn't what I'd planned. I wanted to visit my parents' graves where I could finally tell them once and for all that one of the men responsible for their deaths was dead. I wanted to sit under the stars, reflect on the past months, and plan my next steps. Drawing in a deep breath, I attempted to stay calm while giving a piercing look to Felton. He narrowed his eyes and returned the glare with equal venom. An argument was definitely in our future. Luckily, Robert's attention was on the computer monitor in front of him and he missed our exchange.

His voice stopped our stare down. "I have a room Officer Yates can stay in here in the administration building. I must insist that you not go anywhere on the base unescorted. Your presence here must be kept as quiet as possible. If you need access to any of the buildings or services, please let your escort know and we'll get it arranged."

"Understood, sir," I replied with a nod.

"Private Gomez is outside and will show you to your room and will be your escort for the duration of today. If you have questions or need anything, please speak to him."

"Thank you, sir," I nodded, recognizing I was dismissed.

Shooting Felton another glare, I left the room. Private Chris Gomez wasn't one for conversation, as it turned out, so the walk to my room was quiet. Once we reached our destination, he told me he would be in the hall if I needed anything and reminded me I wasn't to go anywhere alone. I nodded and closed the door, welcome to finally be free from all human interaction.

I plodded to the small light brown couch and flopped on my back. The trip was long, grueling, and included boats full of rowdy tourists and smelly cargo ships. By the time I arrived at the Homestead Air Reserve Base, I was ready to just lay down on the runway and take a nap, no matter who it offended.

My body jolted at the loud knock on my door. I brushed my hair out of my face and slumped to the door. "Yeah?"

"Stephanie, can we please speak for a moment?"

I groaned. Felton was the last person I wanted to talk to, but there were too many matters to address. I was shocked he approved my extraction and part of me dreaded the cost of his good deed. I also knew ignoring him would do no good. He was as stubborn as me and wouldn't leave until he spoke his mind. I said nothing and let him inside. As soon as the door closed, he pulled me into a tight hug.

"Larissa, please never disappear like that again," he scolded, hugging me tighter.

"Not like I had much of a choice since I didn't know who to trust," I retorted. "Though I do apologize for our last meeting. I could've handled it better."

Probably the understatement of the decade. After finding out all the FBI agents in Portland were in Gio's pocket, and that I was a person of interest in the murder of one of the mercenaries masquerading as a student, I went on a bit of a rampage. I grabbed Barton as he left his gym and then held both men hostage in Felton's office. Granted, most of Barton's injuries came from being shoved into the trunk of a car. In my defense, he hadn't needed to put up so much of a fight.

"I actually thought your reaction was pretty measured, given the circumstances."

"I doubt Special Agent Kane would agree with that."

His gaze went to the floor. "No, Barton hasn't been so understanding. He called me every few weeks for the first year or so looking for you. He still calls every few months to threaten me with an obstruction charge."

"Of course he does. That's why I took the less than scenic route back here. What about you? Should I worry why you were so agreeable to bringing me back?"

"I was just so relieved to finally hear from you. You have no idea how worried I was. What if you'd been hurt? Or killed?"

I held up my hand to silence him. "Felton, I'm exhausted. Can we finish this discussion later? I—"

He grabbed my left arm and turned it toward me. "What the fuck is this?" he asked in a low growl, pointing at the scar.

"A battle scar." I pulled away from his grip and tried to step back.

He grabbed the other arm and inspected it. "No, that's a denial of your fucking SF86!"

The SF86 was a questionnaire I had to complete each time I was "re-hired" to keep my security clearance. Now that he had seen clear evidence of my suicide attempt, he'd be required to report it. I fully intended to disclose it. If I didn't, my security clearance would be denied, most likely for life. Once the form was reviewed, I'd have to submit documentation of my treatment and undergo a few assessments before I was reinstated.

I yanked my arm away and moved to the far side of the room. "No, it is *not* an automatic denial. I have the records to show I spent six months in an inpatient facility. A trained psychiatrist gave me a thorough examination and declared that my condition was adequately treated. And if you ever touch me like that again, I'll rip your goddamned arm off!"

"I'm sorry." He held up both hands. "Can you please tell me what happened?"

I sat on the couch and motioned for him to sit in the armchair to my right. As overbearing as he'd been since my arrival, I needed space.

My voice was quiet as I recounted meeting Titus and everything that had happened after that. After I told him about the suicide attempt, I watched him closely.

"I'm sorry that happened to you, but you need to see where I'm coming from. It will still be a blemish on your record! What were you thinking? Why didn't you call me?"

I narrowed my eyes. "I was thinking I was in a severe depression because of the miscarriage I'd just had on top of all the other shit that happened. As for why I didn't call you, maybe because things weren't so good between us at the time and I knew you'd be an insensitive prick about it. And I see I was right."

"I'm sorry. I realize it probably sounds really shitty of me. But you need to understand the career implications of this!"

"Probably?" I yelled.

"And who, pray tell, was the father of this baby?"

I took a deep breath and braced myself for his anger. "John Martinetti."

"What?" he shouted, standing up. "The man who was nothing but a stain on the intelligence community from the time he started until he was forced out?"

"Yes, Felton. The same one who is the nephew of the mobster I've been hunting for the last twenty years. What's more of a stain, the man himself or the fact you hired him? Because I would love to hear your explanation, especially to your bosses, about how you didn't know he was related to the Sardi family."

He recoiled at my words. "You're right," he conceded quietly. "I completely failed to vet him and was put on probation for a year for my carelessness. I'm still under a great deal of scrutiny. But you must understand that him and his issues are the reason so many rules were put in place so that you could work for both agencies. To prevent things like this from happening!"

"Well, I'm sorry to make life difficult for you, Felton. How selfish of me to be a fucking human being and have a mental breakdown! It's not like I planned for any of this to happen!"

"Lissa, I'm sorry."

"Clearly," I snapped. "Look, my situation results from the choices I made and has nothing to do with you. I know some of them weren't the best choices, but they were made by me and therefore I'll take responsibility for them. And since you're more worried about protocols and appearances than about my actual wellbeing, this subject is closed."

"I care about your wellbeing. I'm just trying to be realistic. It's great to have you back, but there might be a delay in getting you fully reinstated."

"I'll just wait for my review. So, just give me the damn SF86 on your way out."

"What do you mean?"

"I mean, I want you to leave the form and get the hell out. It was a long trip. I'm tired, and I just can't stand to be around you right now. You treated me like a goddamned child in the commander's office when you dictated I was stuck here with you until you decide to head back to Langley. I planned to stay for a couple of days and then go to Alexandria to see my parents' graves. It seems you are now more interested in lecturing and complaining at me for having a moment of weakness. So, thank you for approving my extraction, but I don't feel like being lectured anymore. Please leave."

"Let's talk about this. Please."

I stomped to the door and threw it open. "Get out. Now."

"Is there a problem, Ms. Yates?" Private Gomez asked from the hallway.

"Not anymore. Mr. Lynch was just leaving."

"Stephanie."

"We will speak later."

We exchanged glares as he walked past. Once he turned down the hall, I went to close my door when I noticed Private Gomez's wide brown eyes and raised eyebrows.

"Bosses," I said as casually as I could muster.

"At least you can yell back at yours, ma'am," he replied with a nod. "Are you okay? Is there anything I can get you?"

"Not unless you've got a pack of cigarettes and a bottle of liquor I can buy off you."

"No, but there's the commissary."

I found my wallet and handed him a fifty. "One pack of the cheapest, grossest cigarettes you can find and then the rest on some good tequila and a couple of limes."

His brows creased. "You want *bad* cigarettes?"

"If they're gross, I won't enjoy them and if I don't enjoy them, I won't smoke them all. That said, no menthols. I do have my standards."

"Fair enough, ma'am."

Another man, who was tall and slender, joined us in the hall and Gomez gave him a nod. He briefly introduced me to Private Charlie Myers, who handed me a bag from a local fast-food restaurant. I was confused until Charlie explained Chris figured I was hungry and asked him to grab me some food. Chris then left, promising to have my purchases when he returned

I wolfed down the cheeseburger inside and soon it felt like my eyes couldn't stay open another moment. I crawled into the twin sized bed and pulled the blanket over me with a deep sigh. Exhaustion provided relief from the ache in my heart. I missed Lucas terribly, and hated leaving without telling him goodbye. Hopefully, I'd be able to get in touch soon.

My thoughts wandered to John. I'd tried to avoid thinking about him at first, but it was impossible. Instead, I let my hurt and sadness wash over me. Maybe if those feelings ran their course this time, I'd finally be able to move on. Until then, I was stuck in an emotional hell where thinking about him hurt, but I also couldn't stop.

I remembered our conversation one night about fate, and how he had made our meeting at that party sound like being together was written in the stars. Thankfully, I didn't believe in fate, so the fact it was all a lie didn't hurt as bad. That's what I kept telling myself anyway. Thinking of the sparks between us at the party made my chest ache. When I closed my eyes, visions of him and Nicole taunted me. I felt sickened at the realization that our first kiss had been mere hours after he fucked her.

I spent hours flopping around in bed and staring at the ceiling. Eventually, I finally fell into a restless sleep filled with horrible dreams featuring the two of them. I woke up in the early afternoon and by then Chris had returned with my cigarettes and booze. Sick of feeling like shit, I decided to just numb myself and after several shots of what turned out to be probably the best tequila I'd had in a very long time, I passed out. To hell with the hangover.

Over the next few days, I threw myself into training and getting my reinstatement paperwork in order. I provided the documentation of my hospitalization and recovery in Rome, and my case manager said my clearance would be approved in the next few days. I hung up the phone after that conversation with feelings of relief and accomplishment. Being back on track felt great.

Felton and I avoided each other. Private Gomez made it clear to the other MPs that I didn't want to see him. He tried to contact me several times, but soon gave up. On my fifth day on the base, I found my access to the gym and other facilities was suddenly limited.

I interpreted that to mean I was no longer the only CIA officer on the base.

I'd never met Marianna Chambers, but I knew her reputation as an expert in covert operations in the Caribbean and Latin American countries. The rumor was that her upcoming assignment was an extremely delicate mission with serious political implications. I would've been lying if I said I hadn't been curious.

The next day my access to the facilities was restored, though only when the buildings were closed to the troops. After a very early morning jog, I headed to the shooting range. It was a little after three in the morning, but the quiet was a relaxing escape from my already overcrowded mind. Did I envision John and his traitorous balls as a target at any time? Maybe.

"Mind if I practice with you?" a soft voice with a hint of an accent asked as I fixed a paper target on the clip.

I turned and found a very tall, slim woman close to my age in the doorway. Her dark brown eyes were wide as she strolled into the room hesitantly. Her short platinum blond hair was pulled into a tight ponytail at the nape. I could tell it wasn't her natural color, but it didn't clash with her tan complexion.

"Sure." I offered my hand. "Stephanie Yates."

"Ah, the other CIA distraction," she laughed as she shook it. "I've heard about you. Marianna Chambers."

"Heard of you as well. Apparently, the fact that we're both here means the base is being overrun by the CIA, according to the base commander.

"Well, I'm sure he was even more annoyed when I arrived with three additional people. Fortunately, we're only here for a couple of days and then they're headed to Cuba."

"Cuba? Wow." In all my travels around the world, I'd never been there. It certainly wasn't by choice. The powers that be decided that my background and skill set was better suited to Europe. Perhaps I'd found an opportunity to change that.

"Yeah, it should be a pretty straightforward case. However, since it's Cuba and the political situation being what it is, we still have to exercise some caution. That's why I'm sending two officers instead of going myself."

"In my experience, the supposedly easy cases have the greatest chances of going sideways," I said.

"What brings you to Florida? Are you on a case?"

"I just returned from extended leave. I'm waiting for my clearance to go through and then I'm hoping to get back to it."

"That's a shame. If you were able, I'd ask if you'd like to accompany my team. Because you're right. The simple cases can get derailed so easily."

"If you don't mind me asking, what's the job?"

"Sounds like a bit of a cliché, but we're returning a general's wayward daughter. There's more to it than that, of course, but I'm not at liberty to give the full details unless you're officially on the case."

I nodded ruefully. "Sadly, it's not an option until my clearance is approved. The case manager said it should be done in the next couple of days."

"I could see about moving it along," she offered. "I can make the argument we need you on the case. But I'll need approval from your handler."

I hesitated. That meant talking to Felton, and probably another argument. On the other hand it would be a perfect opportunity to return to work, to prove I was ready. Being idle at the base was wearing on me. My return to Virginia could wait, I decided.

"I'm definitely interested. I'm supposed to meet with him today, so I'll see what he says. I'll let you know."

"Perfect! I'll see what I can find out about your clearance."

"Ms. Yates, we need to get going," Chris suddenly interrupted.

I nodded and after exchanging a quick goodbye with Marianna, we left. We walked in silence for a few minutes before he suddenly spoke.

"Are you going to ask him?"

I shrugged. "We've avoided each other long enough. And I really want this."

"Do you think he'll let you? You two didn't part on the best of terms."

"I'll use my powers of persuasion," I joked.

"That's what worries me," he laughed. "Were you planning to go up to the roof tonight?"

After two days of being cooped up in the small guest room, I'd begged him to let me go outside and sit under the stars. He grudgingly unlocked the door and let me sit out on the roof. I guessed he thought I would cause trouble and seemed relieved when all I did was sit and stare at the stars for a few hours while smoking my shitty cigarettes.

"If that's okay. I don't want to cause any problems."

He shook his head. "Nah, you'll be fine. I'll just let Charlie know when he takes over."

"Thanks."

Later that afternoon, Charlie escorted me to Felton's room. I stood in the hall for a few minutes before knocking. Finally, the door opened after what felt like an eternity. His eyes widened when he saw me.

"Ms. Yates?"

"Can we talk in private?"

His room was like mine, with the only difference being a different shade of boring, neutral colors. My room appeared to be medium beige while his was light beige.

"First, I wanted to apologize for the other day," I said as I sat on the couch. "I get that you were concerned and I should've handled it better. So I'm sorry for that."

He exhaled. "I'm sorry, too. When I heard Gio was killed, I knew it was you and it worried me because I knew that meant his brother would be hunting you. I thought I would've heard from you sooner, and got scared when I didn't. You have no idea how relieved I was to finally hear your voice and know you were still alive. And when I finally saw you, saw the scars, and heard what you had been through." He shook his head. "I know I'm not Seamus, Lissa, but I think in that moment I got an idea of what it felt like to be a parent. I was scared, angry, disappointed, but relieved all at once about everything you told me. And I could've handled that better, too."

I crossed the room and gave him a hug. He hesitated, but soon his arms wrapped around me. "What was Karina's response to hearing that I was back in the States?"

His arms dropped to his sides. "Oh god, Larissa. You don't know."

"Know what?" I asked slowly. I looked up and my stomach clenched at the sadness on his face. "No! What happened?"

His eyes shone with unshed tears. "There was an ice storm, and she took a nasty fall down the front steps. Broke her collarbone. She made it through surgery, but a few days later she started having trouble breathing. By the time they found the blood clot in her lung, it was too late."

"Oh my god! When did this happen?"

"Middle of November, just before last Thanksgiving."

"I'm so sorry!" I cried, embracing him again. "If I'd known I would've been here."

"I know. She knew you loved her and she loved you, too."

I nodded silently, keeping my opinion to myself. Karina and I had a complicated relationship. She and Felton were childless by choice, only to suddenly have a traumatized six-year-old in her home. While Felton had welcomed me with open arms, refusing to listen to anyone who suggested sending me away, Karina hadn't been so generous. She was never abusive, but she'd made it clear it wasn't her choice to take me in. Our relationship didn't improve until after I left home for college, but even then we were never very close.

"Are you okay?"

He nodded slowly. "It was rough at first, but it's gotten better. I threw myself into work. Probably not the healthiest way to deal with it, but it helped."

"I know how that goes. In fact, I'm hoping I can do the same."

"What is it you're wanting to do?"

I took a deep breath. "I ran into Marianna this morning and she told me a bit about Cuba. I want in."

"You haven't been reinstated yet."

"It should be approved in the next couple of days. She's calling my case worker to see about moving it along. I just need your approval."

His jaw clenched. "Absolutely not. I'm sorry, Larissa. I know you want to return to work, but I cannot authorize this."

"Why not?"

"It's too soon. Less than a week ago, you were still on leave. Once you get your clearance approved, you'll be back to work soon enough."

"What if my approval comes through before they leave? She said it would be simple. I haven't been back long, so an easy job would be perfect for me. Right?"

"No. I refuse to approve this. Let it go."

"Not until you give me a legitimate reason. I want to get back to work! What's the problem?"

"I don't feel you're ready."

"And what makes you feel I'm not ready?" I challenged.

"Your defiant attitude, for starters," he bit back.

"I have a caseworker who feels I'm ready. Since you don't agree, I'd like to hear your *professional* opinion why you won't approve this."

His face hardened. "Look here, young lady. I know we have some differences we need to work through, but suddenly opposing everything I say reflects your state of mind. And that, coupled with your prior psychiatric issues, makes me doubt your fitness for duty."

"You are unbelievable!" I raged. "Langley doesn't doubt my ability to do my job. They have every single file from Rome, and I passed their assessment. So your doubts are contradictory to the professional assessment of the CIA."

"Langley might approve your clearance, but I have the final say in what job you can or cannot do. And I still say you're not approved."

"You know what? Fine. I'll call headquarters and ask for a new handler."

"On what grounds?" he challenged.

"Your lack of professional integrity for starters. How about hiring the nephew of a mob boss without vetting him? Remind me how long you were suspended for that? And since you also appear to have a personal bias against me, I no longer feel you're acting in my best interests or the interests of the agency."

His eyes widened. "Do you have any idea how much damage that kind of complaint would do?"

"Just giving my professional opinion."

"You ruthless bitch!" he roared.

"Just as you made me," I shot back. "You must be so proud." Spinning on my heel, I stormed out of his room without another word. I was halfway down the corridor before Charlie caught up to me.

"I take it that didn't go well?"

"He's a fucking asshole," I raged, stalking down the hall.

Felton's words repeated in my head once I was alone in my room. Was it too soon to go back to work? Was it so wrong that I wanted to get back to what I was good at? I refused to allow him to question my motivation. Instead, I would defy his doubts and prove him wrong. A soft knock on the door stopped my pacing. Knowing it wasn't Felton, I scurried to answer, curious to find out who it was.

"Hey!" Marianna chirped as she breezed into the room. "Your case worker told me your clearance will be approved within forty-eight hours. It's cutting it close, but it should be approved by the time the other two leave. Did you talk to your handler?"

"He's not signing off on it. According to him, it's too soon and he doesn't think I'm ready since I just got back from leave."

"Do I need to speak to him?"

"Thank you, but no. That will just make it worse. I'll talk to him again and see if I can get him to reconsider."

She nodded. "I understand. Just keep me posted."

I closed the door and sighed. Deciding to take my mind off my conflict with Felton, I sat down at the table, grabbed a pad of paper and started writing. For such a short letter, I struggled with the words that fully expressed how I felt. Once it was done, I stuffed it into an envelope and gave it to Charlie to mail as soon as possible. I begged him to keep it secret, and after a few seconds of scrutiny, he nodded.

Returning to the table, I opened the laptop loaned to me by the IT department. I navigated to the CIA's employee system and updated my personal information, adding a new emergency contact. In the future, if I were to be injured or killed in the line of duty, the agency would notify Mr. Lucas Luccetti, my spiritual advisor. I closed the lid with a small feeling of pride. It felt good to have a family who cared and worried about me just as much as I cared and worried about them. I fought the urge to call him, reminding myself he'd have a million questions I wasn't ready to answer.

"Soon," I whispered, casting one last glance at the laptop before I grabbed a book from the shelf and flopped on the couch.

. . . ● . ● ● . . .

"Why the hell are you smoking, young lady?" I heard footsteps approach and soon Felton took his place directly in front of me with a disgusted look on his face.

"For starters, I'm almost thirty years old. Hardly a young lady." I exhaled a puff of smoke at him. "And if you must know, I'm smoking because my ex-boyfriend is a lying piece of shit and my boss is a controlling asshole."

"I heard your clearance was approved."

"Yep," I nodded, taking another drag. His eyes were on me, but I refused to comment further.

"I'm approving your request."

"Thank you."

He opened his mouth several times, only to shake his head and stare at the ground. I finished my cigarette and watched the sky. We both endured the painfully awkward silence, unwilling to break it.

"Larissa, what happened? I know when you left we weren't on the best of terms, but it seems like things only got worse now that you're back."

"A lot has happened, Felton. I could tell you, but I'm in no mood for any further judgment or criticism."

"I'm sorry things are still so fractured between us. But we need to find a way to repair our working relationship."

I quirked a brow. "Do we?"

"What are you trying to say?"

"When I get back, I want to discuss my future with the agency. I think it might be time to make some changes." I stood and headed toward the door when his voice stopped me.

"Can we talk about this now?"

"Not until I get back. If you force the issue, you won't like the result."

"Please be careful," he called after me softly.

"Always," I replied, turning back to face him. I looked into his eyes and saw something I had never seen in all the years I had known Felton Lynch.

Fear.

Chapter Fifteen

Rio Cauto

Larissa

Once my participation in the Cuba mission was approved, things moved quickly. The following morning, I attended a briefing with Marianna and met the rest of the team. She originally planned on being the lead but that changed, and Olivia Cordero was named as her replacement. Olivia's father lived in Havana and had connections to the country's military leadership. This was especially important, I learned, as the mission had severe political implications if we weren't successful.

Former General Rafael Olivares was a high-ranking member of the anti-government movement. Despite being removed from the national army, he still had many troops who were loyal to him and a great deal of political clout. As a result, the government watched his movements but knew engaging him would only further galvanize his crusade. That just meant they resorted to other measures. Unofficially, of course.

Nevara Olivares, aged twenty-two, graduated from a college in Florida with a degree in finance. On her way home to her father's compound in southeast Cuba, she was abducted in Miami. The FBI apprehended her captors before the media got wind of the situation, but the new problem was how to return the young woman to her father. Havana suspected something was amiss with the general, but had no concrete proof. The State Department was leery of using the standard diplomatic means, as that would hand the government a powerful tool they could use against one of their loudest political opponents.

It was decided the CIA would oversee the return, basically sneaking her back into the country. Needless to say, it was absolutely imperative our team wasn't discovered. Since Olivia's father worked for the government, he was able to give us a ton of valuable information. The team was set to leave the following evening. Heading toward Haiti to avoid detection, we'd travel to the island by boat, where a car would be waiting for us in a hidden location. After that we had a long road trip to Rio Cauto ahead of us since we'd have to avoid the main roads and cities. If all went as planned, Nevara would be home in a few days. Easy peasy, Marianna said. Too easy.

I shoved my doubts aside; the only reason I was so cynical was because my last "simple" assignment turned into a shit show. Granted, that was partially my fault since I slept with my target. Scolding myself, I did my best to shake off the negative thoughts. It was time to stop dwelling on the past and get back to work.

"All right, it's imperative that one of us is by Nevara's side at all times," Olivia instructed. "She's not exactly thrilled to be returning home, so she's considered a flight risk."

I held up my hand. "Surely she knows the danger if she escapes our custody once we arrive in Cuba? Why does she not want to go back? Do we know?"

"She refuses to speak to us," Marianna replied, writing on her notepad. "And, to be perfectly candid, it's not the CIA's problem. We've been tasked with returning her, and that's what we'll do."

"My family has put word out to the villages between Uvero and the compound," the fourth person in our meeting, Annalisa Torres, offered. "We should be fine as long as we don't draw too much attention and stay away from the cities."

"And this is where I'm thankful we have one more person on this mission than we originally planned," Olivia said, glancing at me. Her gaze shifted to the clock on the wall. "All right let's bring this to a close. We'll meet at the lockup tomorrow at 1900."

We all rose and gathered our things. Marianna and Olivia quickly left the room. I turned to Annalisa. "The lockup?"

Annalisa seemed to be the friendliest of the bunch. We were both of similar height and had the same curvy build. She was very young, having joined the CIA directly out of college. Most of her family remained in Cuba. In fact, her grandmother's village wasn't far from the general's home.

She nodded, looking uncomfortable. "Nevara had to be placed in a holding cell when we arrived because she was so combative. She is adamant she doesn't want to go home."

"And that isn't a red flag to you? I know what our mission is, but the fact our payload doesn't even want to be returned concerns me."

"It concerns me, too. But you know how it is. We just do what they tell us."

"Who's insisting she be returned home?"

"Her father. And he knows enough people to make any future CIA assignments in the region difficult for us."

"Get some rest so we can kick ass tomorrow," I said as we stopped outside her room.

"We've got this."

Max permitted me to go upstairs to the roof, to spend one last night under the stars. The silence soothed me as I smoked my last cigarette and wondered how Lucas was doing. It was almost four in the morning in Verona, so he was most likely asleep. I giggled when I wondered with whom.

I thought of John next, knowing everything related to him had to move to the back burner while I was on assignment. My mind replayed our short and rocky relationship. The joy, the pain, and all points in between. I wasn't naïve enough to think dishonesty didn't happen in relationships. The depth of those lies, however, was my problem. I wouldn't find any answers that night, so I stood and trudged toward the door. Before retreating inside, I turned and faced the sky one last time.

"Good night, boys," I whispered. "Take care of each other."

Several long hours later, we arrived on the Cuban coast. Choppy water made finding a place to bring the boat ashore difficult, especially at night. In the end, we finally made landfall just as the sun peeked over the horizon. The driver of the boat sped away almost as soon as our feet hit the sand.

Annalisa's description of Nevara as combative was an understatement. She was a petite woman whose hatred toward Olivia knew no bounds. Her brown eyes showed equal contempt as she stared at the three of us. Asking even a basic question was met with rolled eyes and a toss of her long brown hair. She tried to jump from the boat no less than three times during the voyage from Miami to Cuba, and it was only after Olivia threatened to handcuff her to the seat that she finally relented. For the sake of harmony, Annalisa and I agreed to take turns escorting her.

"I will pay you bitches fifty thousand American dollars to leave me on the beach and walk away," Nevara grumbled as we followed the narrow trail ahead of us.

"Split three ways isn't even enough for a car," Olivia scoffed. "Move it."

She muttered in Spanish, her eyes murderous. I glanced at Annalisa, who shrugged. "She probably knows Olivia's father works for the government."

Once we found the car, we checked for any traps or trackers before heading north. Annalisa drove, engaging in soft chatter with Olivia while I sat in the back with our charge, who was resolutely silent as she watched the scenery from her window. We'd been on the road barely ten minutes when an old pickup truck suddenly swerved in front of the car, trapping us. The other two officers quickly abandoned the front seat and headed for the forest on the right side of the road. Three armed men climbed out of the truck as I looked up. I grabbed Nevara by the shoulder and pulled her out of the car to join everyone in the forest. She attempted to break free from my grasp just as we approached the trees, but I grabbed her arm and dragged her to safety.

"Do you want those guys to find you?" I hissed as we ducked behind some old bushes.

She opened her mouth to speak when Olivia's whispered voice beckoned us forward. I clutched Nevara's wrist and followed until all four of us ran inside a church on the outskirts of a small village. I sat down in the first pew and pulled her down to sit next to me.

"Are you ladies all right?" An elderly man in his black priest's robes walked down the aisle. He watched us with a kind but guarded expression, unsure of what to make of the four young women who had stormed into his church.

"Hello, Father," Annalisa answered. "I'm afraid we ran into some trouble on our way home and we're stranded."

"How did they know where to find us?" Nevara demanded, glaring at Olivia.

She closed her eyes and sighed. When they reopened, she looked inexplicably weary. Unease filled my gut. "Olivia?"

"My father picked up some chatter just before we left that a couple of pro-government groups learned of your disappearance and may have had knowledge about your return."

"So, when were you going to tell the rest of us?" I fought to keep my voice low so the priest wouldn't hear.

"We didn't know how valid the intel was."

"Bullshit," Nevara retorted. "For all I know, you and your father are leading them right to us."

"Miss Olivares, do you realize how much heat comes down on us if you aren't returned to your father?" Her eyes narrowed. "We can pretty much kiss any support goodbye in the region if this mission fails. I hate to sound cold, but you're worth more to us alive and in your father's care."

"Yes, I'm worth more to my father alive and I'm worth more to the government dead," Nevara spat. "That's all I am anymore...a piece of property to barter."

Olivia and I exchanged looks but said nothing as Annalisa approached with the priest close behind her.

"Father Marquez has room so we can sleep here overnight, and in the morning he has a trusted parishioner who can take us to El berjel, which is about halfway. From there, he said we should be able to find a car to get us the rest of the way."

Nevara turned to the priest and spoke in rapid Spanish. After several minutes, she nodded. He showed us to our rooms and then left us to rest. Olivia excused herself to check in and provide an update on our location while Annalisa agreed to sit with Nevara so I could rest for a couple of hours.

The next several days were spent traveling the countryside and avoiding major roads on our way to the general's compound. We got a small, crappy car once we arrived in El berjel, but with travel limited to the narrow and unpaved back roads, our progress was slow. The three of us took turns driving, sleeping and watching over the general's less than cooperative daughter.

She'd become quiet and agreeable the past two days, which made me nervous. The change in her mood was welcomed by the others, but it made me skeptical. Maybe because I had done the same thing a few months ago. With each passing mile, I enjoyed the quiet, but remained watchful. If she had any hidden intentions, time would reveal them.

My suspicions were confirmed when we stopped for dinner. Annalisa had just walked toward the small diner to order our food when Nevara suddenly pulled Olivia into a headlock from the back seat and tried to grab the gun from her waistband. In a flash, Annalisa raced back to the car and broke her grip by pulling the fingers around the gun backward. I clapped my hand over her mouth when she let out a screech, then grabbed her by the neck and slammed her back down on the seat. As Olivia slapped the cuffs on her wrists, I leaned over her, my face upside down to hers.

"Now you're going to listen to me very carefully," I threatened as my hand tightened slightly around her throat. "We get it. You don't want to go home. However, unless you can give me a damn good reason why we shouldn't complete this mission, we will proceed as we have been directed to do. And if you don't knock it the hell off, I'll take you to Havana and march you to the Presidential palace my goddamned self. Are we clear?" I released her throat, but kept my hand over her mouth. I glanced at the other two, and they both nodded.

Olivia stepped forward. "Is there a reason we shouldn't take you home? Is your life or will our lives be in danger if we continue?"

She shook her head sadly. "Your lives won't be in danger, no. I love my father, but he is forcing me to marry one of his ally's sons, and he is a cruel man."

My eyes widened. "Has he abused you?"

"No, he promised my father he wouldn't," she paused, looking fearful. "But I know he's killed at least three of his girlfriends and mistresses."

"Nevara, I'm sorry, but we can't get involved," Olivia responded. "Our orders are to return you to your father as soon as possible."

"I know," she replied, her voice cracking. "Nobody can help me. I met with a lawyer so I could apply for asylum and that's when I was nabbed by those people."

"And it would've been worse if they'd brought you back here," I explained. "I know this man is dangerous, but you have to understand that it would be so much worse if anyone sympathetic to the government gets a hold of you. I realize it's a terrible position, but your safest place is with your father."

Her eyes brimming with tears, she nodded. I felt terrible about her situation. She was a pawn in a political chess match without her consent, and neither side cared about her wellbeing. In the end, any harm that came to her would simply be written off as collateral damage, and no one would give it a second thought.

"We should get going." Her voice trembled. "This area isn't safe."

We all climbed into the car, deciding to grab food down the road. After our conversation, Nevara was quiet and seemed resigned to her fate. We drove in shifts through the night and arrived on the outskirts of the small village about five miles from the general's estate. It was like driving through a ghost town. The shops were all closed and boarded up, and according to both Annalisa and Nevara the outdoor market was gone.

"Something's wrong," Annalisa said as she glanced around the fountain in the center of the village. The water still ran clear and cold, as if waiting for residents to pass by.

Olivia looked around and shook her head. "Should we notify the relay?"

I leaned against the car and scanned the few buildings surrounding us. Sweat trickled down my neck, but the silence was so eerie I feared making a move to wipe it away. The longer we stood out in the open, the faster my heart thundered in my chest.

"We should get in this car and keep moving," Nevara whispered. "We can call if we need to once we get to my father's house."

Reluctantly, I climbed back into the car. Olivia raised her eyebrows when I insisted on driving and then placed my agency-issued pistol under my leg. I quickly drove through the village, but reduced my speed once we reached the narrow road that led to the tall fence we all saw in the distance.

"I have a bad feeling about this," Annalisa said.

Nevara was seated behind me so she could enter the code for the gate. When I came around the last curve and found the gate open, however, I swore under my breath. Parking the car, I killed the engine, and my ears nearly ached from the lack of sound.

I turned to Olivia in the passenger seat. "Did they know when we would be arriving?"

"No. We gave them a twenty-four to forty-eight hour window."

"Grab the satellite phone and everyone stay quiet," I ordered softly.

"I'm going to call the relay," Olivia whispered, trying to keep calm.

I nodded. "Annalisa, I want you to take Nevara and find a hiding spot near the entrance and wait for one of us to come get you. Olivia and I are going to look around and see if we can get an idea of what's going on in there."

Once Olivia left her recorded message with the relay, we all quietly exited the vehicle. After grabbing my Colt and checking to make sure I had mags for both weapons, I threw my knapsack over my shoulders and kept my pistol trained ahead of me. I scanned the area and motioned for everyone to follow. Olivia brought up the rear, her gun also drawn and ready for whatever might happen.

I crept along the perimeter of the fence and scanned the surrounding terrain. The hot, humid air made it difficult to breathe, and the only thing that made it worse was the pressure in my chest. The unnatural silence almost made my head swim. For an area deep inside a rain forest, not a single nature sound was heard. Nevara told us of a secret entrance into the compound around the back of the property, so we proceeded along the western perimeter of the fence to find it. Through the lush vegetation I saw several buildings, but those seemed just as empty as the rest of the property.

A single gunshot brutally shattered the silence. It was likely a large caliber based on the loud boom it made, which was confirmed when the back of Olivia's head exploded into a spray of blood and fragments as she dropped to the ground.

"Fuck!" Annalisa screamed.

Her voice was drowned out by the roar of gunfire and voices yelling. Nevara grabbed my wrist and ran toward what looked like the crumbling remnants of an old building. She dashed around the side and pushed a wall out of the way to reveal a dark cavern that appeared to lead underground.

I hesitated. "How do we know it's clear?"

"Only family members know of it," she answered, pulling us inside.

The walls and floor were made of dark stone and the air was a lot cooler. I grabbed a glow stick from my bag and once it was lit, I held my gun in front of me and we moved slowly down the path. Annalisa joined us moments later and I gave her my spare pistol since her gun had jammed.

"Could those be enemies of your father?" I whispered.

"I don't know," Nevara answered, still out of breath. "When I left, there weren't any threats in the area, but I haven't been home in a while."

"Hopefully relay picked the call up. Though I'm not sure how that will work since we're not supposed to be here."

"My father should be able to get you guys out."

I nodded silently, refusing to verbalize my suspicion that her father was already dead. My conversation with Marianna suddenly rang through my head. I hadn't wanted to be such a cynic, but another easy case was now officially sideways.

The path ended, and Nevara pushed a stone along the wall. A door swung open to reveal a massive rose garden. I held my hand up and scanned the area. We crept toward the house, listening to yelled voices that moved closer. I silently prayed we were alone since we had little to no cover in our present position.

The pool's cabanas were empty and the air remained still. We saw the covered patio by the pool. My stomach churned, imagining what awaited us inside. A sharp movement to my right caught my eye as a man jumped out. He'd barely lifted his rifle when I shot him. He grasped his throat and fell to the ground.

"Never lower your gun, moron."

Three more men were shot by Annalisa and me on our way to the house. Once we reached the patio, Nevara broke from us and ran inside, yelling for her father. Several moments later we heard an ear-splitting scream and ran to find the source. We rounded the courtyard to find Nevara trying to climb a fountain in the courtyard.

"Oh my god," Annalisa breathed in horror.

Balanced on the top tier were two severed heads. I recognized one from the photos as General Olivares, but the identity of the second middle-aged man was a mystery. The water in the fountain was a deep red, and the two heads were in such a state it was hard not to vomit.

"Papa, no," she sobbed.

Annalisa helped Nevara down from the fountain and hugged her as she cried. My body tingled with unease. What else would we find in this house of horrors, and who else was waiting for us?

"Who was the other man?" I asked gently.

"Raul, his second in command."

"We need to find a safe place to hide her," I said to Annalisa, who nodded.

"The closest panic room is hidden in my father's bathroom," Nevara offered.

We crossed the courtyard into the great room. She gasped at the discovery of two headless bodies seated in the armchairs on either side of the large sofa, no doubt belonging to her father and Raul. A bloody machete was stabbed into the coffee table like some sort of macabre centerpiece. She pointed to the left, and I crept along the wall to the next room. I nodded to Annalisa, who raised her gun and followed.

The kitchen was a large, open room that included a small breakfast nook to the left and a formal dining area to the right, which now included several dead bodies seated around a large table. Based on the bugs and the smell, the eight men had been dead for several days. It looked like they'd all been shot execution style in the middle of dinner. I tried to control my rising panic.

If not for the bullet piercing my upper right arm, I would've thought I imagined the next few seconds. Two of the corpses suddenly moved, one shooting Annalisa in the chest before I shot him in the head. The second body, seated at the head of the table, picked up the napkin to his left and wiped the blood from his face.

"Nevara, my beloved. Welcome home." His voice was like ice.

"Ernesto," she whispered.

He stood and kept his gun trained on me, pointing it at my head. His cold, black eyes narrowed as his lips curled into an evil smile. "Larissa Donovan, the elusive assassin," he intoned with a heavy accent.

There was only one way he knew my identity. "Please don't tell me you're another Sardi lackey."

His smirk transformed into an angry sneer. "Lackey? Hardly, bitch. I'm his main drug distributor in the Caribbean."

"And how did you know I'd be here?" I challenged. Not many people knew I was on this mission. Was there a mole in the CIA?

"There's a five million dollar bounty on your head. Ten if you're brought to him alive. Let's just say those of us connected to the family have been keeping a watchful eye. I truly didn't know you'd be here. I guess it's just my lucky day."

"Ernesto, why did you kill my father?" Nevara cried, interrupting our exchange.

He shrugged. "He was a weak old man who refused to recognize a great opportunity. Massimo Sardi has now entrusted me with weapons distribution in this area, but your father was a fool who refused to allow the family to be his new supplier."

My arm burned and throbbed. I slowly extended my elbow to test my range of motion. It hurt like a bitch, but it was still mobile. When I slowly stepped backward, he shot a hole in the wall close to where Nevara cowered behind me.

I pointed my gun at his head. "Not a good idea."

His eyes narrowed. "You really think you're that good?"

"Is it worth five million dollars to find out?"

A loud gasp from the floor interrupted our standoff. Annalisa rolled onto her back, causing Ernesto to point his gun at her prone body. It was the few precious seconds I needed.

"Run!" Annalisa's scream tore through the air. He shot her in the middle of her forehead and she was once again silent.

I followed Nevara down the hall, dodging a bullet that hit the wall less than an inch from my head. She made it to the bedroom and was headed toward the bathroom as I nearly caught up to her. "Get yourself inside and stay there!" I yelled. "Do not wait for me!"

The closed bedroom door splintered as it flew off the hinges and a searing pain tore through my ribs. He was a fast bastard, I'd give him that. Blood flowed from his shoulder and forearm but did nothing to slow him down or calm the pure rage in his eyes.

"It'll be worth losing five million dollars just to watch you die!" he roared, charging at me.

He knocked me to the floor, and all the air left my lungs in a painful gasp. Kicking the gun away, his hands flew to my neck and closed like a vise. My fingers moved to his face and clawed madly at his eyes. He let out an angry sound and backhanded me. I scratched at every part of him I could reach until his fist connected with my face.

"You're a fucking idiot," I rasped.

I grabbed his dense black hair and pulled. He ground the palm of his hand into the bullet wound in my ribs. Pain seized my lungs, and I gasped, dropping my hands. His slaps and punches were rapid and without mercy. My limbs refused to budge, no matter how hard I tried to will my body to fight. His hands returned to my neck and my vision blurred. All other sounds drowned out except for my heart hammering violently in my ears.

Seconds later, a warm liquid sprayed across my face and the hands around my throat fell away. Precious air invaded my lungs, but the relief was short lived when a heavy weight fell against my ribs. I tried to cry out from the pain, but nothing more than a harsh rasp came out. Through my swollen eyes, I saw a figure moving closer. At the sound of a shotgun, my heart stuttered. I tried to free myself from under the weight, which I then realized was Ernesto, but I couldn't get my limbs to move.

"It's okay," a soft voice murmured. "You're safe now."

Tears welled in my eyes. How I wanted to believe that. Instead, I was stuck under a dead man, in a country where I wasn't supposed to be, doing work for an agency that couldn't even acknowledge my death. I tried one last time to move, but my body couldn't, or wouldn't, respond.

I felt the darkness as it seeped into my psyche. It was a familiar feeling, the same despair I felt back in the bathroom that awful New Year's Eve in Rome. Death was coming for me. I heard a frantic voice pleading for me to stay with her that grew more distant until everything faded away into nothing.

Chapter Sixteen

Tampa Tempest

John

"So, I'm going to ask again. Why were you following me?"

Marino gasped and did his best not to scream. Granted, his hands were both impaled on the table between us with two of my sharpest knives, so his pain was understandable. Sweat poured from his forehead as he continued to whimper. I kept my feet propped up on the table and stared at him expectantly.

"Gianni, I swear to god I have no idea—"

"Don't bullshit me!" I sprang up and yelled in his face, twisting the knife in his right hand for emphasis. "What are you doing here? And what were you doing at my aunt's house?"

His shallow breaths increased. "There's been chatter. Your uncle was trying to see if it was true."

"What chatter?"

"That she left Italy and might be stateside. But he also thought there was a chance she was hiding out in Venice."

The tightness in my chest eased. It was no surprise that Massimo knew she was in the wind. In truth, I'd expected him to send his spies to chase down the intel sooner, but I was almost insulted that he'd sent the slimy piece of shit in front of me. Marino had worked for my uncle for a couple of years, and probably thought he'd been sent on an important mission. Lucky for me, he was dumber than a pile of sheep shit and bragged about working for the family at one of Lucas's favorite bars.

"Gianni, I'm sorry. You know I had to do it."

I chuckled softly. "Yeah."

"You believe me, right?"

"Of course I do." Smiling, I stood and pulled the knife in his right hand free. He let out a relieved sigh as he held his mangled hand to his chest.

"Thank you for understanding," he panted when I removed the blade from his left hand. "I really hope—"

He shifted in his seat and stared at my hand clamped around his wrist. Licking his parched lips, he gently tried to move the limb away. My smile widened when I brought the blade down. The crack and crunch of bones as I cut off four of his fingers was drowned out by his scream.

"Sorry, Marino," I said once he quieted. "You know I had to do it."

Staring at the stubs and the mess on the table in front of him, he gasped for air. He tensed when I used the back of his shirt to clean the blood from my knife. I considered cutting his throat. If he'd known where she was, I would've done it without a second thought. Satisfied with my work, I strolled to the door of the holding cell.

"Gianni! You can't leave me like this!"

"But yet that's exactly what I'm going to do, Marino!" I laughed maliciously. "And the best part is that you'll have to explain this to my uncle. I imagine he'll be thrilled shitless when he finds out that not only were you easily caught, but that you squealed like a pig."

I slammed the door behind me and nodded to Paolo. He sat at the security desk watching the cameras and smirked when he heard the little bastard crying to be let go. I washed my hands in the sink across the room, then asked him to clean Marino up and send him back to

Bari. My uncle was free to do whatever he wished to him. I raced back to the main house and to my office. Lucas sat on the couch typing on his phone. His head snapped up when I opened the door.

"Well?" he prodded.

"Massimo knows she left but doesn't know where she is."

His tense shoulders dropped. "Thank god."

"Have you heard anything?"

"I'm supposed to call Marcus back in about an hour. The first one was easy, but you know the other one is going to be a bitch to track down."

It had been two and a half weeks since Liss left the estate. Lucas tracked the burner phone she took with her until the signal stopped somewhere in the middle of the Adriatic Sea. He'd been able to get footage that showed she'd made it to Slovenia before vanishing without a trace until three days ago. A letter addressed to him arrived with a postmark from an Air Force base outside Miami. After he read it, he shut himself in his room for the rest of the day. I stood by the windows in my office, staring out into space and thinking of her when he handed it to me the next morning. I stared at the small, neat handwriting on the paper for about ten minutes before reading her words.

Lucas,

Two and a half years ago, I signed on for what I intended to be my last job as a spy. It seemed simple enough, but you and I both know things are never as easy as they seem. There were plenty of things during that job that I could and should have done differently. Yet, I have no regrets, for I gained the most precious thing. You.

I know we didn't meet on the best of terms. I'll admit I tried to kill you probably as many times as you tried to do the same to me. (That's right, shithead! Rocco talked! Haha) When we learned the truth you could've easily turned your back on me, but you didn't. You immediately accepted me as family, and for that I will always be grateful.

I'm sorry I left without saying goodbye, and I'm sorry if I worried you by disappearing. But please know that no matter what happens, I will always be thankful our paths crossed. You'll always be an important person in my life and I'll always love you.
Please give Nonna my love and tell your cousin I'm okay.
Love,
Lissa

The tone of the letter seemed pleasant enough. It was enough to fool Nonna into thinking she was doing well and simply traveling, but Lucas and I knew better. She was back to work, about to head out on an assignment, and sent him the letter in case she didn't make it back.

Lucas was now obsessed with figuring out where she went and which agency she was working for. She had covered her tracks well, but Lucas was just as stubborn as her and chased down the few leads we had. When those didn't pan out, he went back to the drawing board and came up with a few ideas that seemed unlikely but worth looking into.

In the meantime, I spent my days poring over the limited information we had on Soren Luccetti. Like his daughter, finding him proved to be just as difficult. I stared at the file on my screen, willing it to reveal some kind of deep secret when Lucas rushed into the room.

"So, this is an interesting bit of info," he began. "Barton Kane, her FBI handler, calls the CIA at least once a month looking for info on her. The rumor is he's looking to bring charges against her."

"For what?"

His eyebrows were sky high. "Kidnapping and assault."

"Anything else? How aggressively is he looking for her?"

"No movements from Kane in the past six weeks. No untraceable phone calls, no travel. His last trip was to Boston to visit family. Nothing that would be a red flag. So it sounds like he's waiting for her to give him an opportunity to nab her."

"Which she won't do until she's damn good and ready," I concluded out loud. "What about Felton?"

"Marcus had nothing on Felton. Not that I expected him to. You still think she called him?"

"My gut says yes. If she's back at work she went to him, especially if she's not friendly with Kane."

"On it." He motioned to the computer. "What are you looking at?"

"Massimo's financials. Trying to find something that can give us a location for Soren, but he's just as difficult to pin down as her."

He stared at the screen. "Strange as it may sound, have you checked into Lissa's parents?"

"No. Why?"

"Soren followed her mom all the way to New York. He might have kept tabs on her after they broke up."

"I thought Nonna said Sera made sure they kept her paternity quiet. If they weren't together anymore and he didn't know about the baby, why would he care?"

"Mom said he was damn near obsessed with Sera. She never took it personally because of the circumstances of their marriage, but the first chance he got, he left the country to be with her."

I leaned back in my chair. "It's not like I have much else to go on."

The next few days were spent combing over the lives of Seamus and Serafina Donovan. At first, it was damn near impossible to track their residential movements in New York. Neither owned any homes, nor did they appear on any rental contracts. Seamus owned several commercial buildings in Boston, New York, and Philadelphia. I found a marriage license issued by Arlington County, Virginia about six months before Liss was born, but nothing else was found on her parents until her birth in Manhattan.

The Donovans purchased their first home together in Falls Church, Virginia when their daughter was about a year old. Prior to that, the best I could piece together was her mother stayed at a friend's house in a small township in New Jersey while her father traveled. Seamus made regular trips to New York and Boston during that time, but the Boston trips stopped when Liss was almost two years old. Financial records showed he sold all his Boston properties to an anonymous third party connected to an offshore account. The Philadelphia properties sold by year-end, with proceeds going to the same account. Six months before the raid that destroyed the Westies, Seamus's old gang, the family moved into a condo in Georgetown across the Potomac River in Washington, D.C.

The family remained there for nearly three years before moving into their home in Alexandria where they lived until that horrible night that claimed them both. Upon their deaths, everything was sold and placed into a trust for their daughter that would become payable when she turned thirty in a few months. I combed through business records in search of the mysterious third party when Lucas ran into my office. The look on his suddenly pale face worried me.

He wrung his hands. "I just got a call from a VA Hospital in Tampa," he began and stopped when his voice cracked. "Apparently I'm listed as Lissa's spiritual advisor, and they called to tell me..."

My stomach dropped and my blood chilled. "No...," I let my voice trail off, refusing to finish that sentence.

"She's alive, but it's pretty serious. They wouldn't tell me any details over the phone. All they could tell me is that she's in critical condition but stable."

I inhaled sharply, feeling as if I'd been punched in the gut. Stable but critical. What the fuck happened?

"John?"

"Shit," I whispered. "I was right. She went back to Felton and his CIA bullshit."

"Fuck!"

"I'm guessing you already called to get the plane ready?" I started grabbing files and shoving them into a crude pile.

"We have about half an hour."

The next hour passed by in a blur. Rocco drove us to the airstrip, since we were both too emotional to do so. The next thing I knew, I was gripping the arms of my seat as we taxied the runway.

"What makes you think she went back to the CIA? She's still in the states," he asked once the plane was gliding over the ocean.

"She's at a military hospital. If she was stateside on a Bureau job, she would be at a civilian hospital. When she was attacked in Portland, that's where I took her. Once they secured her identity and spoke to her handler, they were able to treat her. The CIA is another story because those are international assignments. They work pretty closely with the military, so when an officer is injured, they usually receive care from the closest military facility that can accommodate."

"That makes sense," he paused. "So, if she's with the CIA, that means—"

"That means Felton fucking Lynch will be there."

"Which means you need to work on keeping your cool right now, John. This is not the time or the place to be starting shit with him."

Saying nothing, I stared out the window. I'd left the CIA seven years earlier on good terms, or so I'd thought. He blamed me for certain agency failures, I learned later, including the death of an informant. I hated Felton with a passion and wanted nothing more than to knock every one of his perfect teeth out of his smug fucking face. Feeling pain in my fingers, I looked down and realized I'd been gripping the arm of the seat so hard my knuckles were white.

"I'll do what I can, but I make no promises. We need to make damn sure he doesn't find out you're her brother. He's going to be all over you when we get there. He'll want to know why you were notified, and the fact you're with me will just make him want to know even more about how you're involved with her. I'll do what I can to prevent it, but try not to be alone with him. He's a manipulative bastard."

We fell into silence. The long flight did nothing to calm either of us. I fell asleep at some point, but anxiety attacked as soon as my eyes opened. Lucas looked like shit as he guzzled coffee and merely nodded when I tried to talk to him. As we landed in Tampa, I prayed she was okay. Losing her wasn't an option. I couldn't bear the thought and didn't even want to imagine what it would do to him.

"It's going to be okay," I said softly as we rode in the taxi on the way to the hospital.

"You don't know that."

"No, I don't. I'm just as scared shitless as you, man." He turned back to the window, and I joined him in watching the scenery. The sun shone brightly as it crested over the palm trees. A gorgeous day for our horrible mood.

"I'll do my best to distract Felton so you can see her first," I offered in the elevator on our way to the seventh floor.

"As long as that distraction doesn't end with me bailing your ass out of jail."

Tension corded across my shoulders when the doors opened. After checking in at the nurse's station, I turned and found my eyes locked with the icy gaze of my former colleague. His jaw clenched as he stalked toward us.

I didn't even let him get his first question out. "How is she?"

His jaw clenched. "Why are you here?"

"Because I asked him to be," Lucas interjected boldly.

"And who are you?" he challenged.

"Ms. Donovan's spiritual advisor," Lucas quipped. "Now, if you'll excuse me, I'm going to see her."

We watched the door close, and I turned back to him with a broad grin. "Who is he to her?" he growled, pointing to the door.

"He's someone she saw fit to add to her list of contacts, Felton. If you want to know more, you'll need to ask her. As far as the hospital goes, he has every right to be here. In fact, he has more of a right to be here than you or me."

"I don't want you near her."

"And I'm out in the hall. Not seeing her. Again, the person she *wants* here is talking to her."

"Then who is he to you?"

"God, this must be driving you crazy, isn't it?" I taunted. "There are facets to her life that you know nothing about and can't try to control. I bet it just eats at you that she lived her life without you for a while."

"I know enough about that life she lived to know that you're no good for her," he retorted. "You already messed her up once and I'll be goddamned if I'll let you mess her up again!"

His phone rang. He glared at the screen before answering and then stared daggers at me the entire length of the terse conversation before he stated he was on his way and ended the call. "I'm going to go for now. When I get back, you'd both better be gone," he hissed.

"Felton, I hate to break it to you, but it's not up to you and it's not up to me. It's up to the patient and the person she assigned as her emergency contact, who I'm here to support. Now, it sounds like you need to be going, so I won't keep you. It was good seeing you again."

The anger radiating from him felt nuclear as he marched to the elevator. My amusement at his antics shifted as soon as he was gone, and all I could think about was her condition and prognosis. I wanted so badly to barge through that door, but I didn't want to disturb

Lucas's time with her. I feared what awaited me beyond the door. Would this latest incident have left any emotional scars? She was strong, but there was only so much even the strongest person could withstand.

Lucas's eyes were red and puffy when he returned, the emotion clear on his face. We walked to the set of chairs in the hall. His head hung forward as soon as he sat down. "It's not pretty. She's on a ventilator and there's all sorts of tubes and shit sticking out of her. She has a ton of nasty bruises all over her face and neck. It looks like someone beat her up pretty bad."

"Was anyone in there to give you any kind of info?"

"The head nurse was checking her vitals when I came in. They didn't have any details about what caused her injuries. She was stabilized at another facility before being flown here. Officially, she's recovering from what's being described as severe vascular trauma to the upper arm, a splenectomy, a collapsed lung and severe facial trauma."

"Translation, she got shot and someone beat the shit out of her. But they can't tell you that."

"Exactly," he replied. "Where's Felton?"

"He took a call and had to leave. But not without his usual dose of bullshit. Twenty million questions about you and why I'm here."

He rolled his eyes. "Good to see he hasn't changed."

"Yeah."

"Want to go in and see her?"

I straightened in my seat. "Do you think that's a good idea? I don't want to upset her."

"You mean that asshole didn't mention she's unconscious?"

Fucking Felton. "No. He didn't," I bit out.

"Go," he ordered, pushing me toward the door.

It looked like every medical machine and monitor ever made stood behind her bed. Each one made its own series of beeps and noises as they checked every reading and measurement. I slowly walked closer, afraid I'd somehow disturb her, and stopped at the foot of the bed. My eyes scanned her body, seeing the bandages on her upper arm and the padding under her gown on the left side of her abdomen. When I saw her face, my legs nearly gave out, and I quickly sat down on the mattress.

The ventilator tube covered her mouth, but most of the bruises were around her neck and swollen eyes. They were yellowed in some places, but still deep purple and magenta in others. Her hair was matted to the right side of her head and what few tendrils were loose hung lifelessly on the pillow.

"Jesus Christ, what happened to you?" I gasped. I cradled her hand in mine, desperately trying to warm it.

Her eyes remained tightly closed. I watched the lines on the monitors pulse and move for a while with my fingers entwined with hers. My eyes stung when I gently kissed her hand. I'd failed her. Again.

"I am so sorry, baby," I whispered. "For all of it. For not telling you everything when I should have, for lying to you and for not fighting harder to keep you there. I never should have let you leave. I feel like I pushed you into going back to him, and I will never forgive myself for that."

Carefully, I brushed the hair stuck to her face aside, doing my best to avoid the cuts and bruises. My eyes went to the gauze on her arm and then her gown. I said a silent prayer of thanks that she was stable, but I wouldn't relax until she opened her eyes.

My throat tightened. "You've gotta get better so you can kick my ass like I deserve, and then I can make it up to you. Plus, you can't leave me here. I can't marry some nice, *boring* Italian girl. I want my feisty Italian girl who will drive me up the wall and love me as much as I love her."

I sat and watched her sleep, oblivious to my surroundings and the time until a hand on my shoulder jolted me back to reality. Lucas stared at me with a look of concern. "Let's get a bite to eat. We've been here a while."

"Sure. Where's the cafeteria?"

"No, we're going to drop our stuff off at the hotel and then eat some actual food." When I protested, he held up his hand. "You're not locking yourself in her room for days on end again."

"Fine," I conceded in a huff.

We found a small cafe close to our hotel and sat outside after he insisted the sun and fresh air would do us both some good. I hated to admit he was right. The food and change of scenery felt better than anything from the cafeteria and helped to lift my mood, if only for a little while.

He finished his beer and set it down next to mine. "When she wakes up, what's your plan?"

"I don't know. Felton's not going to let her out of his sight, so you can bet he's not going to leave either of us alone with her."

His brows came together. "Is it normal for him to be that closely involved with an employee? Something tells me he wouldn't be as... concerned if it was anyone else in that room."

"No, it's not normal, but he's not just her boss. He raised her."

"How'd that happen?"

"Apparently, he and Seamus were close friends. The night her parents were killed, she escaped and was found hiding in his backyard. Neither of her parents had any other family stateside, so he was able to get custody."

"For being so close, she really didn't talk about him much," he observed.

"I noticed that, too. And when she mentioned him, it didn't sound like they were on the best of terms. I never wanted to open that can of worms, so I didn't pry."

"So?" he prodded. "What are you going to do?"

"I'll figure it out when she wakes up. Let's just hope he doesn't have her transferred back to Virginia. That's his home turf, and he'll have more resources to keep us from seeing her."

I felt more human after showering at the hotel before returning to the ICU. The nurses only allowed one of us in her room at a time, so we took turns sitting with her until Felton returned in the early evening. After that, we sat on the bench outside her room and traded glares with him from across the hall until he left for the night. The night nurse allowed Lucas to sleep on a cot in her room while I stretched out on a bench in the hall.

Felton sat in her room while he ate his breakfast and we sat in the hall the next morning. The scowl and snide comments he made under his breath as he left didn't disappoint. Apparently, we looked pathetic enough for the morning charge nurse to take pity on us. She allowed us to be in her room as long as we promised to keep quiet. We watched shitty TV shows and talked as if we were back in Verona. When Felton came in that night and found us playing poker, his hand shook as he pointed to the hall and ordered us out.

I'd just gotten comfortable enough to fall asleep on the shitty bench in the hall when a hand shook my shoulder. I jolted upright and tried not to snap at the nurse who stood in front of me. "Sorry, but I thought you'd want to know she's awake," she announced in a low voice.

I gave her a quick hug and murmured my thanks before rushing into the room. Lucas held her hand and gently embraced her shoulder. She winced, but smiled as he spoke. Her face became more serious as their conversation continued, and he gave her another gentle hug before walking toward me.

"Don't worry about anything she says right now," he whispered, slapping my upper arm.

"What? Why—," I asked, but he left without another word.

Our eyes met and a knot formed in my stomach. The floor felt like wet cement as I trudged forward and stopped by her feet. The temptation to grab her up and hold her in my arms was too great to move any closer. My heart hammered wildly as I searched for the right words to say.

"I, um...I'm so glad you're okay," I stammered.

"Thank you," she croaked. Her eyes moved to her feet and her lip quivered.

"Are you okay? Do you need the nurse?"

She shook her head and wiped her eyes. When I stepped closer, she let out a sob. I stood frozen and watched her clutch the rail on the side of her bed as she tried to regain her composure.

Holding up my hands, I retreated to the other side of the room. "I promise I'm not going to hurt you, Liss. I—"

"You already did," she whispered, her voice raw.

Her words pierced my heart like a bullet, tearing through me and echoing through my head. My feet were stuck to the floor hoping she'd say something else, even if it was just to scream how much she hated me and throw me out. After a long and painful silence, I turned around and left the room without another word.

Chapter Seventeen

A Touch of Frostbite

Larissa

Getting shot sucked. I'd been lucky to not get shot during my career, but the few times a bullet grazed me was painful enough. The wound in my arm was bad, but the one in my abdomen hurt like a bitch. Another thing movies glossed over was how much pain the smallest movement caused if there's a goddamned bullet wound in an area connected to every other part of your body.

Based on the notes in my file, I arrived at the medical facility at Guantanamo Bay with two gunshot wounds and severe facial trauma. The other bullet nicked my lung and hit a blood vessel in my spleen. I'd lost enough blood to receive a transfusion in addition to a splenectomy. I was airlifted stateside the minute I was stable, no doubt at Felton's barked orders.

When Lucas muttered under his breath for a third time, cursing that I was going to get myself killed and was too hard-headed to admit it, I held his hand in mine. I never thought much about my injuries in the past. That was before I had someone who now stared at me with a determined look on his face.

I braced for his lecture. "What's wrong?"

"You almost died."

"I know."

"You. Almost. Died!" he whisper-yelled.

Footsteps outside my room derailed my reply. Motioning toward the door, we both saw a pair of black dress pants and polished shoes. Lucas slid around the drawn curtain. "Can I help you, Mr. Lynch?" his tone was far too pleasant.

"I need to see her," Felton snarled. "Now."

"I'm sorry, but she's not feeling up to visitors right now. You'll need to come back later. Buh-bye!" he quipped before disappearing back into the room.

"Tell the other one he can go, too," I sighed. "I know he's there."

He hung his head and returned to the doorway. "Dude, she knows you're here. Go!"

I quirked a brow. "Has he been here since this morning?"

"The only time he isn't here is when the hospital makes us leave, Lissa."

I knew I had to talk to both of them eventually, but I wasn't ready. My debrief with Felton would be a shitshow, full of endless interrogations and criticism about my failures. I doubted I'd be able to control my emotions once he started lecturing me that he was right about me not being ready. Because he was right. I'd had no business going out there. I behaved like a fucking child, all because I wanted to prove that I could get right back to work. Even though I owed him an apology, I dreaded his response.

The conversation with John would be a lot more emotional. The emotions that flooded my head and heart seeing him so soon after waking up were overwhelming. I knew I loved him, deeply, and always would. However, there were deeper issues that needed to be worked through before we could even try to repair the damage.

"I know I need to talk to him. Both of them, and I will soon. I'm just not ready."

"And until you *are* ready, it's my job to keep them both out. I'm not taking sides and I'm not here to make John's case for him. I'm staying out of it." He narrowed his eyes. "But now I want to get back to our previous conversation."

"Which one?"

"The one where you almost died!"

I patted the side of my bed and he sat next to me. "Didn't you go through this with John all the times he got injured?"

"I usually didn't hear about his injuries until after the fact. And if he ever called to tell me he was in the hospital, he swore me to secrecy so Nonna wouldn't worry."

"That sounds like him," I mused. "I'm sorry. I'm not used to having anyone worry about me."

"What about Felton? John told me he raised you. As much as we've seen him here, it's obvious he cares."

I blew out a deep breath. "It's hard to explain with him. I know he cares."

"But?"

"But part of me sometimes questions his motives. Like the reason he's here is more to protect a work resource that he needs to do his job than to make sure his quasi-child is okay." I paused. "I'm sure that sounds pretty messed up."

"Maybe it's time to walk away," he offered. "Nobody can deny how much shit you've been through, but if you can't even trust your handler then maybe you shouldn't be doing this."

"I've thought about it. I just don't know for sure. Felton and I need to talk about it at some point."

He grasped my hand. "Please don't go back. I know you're an adult and can make your own decisions, but I'm begging you—," he broke off and shook his head.

"Lucas?"

"Hearing about all your injuries," he shook his head. "It never felt that real whenever John called to tell me he got stabbed in Madrid or got a concussion in Istanbul. But to hear what an awful state you were found in, seeing how pale and weak you are right now scares the hell out of me."

"Like I said, I haven't decided. And after what I learned, I don't know if I can go back."

"What do you mean?"

"Massimo put a five million dollar bounty on me. Ten if I'm brought in alive. The man who shot me was an associate of the family."

"Was?"

I shook my head. "I can't tell you any more than that, Lucas. My point is that the bounty has suddenly made it very dangerous for me to work. It was already dangerous to begin with, but this pushes it to a whole other level."

"I would think that should make it an easy decision."

"Nothing is easy, which is why I'm not going to decide right now."

"God, you're stubborn," he griped, giving me a gentle hug. "But I understand."

I tried to stifle my yawn, but his narrowed eyes when he sat back told me I'd been caught. He lowered my bed and ordered me to rest. I tried to protest, but he simply kissed me on the cheek and told me he'd be back later. It wasn't very long afterward that I drifted off to sleep.

"Hey, Gladys, how's it going?" A familiar voice broke through my mental fog as I woke up. "It looks a little hectic up here tonight."

"Hi, John. The floor's at full capacity, so it's been pretty crazy."

I opened my eyes and glanced around the room for a few seconds to get my bearings before focusing on the two people talking outside my now dimly lit room. Raising my bed up, I released a low hiss when my side throbbed. I listened to the tail end of the conversation outside my door to take my mind off the pain. I'd just realized who the voice belonged to when he appeared from behind the curtain, holding a tray.

"Good evening," he greeted with a wide grin. "The nursing staff is swamped tonight, so I volunteered to bring your dinner. I hope that's okay." He set down the tray and removed the cover.

"Where's Lucas?" I asked, immediately suspicious.

"Passed out at the hotel." He rolled the table closer. "He literally fell asleep in the middle of a sentence."

"So you decided to sneak in since he's not here?"

"Nope. I'm just helping the busy nursing staff." He sat next to me and motioned to the food. "And unless you want to suffer through me making airplane noises with your fork as I feed you, you'd better dig in. It's bad enough he's going to be pissed when he wakes up and realizes I left him behind. It'll be a million times worse if he gets here and your stubborn ass still hasn't eaten yet."

"Fine," I muttered, picking up my spoon and trying the hospital's attempt at potato soup.

"First gunshot wound?" he asked after a few minutes.

"I've had a couple of grazes, but nothing like this."

"How bad was it?"

I shuddered at the memories. "You know I can't tell you that."

"That bad."

"I'm curious to hear how bad it was," a voice interrupted. "And unlike him, you can tell me. In fact, it's required by law."

"Oh, for fuck's sake!" John bit out, looking like he wanted to put Felton on the ground. "Are you serious right now? She's barely able to stand and you want to interrogate her?"

He closed the door, completely ignoring John, and stood on the opposite side of the bed. "The other two agents were killed, so there's nobody else to answer my questions. This is just a preliminary interview. We'll meet a few more times so I can get the paperwork filed for the full debriefing when you arrive back at Langley. My first question is why did it take your team so long to arrive at the compound?"

I raised my eyebrows. "You're okay with questioning me in front of a civilian?"

"Like anyone would believe anything this man says if he were to talk."

John said something under his breath that sounded like "asshole", and I shot him a warning look. The tension between them was unmistakable and not surprising. I'd long come to realize Felton brought that out in people. But it wasn't the time or place to understand the specific reasons these two men hated each other.

"Let's just say our *guest* was less than thrilled about being escorted home," I replied. "It also didn't help that we were ambushed within the first hour of our arrival. After that, we had to be extra cautious, and that slowed us down even more than we'd planned."

His eyebrows raised sky high. "Why wasn't the relay notified of those delays?"

"You'd have to ask Olivia Cordero if she were still alive. She was in charge of reporting our progress, which I watched her do more than once. My task was to keep the guest from escaping, which she attempted several times."

"How was Mr. Saldivar able to disarm you?"

"He shot me in the goddamned arm," I snapped.

John's posture straightened. "Ernesto Saldivar? What the fuck were you doing sending her anywhere near that monster?"

"How do you know that name?" I regretted asking him in front of Felton almost as soon as the words left my mouth.

"Yes, Mr. Martinetti," Felton smirked. "Let's hear you explain to Miss Donovan how you know Mr. Saldivar. He's a known associate of your uncle, is he not?"

"He is, and that's how I know what a sick fucker he is."

"So let me see if I have this correctly," Felton began. "An associate of the Sardi family shot my officer, who is well known for targeting her. And now I have two Sardi family members here in Tampa cozying up to that same officer. Does that sound correct?"

I gripped the armrest of the bed to help me sit up. "You better not be implying what I think you are."

"Liss, baby, calm down," John warned, trying to grab my hand.

"Why is Lucas Luccetti listed as your emergency contact, Miss Donovan?" Felton prodded.

"If you really want to know, why don't you ask me yourself?" Lucas looked ready for battle as he threw the curtain back and burst into the room.

"Ah, there's the other one," Felton sneered. "Mr. Luccetti, are you aware I could have you detained while we check on whether you're visiting this country legally?"

"Get out!" I screamed.

"All right, Mr. Lynch, you're upsetting Larissa and that means it's time for you to leave," Lucas ordered. "You can finish your talk with her once she's calmed down. John, you too. Let's go. I'll be back in a minute, Lissa. Just sit tight."

The room emptied, and I leaned back in bed to enjoy the silence. After a few moments, I sat up and grabbed the spoon, intending to eat my probably now cold dinner. Outside the door, I heard their hushed voices arguing. I turned on the TV to drown them out and then focused on the tray. My soup. I was just going to concentrate on eating my soup.

"What on earth possessed you to send her back into the field after she'd been gone for so long?" John snarled.

Focus on the soup, Lissa.

"It wasn't up to me," Felton retorted. "I denied her request because I didn't think she was mentally fit for duty, but she went over my head."

"What's that supposed to mean? 'Not mentally fit for duty'?" John was trying, and failing, to keep his voice down.

"I saw the scars, saw what you pushed her into doing."

"You son of a bitch!" he roared.

John cursed, his body shifted, and I heard the sounds of a struggle. When a woman's panicked voice yelled for security, I knew I had to act. My legs were still very shaky when they hit the floor, but I held onto the bed and slowly made my way to the door and clung to the wall as I entered the hall. Lucas held John back as he struggled to get to Felton.

"I realized how much of a lying piece of shit you were after you left, but what you did to her was inexcusable," Felton spat. "How many times is she almost going to die thanks to you?"

"You dirty fucker!" John bellowed and lunged at him.

"Stop this! Both of you!" I shrieked, gripping the doorway.

All three men froze. Glaring at both Felton and John, I moved to stand between them. Lucas saw me wobble and wrapped his arm around my shoulders.

"You shouldn't be out here," John quietly scolded.

"Lissa, go lay down. They're both leaving," Lucas said.

"No. I've heard enough. I know I screwed up, and that's why I'm here. I had no business going out there, and that's on me. It's not about either of you or whatever pissing match *this* is. What I do know is that if you two assholes can't act like fucking adults, there's the door."

John reached for me, but I shoved his hand away and set off down the hall as two security guards rushed past. I heard footsteps behind me and rounded the corner, doing my best to ignore the burning pain in my ribcage. By the time I stopped and leaned against the wall, I was out of breath and clutching my side.

"Lissa?" Lucas softly called behind me.

I let out several quick breaths to lessen the pain before turning around. "What?"

When his eyes widened and the color drained from his face, I followed his gaze and pulled my hand away, staring at the blood coating my fingers. "Well, shit. I sprung a leak," I muttered as my head swam and then everything went black.

I was way too warm when I woke up in my hospital bed. Feeling I was being watched, I turned to find Lucas sitting in the chair next to me. His arms were crossed, and he wore a deep scowl. "Hey," I whispered.

"Hello." His voice was flat.

"How long was I asleep?"

His jaw clenched. "Eighteen hours, which is probably a good thing. You popped a fucking stitch."

"Oh."

"They both went apeshit when they saw you being wheeled into surgery. Once you were in recovery, I finally made them leave."

"Thank you."

"An apology for scaring everybody would be appropriate," he grumbled.

"I'm sorry I scared you, Lucas."

"You need to talk to both of them. This has gone on long enough. Security told them they're banned if there's another incident."

I sighed. "You're right. I'll talk to Felton in the morning."

"What about John?"

"Let me talk to Felton first."

"What are you going to tell him?"

"What I should have told him two years ago," I answered.

"Get some rest." He turned to leave.

"Wait." I grabbed his arm. "Please don't leave yet."

"All right. But just so you know, I'm still mad at you."

We watched sports highlights in silence, making the occasional comment about a play or the score of a game. When I noticed him typing on his phone, part of me wanted to ask him to tell John good night, but I resisted. Anything I wanted to say could be said directly. I finally gave up trying to stay awake and closed my eyes.

Things were still quiet and awkward between us at breakfast. Felton watched my every move as we ate, speaking only long enough to ask if I needed anything. The nurse checked on me frequently, understandably wary after the idiot's last visit.

"I wanted to apologize for my behavior yesterday," he said stiffly after the nurse took my empty tray. "I said several things that were out of line and for that, I'm sorry."

"I understand. And now I'm going to say some things that I know you're not going to like, but I need to say them."

"Okay." He looked uneasy.

"All this is my fault. I forced my way onto that mission, and it went bad. That's on me for my own selfish reasons."

"Why did you?"

"I wanted to prove you wrong. I was hurt and angry because of John, and I wanted to throw myself back into work to get my mind off him. When you said no, I got pissed and did what I had to so I could prove to you that I was ready. That was shitty and I'm sorry."

After staring at me for several seconds, he sighed. "I'm sorry as well. I could've tried to understand where you were coming from. But when I saw the scars and heard that John was responsible," he sighed. "He and I don't have a good past. And I let that animosity interfere. When I found out that he hurt you again, all I wanted to do was shelter you. I wanted you to come back home and take some time to heal, get him out of your system."

"And that brings me to the other issue between us. The line where being my boss ends, and being my family begins."

"We've done a pretty good job of that, haven't we?"

"We did, but it felt different when I came back. Maybe being away changed it for me. While I was gone, I had more independence. I didn't have to worry about my next assignment or following all the rules. I had the freedom to make choices, and those choices were my own. Sometimes I didn't make the best ones, and I had to deal with the consequences, but those were mine as well. And I don't want that to change."

"Larissa, what—"

I raised my hand, and he quieted. "I saw and went through a lot of unexpected things while I was gone. A lot of those included John and Lucas. Yes, John and I have a messy history, but anything that happens is between me and him. As for Lucas, all I will say is that he's a very dear friend and my relationship with him is none of your business. All you need to know is both are very important to me. You will *not* interrogate, investigate, or intimidate either of them. Period. Agreed?"

He glared for a few seconds before relenting. "Agreed."

"As for work, I'm giving you official notice I intend to retire ninety days from today."

"What about the FBI?" His brows were pinched.

"Given what happened the last time I saw Barton Kane, I'm pretty sure the Bureau fired me. Once I secure a lawyer, I'll have them reach out to Barton."

"Lissa, can we talk about this? You don't want to make any rash decisions right now. Why don't we wait until after your debrief and then talk about it?"

"I should've retired two years ago when I walked out of your office. This is what I want. Please respect that. You were my family before you were my boss, and I feel that if we were to continue to work together, that relationship will be more damaged than it already is."

"I'll admit I have mixed feelings about this. As your boss, I'm supposed to keep you working. But as the man who raised you and watched you struggle to have some kind of normal life," his face pinched, looking like he'd swallowed a lemon. "I understand."

"I'm glad. Because I'm hoping that means you'll understand when I say I'd like both my parents' complete and unredacted files as my retirement gift."

Chapter Eighteen

Ferme Il Dolore

John

I hung my head. No matter how much I hadn't meant to eavesdrop on their conversation once she made her announcement, I couldn't stop. I'd hoped to bring her back to Verona with me, but knowing she planned to walk away from Felton's bullshit lessened the sting. Between her recovery time and the information I was about to share with Felton, the chances of her going back in the field were slim to none.

When she demanded her parents' files, I had to leave or my laughter would've outed me. Felton had to be shitting a brick. Nobody ever questioned the great Felton Lynch. I'd heard his influence in the CIA wasn't what it used to be, and it made me smile. Served the prick right. My good mood vanished when I saw the deep scowl on his face as soon as he left her room. His eyes narrowed, and I motioned him closer.

"I'm not here to start any shit, Felton."

"Where's your friend?"

"Downstairs making a few phone calls," I answered. "Look, there's something you should know. Massimo put a bounty out on her."

His eyes bulged. "What?"

"Five million dollars. Ten if she's brought in alive."

"Son of a bitch." He scrubbed his hand over his face before crossing his arms in front of him. "How did you find out about this?"

"Ernesto told her just before he tried to strangle her. I guess he only needed five million."

"I'll follow up on it." His phone was out of his pocket.

"Damn right you will. Because if anything happens to her, there won't be a place you can hide that I won't find you."

He rolled his eyes. "Really? She wants nothing to do with you."

"Oh, this has nothing to do with how she feels about me. I'll protect her if I'm a part of her life or not. This has everything to do with you doing right by your friend when you took his daughter in and swore to protect her. We both know what a slimy shit you are, Felton. I sure as hell don't trust you, but for some reason, she does."

"Don't talk to me about trust, Martinetti. It's something you know nothing about."

"No, but I know plenty of things that I'm sure you don't want her to know about you." I leaned in closer so only he could hear me. "Or anyone else."

My gaze held his for a few seconds before he went back to his phone. "Understood."

"I don't want to threaten you, Felton. Just like you, I want to keep her safe."

"And that might be the only common goal we'll ever have." He checked his watch. "I need to get to the office. She was pretty tired and wanted to rest, so you might want to come back later."

"She still gets tired easily. Is that something to be worried about?"

"For now, no. The doctor said popping that stitch set her back a few days. We should see improvement soon."

He left without another word. I stood just inside her door and watched her sleep. Her cheeks had the smallest amount of color, which was encouraging. I'd just sat in the chair next to her so I wouldn't look like some creep when Lucas finally arrived. He watched her for a moment, but the way he clenched and unclenched his fists told me something was up.

Sure enough, his head jolted toward the hall. "We need to talk."

I led him to a waiting area in a quiet corner of the floor. "What's up?"

"The bounty is real. Five million cash, ten if she's alive."

"Fuck!" Desperate to punch something, I paced the floor. "Anything else?"

"They know Ernesto's dead, but according to their intel, the general's daughter killed him after he went nuts and tried to kill everyone. Nobody knows she was there, or that she's here now."

"Well, now we know what happened in Cuba," I said. "I told Felton about the bounty. He said he'd look into it. No doubt he'll find out the same things you did."

Lucas then reported Nonna wanted me to call her for a video chat, and we both laughed. She was nearly eighty years old and refused to eat any pasta that wasn't handmade, but knew the ins and outs of her cell phone. She asked a million questions about Liss and her recovery, scowling and cursing at me in Italian when I told her I hadn't convinced her to come back to Verona yet.

Liss was still asleep when we came back to her room after lunch. The nurse assured us she'd woke up long enough to eat but echoed what Felton said about needing more rest. Lucas headed back to the hotel while I opted to stay. He busted my balls, of course, before promising he'd be back by dinnertime. I sat in the chair next to her bed and watched some horrid, trashy daytime talk show on TV. I flicked through the channels in search of something better before returning to the same show. Before long, my eyes grew heavy. I laid my head on my arm and after stealing one last glance at her sleeping face, I closed my eyes.

"Move his gigantic head out of the way so I can bring the table over," a voice said.

"He's fine. Let him sleep," she whispered. "I'm sure neither of you have slept all that well thanks to me."

"And I'm sure that giant melon of his isn't very comfortable parked in your lap."

"Like your head is any smaller, jackass," I muttered, sitting up.

Our eyes met briefly before she looked away. We hadn't spoken at all since the night she collapsed. Lucas told me she knew we needed to talk, but wasn't ready. I wouldn't push her, no matter how much my anxiety screamed for answers. He tossed me a sandwich from the deli near the hotel. He and I talked and joked around as we ate, but other than a few smiles she was quiet. I snuck glances at her when I could and caught her doing the same several times.

Lucas didn't even bother to hide that he'd noticed. "Well, I think he's probably stared at you long enough, so we'll head back to the hotel so you can rest."

"Actually, I was going to ask if I could borrow him for a little while," she said. "I think it's time he and I talked."

I nodded, regretting that I ate such a large sandwich when it felt like an anvil dropped into the pit of my stomach. He gave her a gentle hug and after whispering in my ear not to screw up again, he left.

We eyed each other awkwardly before I cleared my throat. "Would you like to go outside?" I offered. "I won't be an accomplice, so don't even think about trying to convince me to help you escape."

She giggled. "Sure."

"You also have to put on a hoodie and let me push the wheelchair."

"Fine," she grumbled, rolling her eyes.

We arrived in the garden on the fifth floor. Because it was early evening and sunset was only about an hour away, most of the area was shaded. Her eyes lit up and followed a yellow butterfly as it flitted around. I slowly led her around the path, letting her smell or admire certain flowers. By the time we stopped at the stone bench near a tree bursting with pink flowers, her cheeks were rosy and her eyes almost sparkled as she continued to look around. I held out my hand and, after a pause, she grabbed it and shuffled to the bench and sat next to me. We sat in awkward silence for several minutes, neither of us brave enough to look at each other.

"I'm sorry," I finally blurted out when I could no longer stand the quiet. "I know I should've told you about Cassandra a long time ago."

She nodded slowly. "How long did it go on?"

"She was a drunken mistake that never should've happened."

"Try again. You forget she and I hung out almost every day. I actually felt bad that I left without telling her goodbye."

Fuck, she caught me. "Okay, full disclosure. The first time was a drunken mistake that I regretted the instant I woke up the next morning. Yes, there were other times, but they meant nothing. I swear."

She stared at me, her pale blue eyes giving nothing away. "Is it still going on?"

"*No*," I answered emphatically. "It only lasted a few weeks. It was over before midterms."

"She left early the night I was attacked because she had a booty call, John." She crossed her arms over her chest and narrowed her eyes.

"No, she *told* you she had a booty call. That was her story so she could get out of there and get everything in place for the attack."

"What?"

"This is why I didn't want to tell you about her. She was in on the attack. In fact, she was the ringleader."

She looked like she was going to be sick. "How?"

"She drugged your smoothie. Karl and Trevor stayed so they could grab you when you passed out, but you were taking too long, so they left and kept watch."

"Rachele too?"

"Did you see her at all that night?"

"Fucking bitch," she hissed after a few seconds. "Wait. How do you know all this?"

"When you saw me leave, it was because she threatened to hurt you if I didn't meet with her. She *bragged* about working with my uncle behind my back. After I took care of her, I rushed back to the campus. When I got there, Trevor already had you tied up. He wasn't too thrilled about having a gun held to his head."

"Trevor," she paused and her brows came together. "That was you?"

"I won't give you all the details of what else I saw when I found him with you because that's an image I never want in my head again. But, yes, I killed the sick fuck. And he deserved a more painful death than he got. I didn't get to enjoy his screams for as long as I wanted. I was still trying to find you."

Her eyes widened. "And Cassandra? What exactly do you mean you took care of her?"

"Let's just say I made her see the error of her ways and leave it at that." Liss didn't so much as blink when I said what I did about killing Trevor, but I wasn't proud of threatening to kill Cassandra's twelve-year-old sister.

"She came to see me the next day."

"I was next door in her room and heard every word. She knew if she tried anything, I would've busted down your door and shot her without a second thought and fuck the consequences."

"She came by with food almost every day."

"I bought the food and watched her from either the stairwell or her room. She reported to Gio every day, so I couldn't kill her. But I kept her on a very short leash. Making her bring you food was my way of rubbing it in her face that her sick plan failed. After that first week, she started staying at Rachele so I'd leave her alone."

"Why did you lie to the cops?"

"I needed to explain why I came back to the office that night, and it just popped into my head. It was either lie or tell them the truth, and then I would've been trying to protect you from a jail cell."

She watched the water fountain for what seemed like an eternity. A knot settled into my stomach that got heavier the longer she was silent. "This is your one and only chance to tell me anything and everything else you've been keeping from me, John," she said. "After this, if I find out anything else all bets are off."

"When you were attacked, I told you they were going to smuggle you back to Italy. What I didn't tell you was that Cassandra planned to hand you over to Marco."

"The huge guy at your uncle's estate?"

"Yes, the one who threw you off the pier. To say he enjoys torturing people would be a gross understatement. She was going to hand you over to him, knowing full well what he's capable of. Also, Soren's alive and somewhere here in the US. That's all. I swear."

"Was there anyone else other than her? Anyone else in Italy?"

I took her hand in mine, feeling her tense. "No. After we got together, there was nobody else and there has been no one else since."

"Seriously?" she scoffed.

"I'm dead serious, Larissa. You were the last woman I was with and the last time was the morning you taught the mafia class. Twelve hours later, you took me into custody. Since then, it's been me, my hand, and my active imagination." She smiled and looked at the ground. Encouraged, I moved closer. "I know I screwed up. You have no idea how many times I wrestled with telling you the truth. Lucas kicked the shit out of me the minute he came home after reading your text."

She let out a soft chuckle. "I knew he had it in him."

"What about you? Was there anybody else after you got away?"

"No, much to Titus's disappointment. He'd left one of his men behind in Doolin to watch over me. I think he also hoping I'd be swept off my feet, but I just wasn't ready."

I nodded and silence fell between us. She looked deep in thought as her gaze wandered around the garden. After a while, she slowly got to her feet and stretched her legs before taking small, measured steps to the tree. I watched her every move, ready to step in if she needed it even though I knew she wouldn't want it. She ran her fingers over the bark of the tree as she mulled something in her head. The next time she looked up, her eyes shone with tears.

"Liss? What's wrong?"

She wiped her eyes. "This whole thing has made me realize is that I'm still a mess."

"What do you mean?"

"I want to be mad about the lies, but we're both guilty. When Cassandra told me everything, I could've acted like an adult and stayed so we could talk things out. Instead, I left, crashed your car, and rejoined the CIA. While I was there, I found out about the Cuba job. Felton didn't think I was ready. And yet again, instead of acting like a grownup, I threw a tantrum, was a complete bitch to him and went over his head. I was reckless and impulsive, and it damn near got me killed."

I kept my face blank, but inside my brain was reeling. Seeing her so upset made me want to bury my fist in Felton's smug face. Her actions probably weren't the healthiest, but I knew firsthand how well that asshole riled people up. "We both could've handled that better. And that's something we can work on together."

"No."

My heart stuttered, and I took a step closer. "What?"

"No," she repeated as she leaned against the tree. "I need to fix me before I can even think about trying to fix us. I need to get a handle on controlling my impulses, because I'll be damned if I get anyone else hurt or killed because of me. And it's not fair to you to rope you into this mess. I've hurt me enough. I can't and I won't hurt you, too."

I gently pulled her closer to me, my shoulder muffling the loud sobs as her body shook. She didn't protest when I led her back to the bench and set her in my lap. "I'm sorry. I'm so, so sorry," I murmured in her ear.

"I love you," she whispered, clutching my shirt tightly.

"I love you, too."

I hugged her, avoiding her wounds as best as I could. We sat in silence and after a while, her body relaxed. Her eyes were closed, her breathing slow and even. I carried her back to her room and tried to loosen her hand so I could put her down with no luck. Sighing, I slowly climbed on the bed and pulled the covers over us. A nurse came in to check on her and glared when she found me until I showed her the death grip she had on my shirt. After shaking her head, the nurse told me to be careful of her left side and closed the door.

My phone vibrated. After a few seconds of awkwardly trying to reach my pocket, I saw it was Lucas. I quietly answered and explained I was literally trapped in his sister's grasp. After he stopped laughing, I asked him to text a phone number to me and then told him if I didn't make it back to the hotel, I'd see him in the morning.

The phone number he sent belonged to a security consultant in Lisbon, considered one of the best in the world. My uncle was too quiet, and it worried me. He was no doubt planning something, and I needed to be ready. My conversation with the consultant's office was brief. He wanted to meet as soon as possible and I told him I'd fly out the next day. After sliding my phone back into my pocket, I laid my head back and stared at the ceiling. She nestled her head into my shoulder and her grip on my shirt finally relaxed. Burying my nose in her hair, I committed everything about that moment to memory. I closed my eyes, dreading having to let her go in the morning.

"I know you're staring at me," I muttered, my eyes still closed.

"Sorry," she replied in a soft voice. "You looked so peaceful, and I didn't want to move and wake you up."

I opened my eyes and noticed it was still dark outside. "How are you feeling? I tried to lay you down, but you wouldn't let go of my shirt."

"Shit, I'm sorry."

"Don't be. I just hope I didn't hurt you."

"You didn't," she watched me closely. "I know what I told you last night wasn't what you wanted to hear."

"I'm always going to love you, Larissa Donovan. Even if we aren't together, I will always love you, fight for you, and protect you. Because it's still my hope that one day we'll find our way back to each other."

"You're always going to be my first love. Nothing will ever change that."

"So, what are you going to do once you get out of here?"

Her nose wrinkled. "TBD. I don't even know when I'm getting out of here. It gives me plenty of time to hopefully figure some things out in my mind so I have a coherent plan on how to fix me. I gave Felton my official notice of retirement, so I'll be walking away from that soon."

"Are you serious?"

"I should've done it two years ago. There's still a lot to figure out with the FBI."

"So I heard."

She rolled her eyes. "Lucas is too good at his damn job sometimes. But yes, I need to fix that as well. And then maybe take up yoga or something relaxing."

We laughed and I held her close, loving the feel of her in my arms. Any moment a doctor or nurse would come in, meaning I'd have to crawl out of that bed and it would be all over. I leaned back against the pillow and rubbed her back.

"Will you stay in touch?"

Her eyes met mine and she smiled. "I can't promise I'll call or text every day, but yes. I don't want you or Lucas to worry about me."

Relief rushed through me. "Thank you. And I promise I'll give you whatever time and space you need. In fact—"

"Jesus Christ, tell me you didn't keep her up all night talking her ear off," Lucas said as he breezed into the room.

"Good morning, asshat," she greeted with rolled eyes. "Didn't anyone ever tell you it's rude to interrupt people's conversations?"

"No, it's fine," I said. "The morning crew will be here soon. Plus, I need to talk to the asshat privately."

He caught my eye, and I gave a small nod as I got up and helped her get comfortable. Barely a minute later, the doctor and a nurse walked into the room, followed by Felton. His face hardened at the sight of us, but he remained silent. We watched quietly while the doctor examined her. When he announced she had improved and would probably be discharged in a few days, we all breathed a sigh of relief.

"We'll let you guys have your breakfast," I told her as the nurse entered with a food tray.

Lucas looked like he wanted to ask a million questions, but said nothing as he followed me. By the time we found a place to chat, his face was locked into a scowl. "What's going on? You asked me for that phone number last night and then I find you two cuddled up together this morning? Is she coming back with us? What's up with Felton?"

I held up a hand to silence him. "She's staying here. Once she's discharged, she's going back to Virginia to recover. In eighty-nine days, she'll be officially retired from the CIA."

"Holy shit! And then is she coming back to Verona?"

"That's up to her. She still needs to get shit straightened out with the FBI."

His brows came together. "So, where does that leave the two of you?"

"Nowhere," I answered, and the ache in my chest returned. "She needs to figure some things out, so I'm letting her be. In fact, I'm leaving this afternoon. I don't think Felton will bug you now that she bitched him out for it."

"I don't understand. What do you mean you're 'letting her be'? Where are you going?"

"She needs time and space, and I'm giving that to her. I'm going to Lisbon to meet with Acosta."

"That's why you wanted that number. But why? We haven't heard of any threats."

"And that's why it's the perfect time to talk to him," I answered. "Massimo has been far too quiet. We need fresh eyes on the security of both houses before it's too late. We've already had a few incidents where things have slipped through that shouldn't have."

"When are you leaving? Does she know?"

"No, I was planning to tell her when you came in. So after Felton leaves, I need you to stay here while I go back to the hotel and pack. I'll come back here and say my goodbyes. Since I figured you'd want to stay here until she's discharged, I'm chartering a plane to Lisbon. That way you can take the jet home to Verona."

He looked uneasy. "She's going to be crushed. You know that, right?"

"I know. I also know that if I tell her now, she'll beg me to stay and I'll cave. But I can't. I have to do this. For all our sakes."

I headed back to the hotel, packing quickly. If I stopped moving, I feared my second thoughts would win out. I didn't like leaving her with so many things uncertain, but she couldn't come home to me if that home was wiped out by my fucking uncle. Finishing in record time, I grabbed a taxi back to the hospital to break the news to her.

"Why did he leave, Lucas?" Her voice was suspicious as I approached her room.

"He had to grab something. He'll be back soon."

"What was he grabbing?"

"Something. I don't know."

"Lucas," she warned.

I hurried inside before she interrogated him any further. "I'm back."

"Thank god," he muttered. He closed the door, leaning against it to make sure we weren't interrupted.

Her eyes watched me as I sat on the bed. "Where did you go?"

I took her hand in both of mine, happy to feel her skin was finally warm. "I need to go to Lisbon to talk to a security consultant."

"You're meeting with Victor Acosta? Why?"

"Just as a precaution. It's better to be safe than sorry."

"Tread carefully. His crew is pretty damn scary."

She knew Victor well. Their paths crossed a few years earlier when she was on a job in Lisbon. At the time he'd just joined his family's security consulting firm, but the tech the company provided ultimately helped Liss get the job done and escape without incident. They'd had a brief fling afterward and while it wasn't music to my ears to hear that, I was hardly one to judge. It happened before I entered the picture.

"I've met a few of them and they can definitely be rough. I'm estimating no less than two fist fights and one wicked hangover."

"Working vacation?" she joked.

"Something like that."

She swiped the tears from her face. "Promise me you'll be careful. There's no future for us if you do something stupid and get yourself killed. You hear me?"

"I could say the same thing to you. You *are* my future. I'm just making sure there's a home for you to return to when you come back to me."

She laughed. "Fair enough."

Lucas cleared his throat. "John, you should probably get going so you don't get stuck in traffic."

I bent down and kissed her temple. She clutched my arm and looked up at me. There was a conflicted look in her eyes. She opened her mouth to speak, but she shook her head and smiled despite the new tears.

"I love you," I murmured. "Always have, always will."

"Go," she whispered. "Please. I need you to get on that plane before I beg you to stay."

Fighting every instinct to call the whole thing off, I stood. Lucas pulled me into a hug. "Be careful, man."

"I will. You be careful, too. Don't let her do anything crazy."

I left without another word. My feet protested every step as I left the hospital and climbed into the taxi. When we got to the airport and I approached the plane on the tarmac, my heart screamed for me to turn around and run back. Taking a deep breath, I took a step, followed by another. I hesitated at the bottom of the steps, knowing this was my last chance to escape. It was then that I steeled myself up and did what the woman I loved ordered me to do, and got on the plane.

Chapter Nineteen

Astray

Larissa

I stared at the TV, not paying any attention to whatever obscenely loud action movie Lucas put on. Now and then I glanced at the clock and wondered where he was and if he was okay, which then set off a string of questions I had no business asking myself. Would he come back? Did he miss me as much as I already missed him? What if he met someone else?

It was my decision to let him go, I reminded myself. The pain was intolerable at that moment, but it would be better in the long run...blah, blah, blah. Yes, it needed to be done, but that didn't make it suck any less. I tried to concentrate on the screen again, ignoring the hole in my heart.

"We don't have to watch this if you don't want to," Lucas said, turning down the volume. "If you want, we could sit around and do the girly breakup thing. I could probably be talked into painting your nails, but I can't braid hair worth a shit."

"You're such an ass."

"That's the best you can come up with? Not an asshole or a jackass? Damn, you're a mess!" He leaned against the bed and propped his head up on his hand. "Jokes aside, are you okay? I've seen you look at the clock at least six times."

I nodded. "It hurts, but it was my choice. And he left for a damn good reason. I just miss him."

"He misses you, too. I know you probably don't want to hear this right now, but I know you guys will make it back to each other. I just can't picture either of you with anyone else."

Our heads turned at the sound of a knock at the door. Felton entered, stopping when he saw both of us. Lucas clenched his jaw but relaxed when I put my hand on his arm.

"What's up?"

He glanced around the room. "If I may ask, where's the third musketeer?"

"He had some business to attend to, so he left," Lucas answered curtly.

He motioned to me. "May I have a word?"

"I'll be outside," Lucas announced, standing up.

"Wait." I grabbed his arm. "Is what you need to say classified?"

"No."

I pointed to the chair beside me. "Sit down, Lucas. It's not like you're not going to stand out in the hallway and listen anyway."

Felton pursed his lips and stood by the bed. "I just wanted to tell you I'm heading back to Langley tonight. Hannah wants to see my notes about Cuba, and a few other things need to be handled."

Hannah Myers-Nelson was his boss at the CIA. She'd taken over his section about a year before I left, but my experience with her was limited as I'd been working mostly FBI cases during that time. The rumor was she'd wanted to fire him over the John debacle, and it was only because of leverage he had on some of the senior executives that his job was spared.

"You have nothing to worry about, Lissa. All I'm submitting is your account of what happened. Marianna will ultimately have to answer for what happened since it was her mission."

"I'll let you know when I'm discharged and heading back."

"Were you planning on staying at the house?" His voice was hopeful.

"To be honest, I haven't thought that far ahead. I'll think about it."

"Okay, just let me know," he mumbled, doing a shit job of hiding his disappointment. He glanced at Lucas. "Will you be staying for the rest of the time she's here? If not, I'd like to arrange security. I really don't want to leave her here alone."

"I'm going to stay until she's discharged. But if you'd be more comfortable arranging for security, I won't object."

"No, Mr. Luccetti, I think she'll be fine under your watch. I'm sorry that we got off on the wrong foot when you and Mr. Martinetti arrived."

"I understand, sir," he replied, standing up and offering his hand.

I blinked and stared at them. What the hell was I witnessing? They shook hands and after exchanging a few more pleasantries, Felton gave me a gentle hug and left. Lucas turned around to find me gaping at him with wide eyes.

His brows came together. "What?"

"What the hell was that?"

He smiled. "John told me he raised you, so I understand now. He's worried about you, the same as the rest of us."

I shrugged and checked the clock again, causing him to announce it was time to move around and focus my mind elsewhere. I was finally allowed to leave the ICU, so we went to the garden where he rolled his eyes while I fawned all over the colorful flowers and enjoyed the fresh air. Well, as fresh as the air can be in Florida in June.

Two days later, I was finally discharged. He brought me a change of clothes, which I'd been grateful for until I opened the bag and found an ugly pink t-shirt. I made a mental note to never allow him to buy me clothing again, and also buy him the ugliest Hawaiian shirt I could find as soon as possible. We took a taxi to the airport so I could catch the first flight back to Washington, D.C. Since my flight didn't leave for several hours, we hung out together near my gate.

He stole a sip of my coffee and returned it to the table in front of us. "What's the first thing you're going to do when you get back?"

"Go to my parents' graves. It's been more than two years since I've been there. Are you headed back to Verona?"

"Yeah. I need to check in on Nonna and my mom."

"Please give Nonna a hug from me. Would it be weird to tell your mom I said hi?"

"Not at all. She doesn't hold any of this against you. My parents' marriage," he paused and shook his head. "Just trust me when I say not to worry about how she feels about you. I also want you to know that you will always have a safe haven with us. No matter what's going on, where you are, or what trouble you're in. I know things are tentative with you and John, but he'd say the same thing. If you're ever in a jam, *come home.*"

I willed my eyes not to tear up and gave him a small smile. "Thank you. I will. And I promise to come visit soon."

"It would be okay if you did more than visit, you know."

"All the subtlety of a hand grenade."

His face turned serious. "I want you to promise me you'll be careful. You can roll your eyes and tell me that you're always careful, but I'm still going to worry about you. So just promise me."

"I promise I will, Lucas."

He reached into his bag and handed me a cell phone in a bright red case. "And promise you'll keep in touch. This has both mine and John's phone numbers programmed in. It's a secure line, so it's hard as hell to trace. I don't care what happens or what time of day it is, if you need anything, *anything*, you call one of us. Got it?"

"Got it."

My flight began boarding. He refused to say goodbye, only that he would see me later. I took my seat on the plane and stared out the window. As the plane backed away I waved my hand, not caring if he could see. Once we were in the air I closed my eyes, trying to quiet my sudden unease, and fell into a restless sleep.

· · · ● ●· ● ● · · ·

Two Weeks Later

It was probably the quietest Fourth of July ever. Gone were the days of doing shots and covert debauchery because I was usually on assignment. Instead, I spent the day with Felton, much to his delight. Our relationship was strained, but loosening up a little. While I helped him cook dinner, we exchanged stories about things that had happened over the past two years. I told him about my travels as I hunted Sardi family associates and he told me about all the changes at the CIA. At the end of the night, he hugged me tightly and told me he would miss working with me but hoped to still be a part of my life. I pointed out he was like family to me, so there was no question he'd be there if he wanted to be.

My uncle Titus pulled some strings, and one of his stateside contacts rented me a small cabin in Arlington County. It was in the middle of nowhere, so it was the perfect place for me to stay while I recovered and began training. Every day I jogged the forest surrounding the cabin and practiced shooting in a clearing behind the house.

True to my word, I visited my parents' graves the second day after I got back. Felton knew Barton still had the FBI looking for me, so it wasn't a surprise to find an agent watching the cemetery. I easily dodged her, but knew that meant I needed to be careful of all movements in the future. Thankfully, I was able to attend the counseling sessions required by the CIA following an injury virtually. I'd been lucky enough to find a private therapist also willing to conduct sessions the same way so I could start working on some of my own personal issues. After only a few sessions, I already started feeling some much needed clarity.

Arriving back at the cabin, I headed to the kitchen and grabbed a beer. I tossed my keys on the counter and then flopped on the couch, where I planned to spend the rest of the evening being lazy and watching fireworks on TV. I was thinking about heading to bed when an odd ringtone suddenly blared from my purse. After rummaging around, I found the red phone Lucas gave me and quickly answered.

"Hey," he greeted in a quiet voice.

"What's wrong?"

He paused. "Um, there's no easy way to say this, so I'm just going to say it. John's missing."

"Say that again, please," I whispered, trying to breathe and fighting the freezing cold that invaded my blood.

"I lost contact with him three days ago, and he's always said he's in trouble if that happens."

Tears filled my eyes and I had to lean against the counter to keep my legs from buckling underneath me. "What info do you have?"

"I'm working on getting surveillance now. I should have it in the next twenty-four hours."

"Where's Nonna and your mom?"

"Mom is in Zurich visiting a friend. Nonna is on her way to Verona."

I clutched the counter. "Tell your mom to stay where she is for now. I'm on my way. I'll get you my flight info once I have it. We'll go through everything when I get there."

"Okay."

"Lucas? We'll find him."

He exhaled slowly. "I hope so."

I called Felton on my personal cell as I packed. He wasn't thrilled to hear I was leaving the country and even less so when I wouldn't tell him why, only stating I had a personal issue that needed immediate attention. He gruffly told me to be safe and hung up. I was willing to bet he'd use his connections to get all the info he wanted, but I just couldn't bring myself to care at that moment.

Fifteen hours. That's how long it took to get from Dulles to Verona, and that's how long my brain had to think of every single plausible scenario about why he was missing, who took him, and every horrific detail I could think up. I felt like a zombie by the time I wandered off the plane. Luckily, John's driver, Benny, was waiting for me. An hour later, the SUV stopped at the front door of the estate where Lucas stood waiting for me.

"You look terrible," he observed as he hugged me. "You didn't sleep at all, did you?"

"Nope," I answered hoarsely as we entered the house.

He led me to the kitchen, where Nonna had pots on each burner of the stove and was busying herself stirring the largest one. She ran to me and gripped me in her arms tightly. "Larissa, I'm so glad you're here," she sobbed in shaky Italian, releasing me when I winced. "I'm so sorry. I forgot about your injuries."

"It's okay, Nonna. I'm feeling better. Now we just need to find that grandson of yours. And we will."

In a flash, she put a large white plate piled with food in front of me. "But first you'll eat," she commanded. "You're too pale and skinny."

She set a plate down in front of Lucas and then turned back to the stove. We exchanged glances before digging in. The only sounds in the kitchen came from Nonna as she moved around the kitchen and talked to herself. Once she was satisfied we'd eaten enough, we moved to the library.

"Any new information?" I asked as he powered on his laptop.

"The last time he contacted me was four days ago, when he told me he was meeting someone at a cafe. He hasn't been seen or heard from since. I received the surveillance video from outside that showed him entering but never leaving."

"Did he say who he was meeting at the cafe?"

"No, but I assumed it was Victor. Here's the video."

I watched the screen, my heart hammering wildly in my chest. John entered the building as he spoke to a tall, skinny man with pale hair and even paler skin. The video was in black and white, so it was impossible to see any further details. However, one thing was very clear to me.

"That's not Victor Acosta," I uttered, grabbing the laptop from him and rewinding the video.

"How can you tell?"

"I know him well. Victor is almost as tall as John and probably about fifty pounds heavier. The thing is, he and John know each other. Who the hell is this guy?"

As I continued to watch, he stared at me as he processed what I'd said. "How do you know Victor so well?"

I shot him a quick glare. "In the interest of that agreement we made about not knowing about each other's sex lives, I'm not going to answer that question." I snapped. "Do you have Victor's number?"

He searched his phone and showed me the phone number. I used the red phone to make the call. As I waited for an answer, his eyes bounced between me and the screen. After a few seconds, and apparently no longer able to control himself, his eyes widened and he started gibbering about me and Victor. I smacked his shoulder when the call connected.

"Olá," a thin voice answered.

"Victor Acosta, por favor," I replied in Portuguese.

"*Posso pergentar quem está ligando?*" (May I ask who's calling?)

"Miriam Burnett."

The call ended. I blinked and processed what that meant before tossing the phone next to me on the couch. I gazed at the laptop screen for a moment. "How did John contact you while he was gone? Did he call or text?"

"He texted, but that's normal when he travels."

"Where did you get Victor's number?"

"A friend of John's, but he's trustworthy."

"Yes, but how trustworthy is the source the friend got it from?" I rubbed my eyes. "What do we know about Massimo?"

"He's back in Bari, but I doubt he would do this. No matter how pissed off he gets, he needs John. He's the next in line."

"Yeah, but if something were to happen to John, it would go to you, right?"

He gave a humorless chuckle. "Nope. I'm not a Sardi by blood. My uncle would rather knock up one of the whores in his house. And even if I was, he hates me since I'm not a fighter."

"What an asshole. Okay, so who else knows he's missing?"

"You, me and Nonna. The guys still think he's in Lisbon." He looked uncomfortable, as if preparing for me to disagree with what he was about to say. "We should tell them. We've known those guys, all of them, for a very long time. Some all the way back to when we were kids. Hell, both Rocco and Paolo's dads worked for John's dad in his law office. The security breaches are usually thanks to the household staff, but once Nonna got here, she sent them all home like she normally does. She hates having them underfoot when she's here."

I nodded as I dialed the red phone. There was one person who might help without alerting Felton. "Ginnie Matthews," a gravelly voice answered.

"Ginnie, it's Larissa Donovan."

"Lissa? Holy crap!"

Ginnie was a close co-worker of Felton's, and I usually contacted her if he wasn't around. She was also the kind of person who didn't tell Felton I'd been in touch if I asked her to keep it quiet. I hoped that was still the case.

"It's been a while. How have you been?"

"Same old, same old, I guess. How can I help you today?"

"I need a favor," I paused. "And secrecy."

"You know I have no problem doing that."

"Thank you. I really don't want Felton to worry about me right now."

"That's so sweet of you, honey," she gushed. "He's been really struggling to cope since he lost Karina. It was just so sudden. I really feel for him. He hasn't been the same since she passed."

"I noticed that, too. He definitely misses her."

"So, what did you need me to find out for you?"

"I need to know if you can find out any information about Gianni Martinetti, AKA John Martinetti. Any movement, anything you can find. He's Massimo Sardi's nephew and I need to find him as part of my investigation. Please check all his known aliases if you're able."

"That'll take a couple of days. Doing some research on your favorite mob family while you're recuperating?"

"You know me so well," I chuckled. "I really appreciate you doing this for me. And for not telling Felton. You know how he gets. He thinks I should wrap myself up in a blanket and stay on the couch for the next few months until I'm better."

We chatted for a few more minutes before I ended the call. "The CIA is now doing some of the work for us."

Lucas closed his laptop. "So now what do we do?"

"Call any of John's friends and associates who want nothing to do with your uncle and see if they've heard anything. I'm going to call some of my contacts who might know something."

I lost track of the time calling so many people. It was only when Nonna stormed into the library and demanded we come and eat dinner that I saw it was dark outside. We strolled to the kitchen and gave her limited information so she wouldn't worry more. She hung her head and said a small prayer when Lucas told her we were waiting to hear from everyone we'd called.

"Well, now that you are waiting, you should be resting. You both look like you're going to fall asleep on my kitchen floor. Off to bed!"

My knapsack was still sitting by the stairs when we entered the foyer. Lucas grabbed it from my hand and slung it over his shoulder. I followed in silence until he stopped in front of John's bedroom door.

"What are you doing? That's not my room," I protested.

He placed my bag in my hand and opened the door. "It's your room, Lissa. Trust me."

My eyes watered, and he pulled me into a gentle hug. "We're not going to assume the worst right now," I mumbled. "He just hasn't checked in. For all we know, he and Victor got drunk and wound up in Ibiza or some shit."

"You really think that?"

"That's what we're going with until we hear differently. Get some sleep."

I glanced around the room, and my heart stuttered in my chest. If I hadn't known better, I would've sworn I woke up in the bed that same morning and made it before walking out to start my day. The book and bottle of lotion I'd left on my night table almost two months earlier were still there. I trudged to the table, opened the drawer, and found the ball of yarn and knitting needles I was going to use to make a scarf for him, causing tears to fill my eyes. When I found the small

Italian flag I knitted for him as a joke in the drawer of his night table, I couldn't hold back my emotions any longer. I buried my face in his pillow and sobbed.

Once my tears stopped, I felt all the energy drain from my body. I dragged myself to the closet, grabbed one of his t-shirts and let his scent flood my lungs as I pulled it over my head. I freed my hair from the ponytail and slowly crawled under the covers.

"We're going to find you, baby. I promise," I whispered as I ran my hand over his pillow. "And I promise you that whoever is responsible is going to die with a bullet in their head."

Over the next three days, we talked to an endless stream of people. Each person's response was the same. John hadn't been seen in Lisbon, anywhere in Italy, or anywhere else. Lucas watched me carefully as I finished my call with Ginnie and hung my head in my hands as soon as I thew the phone down.

"Nothing?" His voice was hoarse.

"Not a goddamned thing." My voice cracked. I took several deep breaths, refusing to abandon all hope. Lucas spoke, but the words didn't penetrate. I felt his hand on my shoulder and looked up to see him eyeing me with concern.

"Are you okay?"

I shook my head. "No. He's gone and nobody knows where. Or why."

"So what do we do?"

"We do what we've been doing; keep quiet and keep our ears open because someone will slip up eventually. We'll find him, even if I have to tear this goddamned planet apart to do it."

Chapter Twenty

Sanctuary

Larissa

"Larissa? Are you okay?" Nonna asked, breaking me out of my dark thoughts.

I nodded and looked down at the ball of dough on the counter. When putting me to work in the garden hadn't helped my restlessness over the past few weeks, she dragged me into the kitchen and taught me how to make pasta. While beating the hell out of the dough felt good, it did little to curb my frustrations. Hearing her scoff, I looked up to find her at the corner of the counter less than a foot away.

"Child, don't lie to me," she scolded, shooing me away. "And don't cry in my dough. Wash your hands and keep me company while I finish."

Time spent with Nonna was special. I'd never known my own grandmothers and my relationship with Karina was strained and mostly for show, so my exposure to a female family figure who actually cared about me was minimal. The great thing about Nonna was she always made it clear how important we were to her. When she rolled her eyes and started muttering about the "mess" in front of her, I pursed my lips to keep from laughing. I washed my hands and took a seat on a barstool.

John had been gone for a month, and the pain only increased with each passing day. I'd recovered from my injuries enough to go back to my full training regimen, so I was ready to take on his captors. The only problem was we were no closer to finding them, or him, than the day we realized he was missing.

"Sorry," I replied. "I miss him."

"Never apologize for missing the man you love," she said, kneading the dough she forced me to vacate. "And never think your sadness is a weakness. You can pull an amazing amount of strength and will from sadness."

Lucas walked into the kitchen with a look on his face that told me there was trouble. He spent much of his time holed up in the library, chasing down even the tiniest lead he could find. I opened my mouth to ask what was wrong, but he shook his head quickly. His eyes shot to Nonna. We would talk later.

He sat on the stool next to me. "Nonna, do you think you could call Mama later and try to convince her to come to Verona? I don't like her being there by herself, and she won't listen to me."

"I will ask, but I will not force. If she says no, then I cannot make her," she answered.

Elena returned from Zurich the previous week but refused his repeated requests to come to the estate. He didn't want to tell her about John's abduction until she was in Verona, so she still had no idea. There had still been no news from Massimo's crew that made us think he had any knowledge or involvement. Unless that was the reason Lucas looked worried.

Later that night, after making sure Nonna had retired to her guest room, he led me down the hall to John's office. I pulled away from his grasp when he opened the door. Over the past few weeks, I refused to enter the room. It was John's inner sanctum, where he retreated when he needed time alone. Invading that space felt like I was abandoning hope of his return, accepting that it was no longer his. Lucas gave an impatient look and gently tugged me inside, locking the door as soon as it closed behind us. The room was stuffy since it hadn't been used for a while. I wandered toward the window behind the desk as he grabbed a drink from the bar.

"Lissa?"

I turned and found him seated in one of the chairs facing the desk. I slowly sat down in the high-backed black leather chair next to me. My eyes grazed over the papers and folders strewn across his desk, stopping at the framed picture of the two of us taken before everything got screwed up. The letter I sent Lucas sat next to it, along with a map highlighting my route back to the States. I traced his handwriting on the note stuck to a folder with my finger as I tried to stop the tears from falling.

"Lissa?" he repeated a little louder.

My eyes shot up. "Sorry. What did you find out?"

"Marco was spotted outside San Marino. We don't have any associates there, but…"

"It puts him fairly close to Venice," I finished.

"A lot closer than I would like."

"Do you think Massimo is up to something?"

He nodded. "The family has no associates in that area. Massimo never visits my mom, so there's no reason for him to be anywhere near that area. Gino also told me this morning he saw a couple of low level Sardi men in Verona yesterday."

"Fuck, they're circling," I groaned. "We need to get her out of there."

"Easier said than done with all Massimo's men sniffing around."

"Would it arouse any suspicion if you just showed up and had someone with you?"

"Probably not if I brought Paolo. He's close friends with a couple of the guys. Why?"

"Because it's not safe for you to travel alone and you're going to go sneak her out and bring her back here."

"I'm not leaving you and Nonna by yourselves!" he shouted, standing up.

"Lucas, there's no time." I tried to keep my voice calm. "We need to get her back here and then we need to figure out how to increase the security around this house before they figure out that I'm here and John's not."

"He's too strong. He has enough men to overpower our security and kill us all. And any additional security we find would probably be full of his spies. We're sitting ducks."

Closing my eyes, I placed my head on the desk, hating to admit he was right. If Massimo wanted to take this place, there wasn't a damn thing we could do to stop him. After a moment, I realized I had a solution right at my fingertips.

He stared at the list of numbers written on the sheet of paper I handed to him. "What's this?"

"The Sanctuary."

"I don't understand."

"It's the coordinates to an island. My island, to be precise. It's uncharted and my ownership is untraceable. Tomorrow morning, you and Paolo will head to Venice. How trustworthy are the security guards at your mom's house?"

"I picked every single one, and Paolo is friends with most of them. My mom and Nonna refuse to keep a household staff, so we don't have to worry about that."

"Okay, good. You go to her and we'll take care of things here. In three days, we will meet you at her house. From there you, Nonna, and your mom will head to the island."

"And where will you go?"

"Back to the States. I'll draw their attention to me so you can get away."

"That puts you right in his crosshairs. We need to stick together, Lissa. I don't like this."

"I don't like it either, but at some point, he's going to realize John is missing and go apeshit."

"And he'll come after you."

"I'd rather he come after me than any of you. I will *not* allow the three of you to be in danger or used as leverage again if I can help it. And the best way to do that is to remove you from the chessboard. Period."

Resigned, he nodded and eyed the paper. "How do you have a private island?"

"My dad was in the Irish mob," I answered, looking through the file folder at the top of the stack.

"And?"

I smiled. "And my dad ripped off the Irish mob."

"He did what?"

"Several of their real estate holdings were in his name. Right around the time he found a way out, he was told to sell them, and some of that money found its way into an offshore account. I'm told other money magically found its way there, too."

"Holy shit," he whistled.

"I had no idea until I got to Belfast and my uncle told me. Just before Seamus died, he gave Titus all the info and told him to hold it for me when I got older. One of the first things I did was buy the island, so I would have somewhere to disappear to once I retired."

"Nobody knows about it? Not even Felton?"

"The only people on the island are my security staff. I wasn't even talking to Felton when I bought it, so he knows nothing. My ownership is buried under several aliases and shell companies that nobody knows about, and lead nowhere near me. We'll contact Tavi, my head of security in the morning so he can get your travel arranged. He'll make sure nobody can track you guys. I won't even know the details. Once you're there, you'll have to follow his security protocols. Is that something you can live with?"

"I don't like it, but it's not like I have much of a choice."

"No, not really," I stated plainly, pointing to the folder. "What was John working on before you guys came to Tampa?"

"He was looking for anything he could that might point him to Soren. We found recent financial activity on an old offshore account linked between him and Massimo."

"Interesting," I replied, reading through the papers. After a few minutes, I placed the folder in my lap to take with me.

"So, back to this plan," he began and paused when there was a loud knock on the door. He unlocked it and had to step away quickly when it suddenly swung open.

"Why are you yelling, Lucas?" Nonna thundered as she barged in.

"Nonna, please sit down," he sighed, motioning toward the chairs in front of the desk.

We spared no detail and told her everything we learned about Marco's movements and the possibility of an attack. She listened quietly but tensed when I told her my plan to send the three of them into hiding while I went back to the US. Her eyes followed my every move as I tried not to fidget while Lucas finished outlining our plan to meet at Elena's in a few days. She stared at me after he finished, only increasing my anxiety tenfold.

"Nonna, tell her we need to stick together."

"Lucas, I could do that, but the words would be useless." She turned to me and her eyes softened. "You're going to look for him, aren't you?"

"I have to," I admitted quietly. "He'd do the same for me. In fact, he already did. Somehow, some way, I will find him. Once we leave here, the next time you see me, I'll either be bringing him home to recover or bringing his body home to bury."

She stood up and walked around the desk, pulling me into her arms. "I can see why he loves you so much. You're the only woman strong enough to handle him and this crazy family. I hope one day he's smart enough to make you his wife."

"Thank you," I whispered. "I love him too."

The next morning, Lucas and Paolo headed to Elena's house. While the rest of the men patrolled the grounds, Max and Rocco helped us gather important documents and pack. Gino returned to the city to keep watch for any more of Massimo's spies. On my last night in Verona, Lucas called, and we went over the final details of the drive to Elena's house. He reported his mom was upset to learn about John's abduction and eager for us to get to her house the next day.

Too anxious to sleep, I wandered the property for most of the night. I retraced the route of my daily jogs, sitting on the bench where John tried to get me to talk to him for so long before I finally let him get close again. I looked up at the sky above and said a silent prayer to keep him safe until he was found. My tour of the grounds next found me meandering through the olive grove, one of the few places we could escape from everyone in the house and be alone together. It became a favorite spot for picnics that often turned into the two of us snuggled up for hours. I smiled sadly at the memory before forcing myself to head back inside and try to get some rest. Still unable to settle into bed, I found myself on the balcony outside our bedroom, wishing he'd been there with me to watch the stars as we'd done so many times on sleepless nights.

Everyone was emotional and tense the next morning. Nobody liked the idea of leaving, but knew we had little choice. Rocco and Max would drive us to Elena's house while the rest of the guys secured the grounds. They would then leave in smaller groups so it wouldn't look suspicious. The estate would be empty within three days if all went to plan.

After grabbing a sweater from John's closet, I took one last look around our bedroom to make sure I had everything. I closed the dark gray curtains, hating the idea of abandoning the house. It belonged to John's dad, who brought his new bride to live until a job offer brought them to the States. They returned home with their newborn son a year later and lived as a happy family until their untimely deaths. As I turned off the lights and went to the door, I swore we would return as soon as he was found and everyone was safe.

The ride to Elena's house in Treviso, just north of Venice, was long and uncomfortable for me. Then again, I was hidden behind the front seat of John's SUV as we made the hour-long journey. It wasn't until five minutes before we arrived at the house that we decided it was safe enough for me to sit next to Nonna in the back. She pulled me closer until my head rested on her shoulder and took my hand in hers, squeezing it gently.

Elena's white two-storied house was simple yet elegant looking as it shone in the morning sun. As we slowly navigated the driveway, Nonna pointed out little points of interest on the property, showing me the tree where Lucas fell and nearly broke his arm. She smiled warmly at the basketball hoop, telling me about the highly competitive games John and Lucas had through the years. I couldn't help smiling as I envisioned the two of them hurling insults at each other as they played. I prayed I'd be able to see it for myself in the future.

We stopped next to the other four black SUVs parked in front of the house. Paolo came to the front window and spoke briefly to Rocco before nodding to the other guards to stand down. Nonna stared at the house in front of us. She and her husband, Angelo, had bought the house as a wedding gift for Elena and Soren, only for him to abandon his family less than two years later to chase after my mother.

I fidgeted in my seat, anxious about how her daughter would react to meeting me. Lucas told me she held nothing against me, but I was still the product of the torrid affair her husband didn't even bother to hide. Coming face to face with proof your husband loved someone else was bound to be difficult. As if sensing my apprehension, Nonna squeezed my hand, forcing me to look at her.

"You are family here, Larissa," she affirmed. "You will see."

Rocco opened the door and helped her out of the car. I climbed out on the other side, taking in the peaceful surroundings and looking back at the house in front of us. The dark green shutters adorning each window of the three-storied structure were closed tightly, giving it a look that it too was preparing for a battle it hoped to survive. The excited voices from the front door pulled me back into the present as I looked over and saw Nonna hug her daughter tightly.

Lucas rounded the front of the car and enveloped me in his arms. "Everything okay?"

"So far, so good."

"Thank god," he sighed with relief as he led me to where his mother stood chatting with Nonna. "Mama," he interjected as they spoke amongst themselves. "This is my sister, Lissa."

Elena turned to me and smiled, her dark blue eyes twinkling. She stood barely an inch taller than her mother. They shared the same petite frame and facial structure. Her lush black hair only had a few strands of gray and hung past her shoulders. She was impeccably dressed in a simple dark blue high-waisted dress and matching heels. She carried herself like royalty as she moved closer, but the gentle and calming nature of the smile on her face was completely disarming.

"Larissa, I'm so glad to finally meet you," she greeted in Italian, gently grasping both my hands in hers.

"Likewise, um…," I stammered, unsure how to address her.

"You can call me Zia Elena or just Zia," she said. "You are family, my dear. And I will fight anyone who says otherwise."

My anxiety melted away when she hugged me tightly. Tears sprang in my eyes. "Thank you, Zia," I whispered.

"And I thank you as well, dear. Lucas has told me how much he's enjoyed spending time with you, and I'm overjoyed that you two found each other."

"I'm happy to have found him, too."

We strolled past the SUVs. "You're just as beautiful as your mother," she whispered as soon as we were away from everyone else.

"You knew her?"

"We met several times. My marriage was never about love. Soren's father was looking to make a match to improve his standing, and my brother needed to quiet the rumors about his 'scandalous' sister." My face apparently didn't hide my confusion because she smiled. "One of Massimo's foot soldiers caught me in a compromising position. With his daughter."

"Oh my gosh," I said, censoring the words that would no doubt earn me a slap from Nonna. "So you were forced? I'm so sorry."

"No, don't be. Soren was many things, but he respected that I'm gay. He never forced me. In the end, it was an escape from my brother's household and his abuse. Lucas was conceived to keep up appearances. I am not proud of some things that happened during that time, especially to his birth mother."

"Massimo ordered her to be killed, didn't he?"

"Dead whores tell no tales," she replied with a tight smile.

"Why does Lucas hate Soren so much?" I couldn't resist asking because it didn't make sense. "If he respected your sexuality and never forced you…"

She sighed. "It's complicated. I knew how miserable Soren was after she left, so I told him to go to Sera, and he did. But I then had to deal with Massimo's wrath because, as he put it, there was no man to 'fuck me into compliance'. He threatened to marry me off to someone else until my mother forbade it. It was one of the few times he listened to her. In Lucas's mind, his father abandoned me to deal with the fallout while he lived happily ever after with another woman."

"That woman was my mom."

She raised her eyebrows. "Has he ever said anything negative about Sera?"

"No, which is surprising now that I think about it. We hated each other when I first came to Verona."

"Like I said, complicated. Lucas needs someone to blame because I'm still under the control of the Sardi family and my brother will not allow me to live freely with my love. I can handle my brother. I just stay here out of the way while he lords over his little kingdom in the south. As for Yuna, I visit her in Zurich as often as I can."

Lucas joined us, looking rushed. "Mama, we need to get going."

We followed him back to the front of the house. Elena hugged me one last time before climbing into the same car as her mother. The guards moved to either the back of the house or into one of the vehicles. Soon Lucas and I were the only ones in the driveway. I inhaled deeply to keep the tears at bay, but the ache in my heart refused to stop. Reminding myself their safety was at stake, I shoved all my emotions back.

"Promise me you won't get yourself killed trying to find him. He can't live without you any more than you can't live without him," he ordered, his voice thick with worry. "You both better come back in one piece because I sure as hell can't live without either of you."

"I promise I'll do everything I can to make sure we both make it back," I pledged before hugging him to me as tightly as I could. "I love you."

"I love you too," he sighed. "Safe travels."

I found Paolo waiting for me at the last remaining SUV. He handed me the keys with a small smile. I looked at him questioningly. "I didn't like you at first, but you're family," he said gruffly. "Stay safe."

"I will."

The caravan disappeared through the metal gates and out of sight. To keep them safe, I knew nothing about their travel arrangements. For all I knew, they were on their way to Rome or taking a boat to Athens. I trusted Tavi and knew he'd get them to the island before anyone realized they were missing. I'd questioned and second guessed my decision to send them away countless times, and every time all I could think of was Massimo's rage and the trouble it would mean for the three of them. Tucking them away in a remote corner of the world was the best I could do to keep them safe.

Now it was my turn to make my escape. I stared at the number I'd entered into the red phone and said a silent prayer before pressing the button to dial. It was just after four in the morning in D.C., and I was about to leave a voicemail that would set off one hell of an explosion. The call connected on the fourth ring and a voice I hadn't heard in over two years filled the line. I waited for the irritating beep before speaking.

"Special Agent Kane, this is former Agent Larissa Donovan. I know it's long overdue, but I owe you an apology for my behavior during our last meeting. I was way out of line and that should never have happened. I'll be in touch soon and I would like to talk about this and hopefully come to an understanding. Thanks."

I tossed the phone into my knapsack and stared at the house in the rearview mirror. What I was about to do was a gamble that had to work. There was no alternative. After blowing out a slow breath, I started the car and set out for the next part of the plan.

Piazza San Marco, known to Americans as St. Mark's Square, stood as the heart of Venice for centuries. The area was filled to the brim with tourists milling around and taking selfies in front of the historical buildings. It was a beautiful day and their joy was infectious. I ducked in and out of several shops in the arcade, buying a few small souvenirs.

A man in a dusky blue dress shirt followed me from the gift shop to the gelato store. He stayed off to the side while I ordered a bowl of passion fruit, and when I left after talking myself out of another flavor, he followed. I passed by a man in a deep green hoodie and jeans, who exchanged the subtlest of looks with Dusky before joining our bizarre caravan. I kept my face down to hide the smile until passing by a security camera mounted by a flower cart. Slowing my steps, I looked through the bouquets for a moment before looking at the camera and smiling.

Mala Veneta was the local mafia in Venice. The group was slightly larger than the Sardi family, but their reach was greater thanks to the city they controlled. The fact they identified me and had me followed so soon was impressive. It meant I had to speed up my plan, but still impressive. Slowly making my way across the square, I scanned the building until the small cafe near the museum came into view. Excellent.

A small bell hanging above the door chimed when I entered, and the elderly man behind the counter stepped to the register. His smile was warm and inviting as he rang me up, reminding me of a kind grandpa. As he ground the espresso beans for my drink, I wondered what beverage he served Cesar Basso, the boss of the two men who entered as I grabbed my marocchino and headed for the table in the front corner.

The two men stood at the bar and sipped their drinks as I savored mine. It was the closest I'd had to a mocha since coming to Italy and it was simply divine. Out of the corner of my eye, the man behind the counter held the gaze of my admirers. Hoodie snuck a look at me each time he checked the clock, at least four times in seven minutes. My eyes stayed fixed on the map in my hand, while I tried not to be smug about being out of range of the camera directly above my head. No doubt it was Signore Basso's table I occupied.

At last, my drink was gone and it was time for some fun. After placing my cup in the bin, I asked the owner for the restroom. His face was blank as he gestured down the hall. Dusky's excitement radiated from him as I walked past. The feeling was mutual. Locking the door to the bathroom, I turned on the faucet and dug through my knapsack. Once I had what I needed, I turned off the water and moved into position. Smiling at the shadow I saw on the floor, I released the lock and jiggled the knob.

The door kicked open and Hoodie's tattooed hands came forward with his gun drawn. Clutching my knife, I sank the blade into his wrist all the way through both hands. He let out a wail and I dropped to my knees when I heard the click of Dusky's gun. A blast rang out and splintered the door, followed by a curse when he realized he'd missed. Hoodie swung at me with his bloodied hands. I dodged the blows and stabbed his inner thigh, running the blade all the way down to his knee. Blood erupted from the wound and he crumpled to the floor. He screamed and gripped his leg as I raised my gun and shot Dusky in the throat.

I blew out a breath and lowered my gun. Looking at the carnage, I was thankful I wore my black boots. All the easier to climb over the bodies with. It took a moment to scramble over the large dead lumps on the floor. The shopkeeper's eyes bulged when he saw me, but said nothing as I walked to the sink behind the counter. Once my hands, nails, and the knife were scrubbed clean, I grabbed the towel from his apron. After admiring the pale pink streaks on the fabric, I placed the knife on the neatly folded rectangle on the counter.

He gasped, stepping back when I turned my narrowed eyes on him. Closing the gap between us, I placed several euro notes in the pocket of his apron. Ignoring his mumbled words, I placed the cups used by the now dead men in the bin. Nodding to the security camera I'd hidden from minutes earlier, I then left the bar without another word.

Foot traffic in the square had thickened since it was closer to lunchtime. My black clothing hid most of the blood on me, but my boots left a few obvious tracks on the pavement. Tossing them into the first trash can I found, I then ducked into a public bathroom to put on the clean clothes in my knapsack, a pair of khaki capri pants, a black tank top, and a pair of soft black ballet flats. Checking the time, I hustled to the pier and hopped aboard the crowded water bus.

I watched the water sparkle in the sun, wishing I'd had a camera to capture the beauty surrounding me. My impending retirement made my dream to travel the world as a tourist closer to reality, but it meant nothing until John was found and brought home. Closing my eyes, I said a silent prayer that even the smallest of leads would show itself soon. Afterward, I raised my face to the sun and enjoyed the smell of the salt air.

Before I knew it, the red brick columns of the pier at the airport appeared. I breezed through the gate and into the light-filled lobby as soon as we docked. Clutching my knapsack tightly to my body, I navigated through a sea of people eager to find and reach their destinations. Once I got to the departure deck, I strolled around as if I wasn't a spy and assassin who spent much of my life hiding in plain sight. Staring and nodding at several security cameras in the hall gave me a small thrill, so much so that I was nearly giddy when I handed my passport to the ticket agent.

"Hello, Ms.…Donovan," she greeted, glancing at the name on the document. "How can I help you today?"

She entered my ticket into the system. Her smile faltered for a fraction of a second when I presented my CIA paperwork authorizing me to fly armed. I did my best to keep my face blank as she ran my info through the operations system, relaxing when she gave a small nod and handed me my ticket. Protocol dictated that Felton be notified of my travel, but I knew the phone call I'd receive from him asking a million questions was several hours away. No, the real test was down the main corridor and to the left according to the friendly agent.

The Passport Control Office looked small, but the staff was fast and efficient. I entered the line for my destination, which snaked out the door toward the neighboring shops. The smells from the candy store were mouthwatering, but thankfully my torture was brief and soon I was next in line. A young man smiled as he called me forward. He read my firearm paperwork and nodded before scanning the bar code for my ticket. My fingers were icy when I handed him my travel documents. I couldn't remember the last time I'd used my real passport and, to my surprise, the simple beep of the scanner didn't cause any alerts or looks of alarm on his face. He simply smiled and wished me a good day before pointing me to the departure gates.

I grabbed a pastry and a sparkling water on the way to my plane, pausing to look directly at several cameras along my route. A security guard gave me a look of confusion, but I merely smiled and nodded before continuing. I read the magazine I bought at the market until my plane began boarding. Grabbing my knapsack, I shot one last look at the camera and winked before heading down the jetway.

Nobody in Italy knew that when my passport was scanned, it set off a shockwave an ocean away. As the plane reached its cruising altitude, I reclined my seat and closed my eyes, preparing for the chaos waiting for me on the other side.

Chapter Twenty-One

Unsafe Travels

Larissa

The paper coffee cup in front of me was beige with coffee beans made to look like the petals of flowers. It was meant to be cheerful, as cheerful as anything beige colored could be, but it did nothing to mask the burned smell of the sludge inside. Not even cream or sugar could've made it more appealing, but I couldn't even move the cup away thanks to the handcuffs that prevented me from moving more than a few inches.

I'd been in my share of interrogation rooms, and this one located deep in the basement of Dulles International Airport was nothing spectacular. Two squeaky, uncomfortable metal chairs, a cold metal table with a bar to attach said handcuffs, a clock that loudly ticked the day away, security cameras, and the ever famous two-way mirror. I watched the clock for a good ten to twenty cycles of the second hand before blowing out a breath and turning my head toward the ceiling.

"Isn't it funny how all these holding cells look the same? Except for maybe the shade of gray walls. Though I'm pretty sure the cell in Budapest was concrete. Still counts as gray, though."

Tick, tick, tick. Countless more cycles around.

"Why is it that airport coffee is universally bad? I mean, there are plenty of great coffee places *at* each airport. You'd think they'd give the administration a discount or work out some kind of agreement. It would be a hell of a way to support local businesses."

I stared at my own horrid beverage, knowing exactly who was behind it and why. There was no denying what I'd done to earn her wrath. The real question was if she was alone as she watched me squirm. That would help determine how much trouble I was in, and the likelihood of being able to make a deal to buy myself some time to do what I needed to do. There was only one way to find out.

Sitting up in my chair, I turned to the mirror. "Greetings, Agent Kaplan."

The door next to the mirror flew open and my friend and sometimes colleague entered. In the two years since I'd last seen her, her hair was now in braids that hung to her shoulders and was a little grayer. Her eyes narrowed from behind her clear blue square glasses before she closed the door behind her and tossed the folder in her hand on the table.

"Ms. Donovan, fancy meeting you under these circumstances."

"Wish I could say the same. What am I being charged with?"

"Kidnapping a federal officer and three counts of assault and battery on a federal officer."

"Wait," I started to protest, but paused as I remembered that fateful day. "Okay, three sounds about right. I've gotta say I was impressed with how quickly you got an air marshal to intercept me. I figured it wouldn't be until I got to New York. Imagine my surprise when we landed at Heathrow and there he was. He was a decent enough guy. Shit taste in basketball teams, though."

"After the performance you put on for airport security, could you blame us? Interpol is looking into the murder of two men in the bathroom of a coffee shop in Venice. Would you know anything about that?"

"Can't say that I do," I replied. "Venice is a great city with a lot of places to grab coffee. Unfortunately, a woman traveling alone has to remain vigilant in case she encounters those who would do her harm."

She placed her hands on the edge of the table. "What in the hell were you thinking, Larissa?" I pursed my lips and shook my head before saying anything to put me in even deeper trouble. At my hesitancy, she slapped the surface with her hand. "Answer me!"

"Since I'm going to assume you didn't read the full file on what happened in Portland, don't be surprised if you don't like my answer. I'd just been on a job that went so sideways that even two years later I don't know if I'll ever fully recover from it and be the same again. I was thinking that I escaped being kidnapped and beaten after being in a house full of dirty FBI agents. I was thinking that the same agency tried to pin a murder on me and I didn't know who to trust."

With the gift of hindsight, I knew Barton was someone to be trusted. At the time, when I was nursing a broken arm and deep emotional trauma, nothing made sense other than running far away from anyone and anything capable of hurting me. Did it justify my actions? Absolutely not, and I struggled with that for a long time in the aftermath.

Her eyes softened for a moment. "I read the file, and I'm sorry that happened to you. And while I can sympathize that you were upset and confused, you should have let the investigation run its course."

"Are you serious? Did you not hear that I was in a house *full of sworn FBI agents who were all dirty as sin*? Gio Sardi bought and paid for every single one of them, along with four fake graduate students. With those kinds of odds stacked against me, you think I was going to *stick around* while you tried to figure out how far and wide the corruption went? There was no way the Bureau was ever going to fully expose everyone in his pocket."

"Well, it sure as hell wasn't up to you to kidnap two agents, threaten them, and then skip off into the sunset to live happily ever after!" she yelled.

I closed my eyes and counted to ten. And then twenty, thankful that Georgia apparently saw my distress. "It was more like a hellish ever after." I held up my arms to show her my scars. "By the grace of whatever force in the universe decided to smile upon me, I survived. But don't think for a second I wasn't feeling the consequences of my actions."

Her eyes lingered on my arms and then met mine, filled with questions and concern. I nodded, answering the most important one she couldn't ask. She looked at the folder between us for a moment before raising her head, her face blank. "Again, I'm deeply sorry for everything that happened to you, Larissa. I can tell you that the US Attorney will take those events into consideration when they review the case."

I couldn't fault her for doing her job, but my eyes filled with tears anyway. "So you're going to charge me?"

"That's correct. You're scheduled to be arraigned tomorrow morning, where you'll be formally charged, along with anyone who helped you into the country."

I threw my head back and laughed. The look on her face showed she had no patience for my humor, but it still took a moment to recover. "Agent Kaplan, this is my third trip back to the US. The first time was as an officer of the CIA. Second time was because I was injured in the line of duty, again as an officer of the CIA."

"And what about this time?" she challenged. "Was Felton behind the paperwork you showed to the Italian Civil Authority so you could get your gun through?"

"Agent Kaplan," I began with a small smile. "Can you please tell me what name is on my plane ticket?"

Her brows knitted together after staring at the manifest. "What the hell? You...*planned* to get caught? But why? Why are you here?"

"Someone very important to me, someone I care about, is missing and I need certain people to know I'm here. I'm a distraction."

"For what? Who?"

"It's related to the Sardi family. That's all I'm going to say."

"Okay, can you tell me why you didn't reach out to Felton for help?"

"For starters, I want to do this on my own, and it might be a little awkward if I ask him for help since I've submitted the paperwork to retire from the CIA."

Shaking her head, she sat in the chair across from me and rested her hands on the folder. "What are you hoping to accomplish here? What, specifically, is it you're looking for?"

"I need intel on Marcus Vargas. Once I've found who I'm looking for, alive or dead, I will surrender without incident and face whatever charges Special Agent Kane would like to bring against me."

"Why are you looking for intel on Marcus?"

I raised my eyebrows. "Why do you care that I'm interested in Marcus?"

The door next to the mirror opened once again and Special Agent in Charge Barton Kane strolled into the room. "Because finding Marcus Vargas just became the key to your freedom, Agent Donovan."

• • • ● • ● • • •

John

The plane taxied the runway and every cell in my body was on edge. My brain battled itself, at war over whether leaving her behind was a good idea. The irrational part of me wanted to race back to that hospital room, throw my arms around her, and never let her go. I knew that would be a mistake; she needed to figure things out on her own. I fidgeted with my seat belt, unable to calm down. As soon as the flight attendant came by, I begged her for a drink.

Leaning my head against the headrest, I looked at the ocean below. Maybe when this was all over, I'd take her to a tropical island for a vacation. Better yet, our honeymoon. I closed my eyes and smiled at the thought of her in a bikini. My head fell against the window and my eyes blurred. I stared at the now empty glass in my hand and swirled the ice around, trying to calm my rising panic. As soon as I felt the residue on the inside, I realized too late that I'd been drugged.

My eyelids drooped, and I shook my head to try to clear the fog. I reached for the button to contact the cockpit, but my arm felt like it was full of cement. The door at the back of the plane opened and a familiar looking woman sat in the seat next to me.

"You had black hair the last time I saw you," I mumbled.

"I'm surprised you remember. That was a crazy assignment," she laughed softly.

"I'm guessing this isn't a social call, judging by the amount of GHB I'm only just now realizing you put in my drink."

"That's correct. I feel bad about this, John. I really do. You seemed like a nice enough guy when we worked together, but I've got my orders. You're getting in the middle of something you can't even begin to understand."

"Hey, I said something like that to Liss once," I slurred, my eyes getting heavier by the second. "She shot me."

"Just go to sleep, John," she whispered.

I snapped awake. My arm twitched, sending a dull wave of pain up my shoulder, all but confirming it was dislocated. I would've tried to pop it back into place, but the zip ties used to keep me secured to the old metal chair were painfully tight. The fact that at least two of my ribs were broken didn't help, either. Every move-ment was pure agony.

The room was pitch black and completely silent except for my desperate gasps of air. It smelled of old wood and paper, not made any better by the heat and humidity brought on by wherever the fuck I was. My surroundings were hellish, but nothing compared to my daily activities.

I was in Hell's Amusement Park. Each day, after a ration of barely edible food and minimal water, I was brought to a different room and subjected to new and creative ways of torture. I'd been placed in a freezer, beaten, electrocuted, and several other gruesome things the sadistic asshole running things seemed to enjoy.

When my injuries became too severe, he moved me to a small infirmary to recover. Right after I felt better, back to the rooms I went. It was a sick, painful cycle that soon melted into one long, hellish day that never ended. I had no idea how long I'd been there, but my best guess was a little over a month.

I leaned back in the chair, shivering when my bare skin touched the cold metal. After complaining about the heat, my shirt was cut off and I was doused with water. The now filthy and threadbare jeans I wore when I left Tampa barely covered my legs. I blinked slowly and tried to fight my exhaustion. Sleep was rare and filled with terrible images. Even as I sat there and my eyes grew heavier, I tried to fight it. The fight was over before it began and soon I felt myself slide back into a slumber.

Liss's smiling face swam into view above my own. We lounged on a blanket in the olive grove after one of our many picnics. I leaned forward to give her a kiss, only to be greeted with a mischievous smirk. She leaped up and giggled, silently daring me to chase her through the trees. I laughed and shook my head before racing down the aisle and thought of the extended make out session we'd have once I caught her.

I didn't think about not hearing her laugh until I rounded the corner. Her face was full of terror as she tried to struggle out of the rope that bound her arms to her sides. The faceless man in black held a knife to her throat, and she froze. "Quick or slow," he hissed, pressing the knife to her skin.

My heart stuttered when I saw the noose around her neck. I raised my hands and slowly walked closer until he pulled the rope hanging from the tree, causing it to tighten. Paralyzed, I was unable to move or speak. "Can't even decide," he scoffed. "Pathetic."

He yanked the rope and her body shot up off the ground. The sound of her panicked choking filled my ears as she struggled to free herself. I screamed and ran closer. The man laughed maliciously as he lowered the rope. I closed my arms around her waist, only to be shoved aside at the last second. I rolled over and watched in horror as he plunged his knife deep into her throat and slashed forward.

I gasped awake and tried to shake the image of her lifeless body on the ground from my psyche. The more exhausted I was, the more horrifying my nightmares were and thus it was nearly impossible to get any kind of rest, physical or mental. I shut my eyes and forced myself to slow my breathing. It was just a dream, I told myself. None of it was real. After a while, my breaths slowed and the pain in my ribs lessened.

There was no chance I was going to survive. It was a shitty reality to accept, but one I embraced if it meant those who mattered the most to me stayed safe. I sat in the dark, stripped of all pretense and vanity, and thought of the things I wished I'd done or said if I'd known I'd never see them again. I never spent enough time with Nonna, listening to her lament that I didn't eat enough and her complaints that I never used enough water in my pasta dough on the rare occasions she let me cook with her.

I never told Lucas how much I appreciated all the times he saved my ass, both physically and emotionally. He'd witnessed the darkest periods of my life, from the day my parents died to the day I read her medical records from Rome. No matter how many times I pushed everyone away, he'd been there to pick up the pieces.

And Larissa. So many things were left unsaid between us when I left. Things I thought I'd be able to say when we found our way back to each other. I never told her I'd planned to get her to a safe house when we went on our disastrous trip to the beach, that learning about what happened to her in Rome caused me to lock myself away for weeks as I dealt with how badly I broke her, or that the reason I acted so cocky around her was because I never wanted to admit that she'd owned my heart and soul from the time she shot me down outside the bathroom at that goddamned party and turned my life upside down. The day she told me she loved me cemented she was meant to be my wife. I closed my eyes and pictured her standing on the balcony of our bedroom back in Verona, desperately wishing to hold her one last time.

Out of the darkness, a burlap sack snapped over my head and a fist connected with my jaw. My head flew back, causing a sharp pain to radiate down my neck. I slumped forward, only to be punched again. The next blow hit me in the side, knocking the air out of my already battered lungs. After a series of kicks to my legs and stomach, everything stopped and it was silent once again. I heard a loud click, followed by a low buzzing sound. The sack was ripped away and my head throbbed at the blinding light in the room. It took a while for my eyes to adjust, and then my heart nearly stopped.

The walls were covered with pictures of my family. My grandmother walking around the market in Verona, escorted by Max. Lucas arguing with someone at the front gate. Liss and Nonna sitting in the garden. Liss leaning against a tree looking worried. The closest wall showed pictures of all three of them, along with my Aunt Elena, standing outside my aunt's house near Venice.

"For what it's worth, they've been searching for you," a man's voice stated from the darkness.

"You gonna kidnap them, too?"

"I understand why you're angry."

I turned away from a picture of Lucas hugging Liss as she cried. "How long have I been here?"

"Does it matter?"

"How long?" I yelled, wincing.

"Two months."

"Are they safe?" I demanded. None of this mattered if this sick fuck was hunting any of them, too.

"They're safe."

My shoulders relaxed. "Thank you."

"You look like hell, John."

"What can I say? The facilities in this place leave a lot to be desired. The bathrooms are especially lacking. More of a bucket and a fire hose, really. But thank you for the feedback. I'll be sure to bring it up with the staff the next time they come to torture me."

"I'm really sorry it had to be this way. You know too much, and I can't risk you telling them right now."

"I'll try not to take it too personally," I replied, my eye throbbing. "Just like I hope you won't take it too personally when I call you a fucking psychopath."

"Apologies for Franz. I told him to keep you under control, not realizing he'd take his job to such an extreme. I'll have a word with him."

"Yeah, you do that," I muttered.

"When did you figure it all out?"

Chuckling, I shook my head. "I'm not saying. I need to have at least one secret to take to my grave. My only wish was that I'd figured it out sooner."

"Do they know?"

"I'm afraid I don't understand the question. You'll need to be more specific."

"Do either of them know I'm their father?" he yelled.

Hearing the rage in his voice, I smiled. "Don't worry, Felton. Your secret is safe. For now."

TO BE CONTINUED...

Bonus Chapter: Shattered

Lucas

"I don't give a fuck, you useless piece of shit!"

A crash drowned out the rest of John's tirade and I stopped pacing in front of his door. I still heard his voice, but it was muffled. Christ, he was already on a tear. The sun was barely up when he locked himself in the office to make phone calls. Phone calls with a heaping dose of verbal abuse thrown in from the sound of things.

The manila folder in my hand felt even more poisonous. His temper the past nine months had been a shade under nuclear, and the news I carried would push him past the limit. I didn't want to tell him, yet I knew his reaction would be worse if he learned about it from someone else. My balls were in a vice either way.

"Then earn the goddamned money I pay you and find out!"

The receiver slammed down on the office phone so hard it sounded like he'd broken another one. I took a deep breath to prepare myself for his rage and pounded on the door. Hearing nothing, I entered and found him slouched in the chair behind his desk. To the side stood two large frames on wheels, one held enlarged maps of Italy and Europe while the other was a whiteboard with bits of information scrawled all over. He stared at the whiteboard as he sipped amber liquid from a lowball glass. I looked at the nearly empty bottle on the desk and cringed. It was barely lunchtime and he'd already been in the Macallan.

Steeling myself up, I sank into a black leather chair in front of his desk. "I'm surprised you didn't bellow out for me to fuck off when I knocked."

"What do you want, Lucas?" His attention was still focused on the board, but he couldn't hide the exhaustion in his voice.

Nine months ago, my cousin came home a broken man. Our uncle sent him to kill an American spy and assassin who was an enemy to the family, but John refused. Instead, he tried to get her away from our family but our uncle made sure Larissa knew that John was hired to kill her before she escaped. Finding and rescuing her became his obsession, and now his life was consumed with the task. He was still expected to kill her, so how he walked the tightrope between those goals was a mystery to me, especially now.

The map of Italy included several round pins that started in Rome and moved south. Two family associates were killed under mysterious circumstances about a month ago, and a trail of bodies followed. A top earning soldier was the most recent victim, the fifth one to die, and both our uncle and the capo of the crew he belonged to were out for blood.

"I have news." My voice was small as my fingernail flicked the tab on the folder. "About her."

Her. Larissa Donovan, alpha level crazy bitch, psycho killer, and the woman he was convinced needed saving. Someone so deadly she replaced John as the American government's top intelligence asset. The same woman who told him she wouldn't hesitate to put a bullet in his head if she saw him again. We'd butted heads over this crazy idea at least a dozen times, and the regret I felt at my harsh words made my stomach churn.

He slammed his glass on the desk. "Lucas? What is it?"

"It's not good." I opened the folder. "This news is out of date, but it explains why she was so hard to find in the beginning. She was in a psychiatric ward in Rome. She, um, tried to kill herself on New Year's Eve."

The crease between his eyebrows deepened and his face paled. "She did what?"

"She was found," I cleared my throat and read the file. "She was found unconscious in a hotel room outside Rome with—"

"No," he bit out. "I want you to repeat that first part. You know the one."

Fuck, he was going to do this now. I could argue, but I was the asshole who mocked both him for insisting she needed his help and her... God, all the names I'd called her, the one he knew and didn't know about. All the times I'd called her heartless when I was no better.

"John."

The sneer on his face was chilling. "No, I want to hear you say it. You look me in the eye, and you repeat exactly what happened to that 'cold blooded bitch' as you called her multiple times a day. Or is she a 'crazy cunt' this time?"

"Look, I'm a giant piece of shit and you're right to be pissed at me. Is that what you want to hear?" He raised his eyebrows before taking another drink as I shuffled one of the papers to the front of the file. "There's more, and um," I broke off, shaking my head. "I can't, man. I'm so fucking sorry."

With shaking hands, I gave him the file. His eyes darted to the first page, and I had to look away when I heard his gasp. That was the second I knew he'd read that she'd suffered a miscarriage just before Christmas. At the time she still wore the cast on her arm from a fracture she received escaping from our uncle. The doctor had been concerned about her emotional state when she was discharged, but she told him she was headed home to recover with her family.

He stood and grabbed his glass. "Leave."

I watched him go to the liquor cabinet in the corner. He filled the glass almost to the top and consumed it in three gulps. After filling the glass a second time, he turned and found me glued to my seat. I rose as he moved closer with slow and measured steps. He stopped well into my personal space and stuck his face dangerously close to mine.

"I said leave."

It was pointless to argue. I felt his eyes burning into my back as I headed to the door. Turning to tell him I'd be there if he wanted to talk, I watched him trudge back to his chair with his head hung low. I grabbed my phone out of my pocket and closed the door.

"Lucas, what's going on?" Carlo answered.

The sound of breaking glass, wood, and fuck only knew what else made me jump. A scream followed, and then the sound of more things breaking. The call dropped. He knew where to go. Joey and Max rounded the corner with their guns drawn, stopping when they saw me. Carlo joined us from the kitchen a few seconds later.

"We just got a lead on Larissa Donovan, and it wasn't good," I explained. Another roar and more crashing came from behind the door. "It's bad. I don't know how he's going to recover from this, and I need you three to watch him."

Joey looked confused. "What about you?"

"I'll make it worse." It tore me apart to admit the truth, but there it was. "I won't go into details other than to say I was very wrong about the situation, and the news he got just shattered his goddamned world."

"Is she dead?" Max grunted.

"No, but she's not the issue right now." I pointed to the door, which muffled more sounds of destruction and sorrow. "Keep an eye on him. Yell through the door if you have to. If he yells back and curses you out, he's fine. If it goes quiet in there, go inside and don't leave until you see him breathing with your own two eyes. *When* he passes out, grab the liquor out of there."

"Fuck," Carlo muttered.

I nodded and blew out a breath. "I fucked up, so just be there for him. He's going to need someone."

"What are you going to do?" Joey asked.

"Talk to Paolo about damage control. The last thing we want is Gio or Massimo finding out about any of this."

Carlo woke me the next morning with a cup of coffee and a plea to follow him down to the office. The destruction that stood before us left me speechless. Two windows behind his desk were cracked and the curtains had been ripped from the wall and left in a pile on the floor. There was no liquor to remove as he'd either drank it or it sat spilled on the floor, along with shards of what looked like every bottle and glass in the bar. John was passed out on the couch near the fireplace surrounded by broken and burnt debris.

My heart sank when I recognized one of the pawns from the chess set that used to sit in the corner. The wood was now blackened with a ring of ash on the floor. Several other pieces, some smashed and others burned worse than the pawn were strewn on the hearth in front of the now extinguished fire. John's grandfather bought the set during a trip to London when he was younger. On the floor directly in front of the couch where John slept, his father's decanter lay in pieces in a puddle of whiskey. He'd be devastated once he sobered up, but that was a worry for later.

"Does he have any cuts on him?" I asked Max, who shook his head. "Get him up to his room and have the doctor check him out. He'll probably need an IV."

"Which he'll rip out," he argued.

"Then the stubborn bastard can have a hole in his arm and only a small amount of rehydration."

He cursed under his breath and pulled out his phone. Carlo motioned me over to where he stood with Paolo, and I knew it was to take control of the chaos. Being without a leader left us on dangerous ground and we couldn't risk anyone finding out about John. I told them I'd handle any calls from Bari. As John's second, the unpleasant task of talking to our uncles fell to me while Paolo said he'd take care of any calls from the port.

"What do we do now?" Carlo whispered as Max and two others dragged John out of the room.

I scratched at the stubble on my jaw. "Get someone in here to clean up the mess so we can use the room. We need to get back to work. Once we get the boards back up, go through his notes and see if there's anything worth looking into. We need to find Larissa before the family gets impatient and decides to take matters into their own hands. And get rid of all the liquor in the house. All of it. I don't want so much as a drop of cooking wine in the kitchen."

Paolo nodded at the ceiling. "Should you call Nonna?"

"Not yet. He needs time to process all of this. Let's give him a couple of days and go from there."

They both left and I sank into the chair behind his desk before dropping my head into my hands. I'd been an absolute piece of shit for what I said about her. When busting his balls and calling him pussy whipped or obsessed didn't work, I hurled gallons of hatred at her. The two names John threw back in my face had been my favorites, but there were so many more that would've kept me black and blue for weeks if Nonna ever found out.

Love had always been a liability in the mafia, and our family was no exception. The only thing my uncles loved was their power and saw human attachments as a weakness to be obliterated. John and I swore to avoid anything beyond casual acquaintances. My resolve lasted for a while, but one wild weekend in Monte Carlo turned me into a bloody hypocrite. However, Valyria wasn't just an entanglement. She was a one-way ticket to war. Keeping John away from Larissa was to prevent him from the same pain, I'd told myself in the beginning. For a time I even believed it because it was partially true. Falling for someone my family wanted dead was insanity. But where Valyria had a family to go back to, Larissa had nobody. Only John.

Paolo returned, and the sound of something on the floor being kicked caused my head to jolt up. He cursed and picked up the item, one of the chess queens, and set it on the desk in front of me. "He's in bed. Dom and Ciro are working on getting all the alcohol dumped."

"Thanks."

He motioned to the desk. "Anything?"

"I haven't looked yet. I'm still digesting all of this and," I shook my head. "It's a mess."

"It is. But like you said, let's give him some time." He grabbed a stack of papers on the corner of the desk. "Let's look through these in the kitchen. Food helps brains work and this room reeks."

Paolo, always the practical one. I followed him out of the room, stopping to pick up the cracked bottom of the decanter. The queen stood alone on the desk, worn and damaged but still standing strong. As I dropped the piece into the bottom of the broken glass, I hoped that was the same condition we found John's queen.

Nonna appeared a week later, almost as if she knew of his distress. She cooked enough food to feed an army and then breezed into his room with a large bowl of soup like she did when we were kids. Her eyes were red and puffy when she returned to the kitchen hours later.

"He mourns, *Tesoro*," she sighed, sipping her coffee. "He doesn't let many people into his heart, but this girl pushed deep inside, and he doesn't want to let her go." Her small hand grasped my arm. "Stop beating yourself up. You couldn't have known what would happen any more than Gianni."

"No, but I know what's expected of him. Zio ordered him to kill her."

After a bowl of soup, she dragged me to the living room and we stayed up all night talking. Nonna knew a thing or two about doomed love. My grandfather killed many men and ordered the deaths of dozens more until her son left him in pieces at the Bari port. She still mourned him and would until her last breath.

According to my uncle his father was a weak leader, and her devotion was traitorous. The only reason she still lived was because killing one's own mother was not only a dick move, but one that would cost him the respect and support of allies he needed. Instead she was used as collateral to force John into doing jobs he would've otherwise turned down. It was still a dick move, but one that was easier to hide since Nonna only got the occasional bruise when his henchmen got grabby.

"Give him time," she advised as we walked to her car when she left the next evening. "He feels responsible for her pain. For this loss."

"I'm trying, but we may not have much time. She's on a killing spree, and it's only a matter of time before Zio gets tired of the lack of progress and sends out his own people after her."

"Then you must push through and make him see, Lucas. He does not hate you. But you and I both know he will forever hate himself if she comes to any more harm."

"How?"

"You will know when and you will know how." She cupped my cheek with her small hand. "He will be angry, but he needs you. Just like you need him."

"Thank you, Nonna."

She softly kissed both my cheeks before letting me help her into the back seat. I nodded to the driver, and he slowly drove away. Once the gate closed, I sent a text to the car at the bottom of the hill that would escort her home.

After a week, not only was John not getting any better, but we'd also found out he bribed one of the groundskeepers into sneaking bottles of liquor to him. It was one of the few times I saw Paolo lose his shit when he forcibly removed the man. It was then that I dismissed the rest of the household staff until things were back to normal. Or whenever we didn't start each morning finding where my cousin passed out the night before.

I found John in a chaise lounge by the pool that morning. He looked like shit. There was no sugarcoating the matted hair, over-grown beard, and sweats I was sure he'd been wearing for at least two days. No, he looked and smelled like dog shit. I sat in the chair next to his and read the text message that the bodies of four Sardi associates were found in a house not far from the port, and knew it was time to act. Standing up, I kicked the foot of his chaise. Nothing. Grabbing the top of the chair I spun it around and overturned it, dropping him into the pool.

I returned to my chair and patiently waited for him to finish yelling and cussing once his head broke the surface. "Good morning."

"What the fuck do I have to do to get all of you to leave. Me. The fuck. Alone!"

"I'm not. It's time for you to pull your head out of your ass and get back to work."

He climbed out of the pool and pulled the soaked hoodie over his head before tossing it on the ground. "I wouldn't expect you to understand. I love her. But I was a coward and let her slip through my fingers. That's all I can think about. If I hadn't been so proud, I would've chased after her. I would've brought her here and they both would've been safe. Instead I turned my back on her and let this happen."

"Are you fucking hearing yourself right now?" I scoffed. "You *let* this happen to her? You're putting a lot of faith in someone you'd only known for, what? Two months? How can you even be sure the baby was even yours?"

He shoved me so hard I stumbled backwards. "Fuck you! It must be so easy to sit there and judge when you have no idea what it feels like."

Something inside me snapped and I stepped in front of him so quickly he took a step back. I poked my finger into his chest. "You need to shut the fuck up about what I would and would not understand. It wasn't long ago that you *forced* me to walk away from the one woman I cared about. She wasn't in the best situation at the time either, but that didn't matter to you. And you didn't give a fuck how shitty I felt."

His eyes widened and he pushed his wet hair back from his forehead. "Lucas, I don't know what to say."

"Good. Because I wasn't finished." I picked up the empty liquor bottle on the ground and shoved it in his face. "If you love her so fucking much, you've got a funny way of showing it, asshole. While you've been drowning your sorrows and losing god knows how many brain cells, Larissa has killed four more associates." I shoved the bottle into his hand. "Go back to your true love. Hopefully our uncles haven't decided to go after her themselves by the time you decide to sober up."

I went back inside the house without another word and didn't stop walking until I reached his office. The room had been cleaned up and looked nothing like the destroyed version two weeks earlier. We hadn't used it since then because it took days to reorganize his papers. John's rampage wiped out everything he'd written on the whiteboard and the maps were ripped to shreds. Recreating everything from his messy and unorganized notes took hours. I had just started adding the latest information about her movements when I heard footsteps behind me. Glancing over my shoulder, I expected to see Gino or Paolo. At the sight of John, I almost dropped the marker in my hand.

He'd shaved and though his hair was now longer, it was clean and combed back from his face. He wore a black t-shirt and old jeans, but they were clean, and his eyes weren't glassy or bloodshot for the first time since his world came crashing down.

I crossed my arms. "Are you lost?"

He lowered his head. "I was."

"And now?"

"I'm terrified. That they'll find her before I can get to her or that she's too broken to recover from what happened."

I studied him for a moment. "I'll admit that I don't know what you two had, so I still can't say I fully trust her, *but,*" I looked at the map. "Let's find her first and then we can worry about the rest."

"Thank you. I've been a complete shit and I don't deserve everything you guys have done for me. And I'm sorry for how shitty I was to you about V. Maybe we can figure out a way to…," his voice trailed off when I looked away.

I didn't have the heart to tell him that I'd tried to talk to her just before we got the news about Larissa, and that she'd made it perfectly clear she wanted nothing to do with me. I didn't want to admit it, but after breaking up and getting back together so many times she was probably right that it was time for both of us to move on. I didn't know what that looked like, but I'd figure it out someday.

"Lucas?"

"One miracle at a time, man," I replied. "Because that's what it's going to take to find Larissa. And it'll be another miracle if she doesn't kill you if we find her."

"When," he said. "*When* we find her."

"Either way, it'll be a miracle if she doesn't shoot your ass."

"Such a pessimist."

"What? I'm looking forward to that part. Let's get to work."

Thank you!

Thank you for reading Mutual Assets! If you liked the story, please consider leaving an honest review here.

Acknowledgements

First of all, I want to acknowledge all readers who have made it to this point without throwing your book/reader across the room because of the cliffhanger. I know! Please feel free to curse my name all you want, but please don't actually curse me since I still need all my faculties to finish the series.

My family has been my rock throughout this journey, perhaps even more so this time around. To my kiddos, bragging that your mom writes books on your social media means more to me than you'll ever know. Damien, my husband, you officially have the patience of a saint and I'd like to promise that I won't keep sending you pics and snippets at random times with nothing more of a message than "???" but you know that's a fib. And I appreciate you loving me for that.

To Karolina, THANK YOU for an amazing photo shoot. This cover... *chef's kiss.* And it's all thanks to you!

Finally, to my Indie Author Club, aka the Mankini Cartel...I don't know if I'll ever find the right words to express how much I love all of you. Thank you for accepting me, letting me lurk, embracing my social awkwardness, and for all your kind words of encouragement. You've helped make this a less scary place and I'd gladly go into battle with each and every one of you.

The Asset Series

Mutual Assets: Prequel to The Asset

"Do you know why your employer would pay me half a million dollars to kill you?"
That's the question posed to secret agent Larissa Donovan after a date with her boss's business associate, Victor Acosta. After working undercover for weeks as an au pair, the case certainly hasn't gone as she'd hoped and now someone wants her dead. Is it the wife who steals industrial secrets or her art thief husband?

Victor reveals his own issue with the couple and proposes a crazy idea: pretend they're dating and work together to bring the couple down. Larissa is skeptical at first, but reluctantly agrees. Convincing their targets that Victor is using her before carrying through on the hit is easy enough. But is it really pretending when she finds it harder and harder to resist the sexy security consultant?

Mutual Assets is a 28k word short story that takes place a year before The Asset.

The Asset

The (possibly last) job: Spy on a college professor. How hard can it be?

Larissa Donovan has one of the most interesting jobs in the world: travel to new locations, take in the sights, meet the locals, and sometimes kill them. Foreign or domestic? Depends on who's signing her paycheck. Such is the life when you're The Asset, the country's most elite intelligence operative. After twenty years of murder and secrets, however, Larissa is considering retirement. She agrees to one (maybe, okay probably) last job for the FBI: go undercover and gain intel on a college professor with ties to the same mobster responsible for her parents' brutal murders. From the time she arrives on campus, the seemingly simple spy mission is fraught with unanswered questions and countless complications. How is a college professor connected to a mobster? Who's responsible for the mysterious phone calls and threatening packages delivered to the office? And why can't she stop thinking about the professor's sultry voice and devilish grin?

As Larissa digs deeper, she finds herself tangled in a web of dangerous secrets and lies. When one of those secrets leads back to her family, she learns there's more to father and her parents' deaths than she ever imagined.

Family Assets

Larissa's story concludes in Family Assets, the third book in The Asset series

First they came for me and my family. I survived and lived my life peacefully in the shadows.

Next they forced me from the shadows and came for me again. I survived, but now even the shadows have turned against me.

Now someone has taken the man I love. Once I find those responsible, not even the shadows will be able to save them.

• • • ● ● • ● ● • • •

Warning: the following excerpt contains violence.

<u>Excerpt</u>

I smiled and turned to the black case next to me, unzipping it slowly. Her eyes widened as soon as she saw the contents. I picked up the blue marker next to the case. "Okay, hard way it is." I drew a line on both her forearms and the middle of each thigh.

"Stephanie, honestly. I don't know what you're talking about."

"When I was a kid, I really enjoyed watching medical shows on TV," I began, ignoring her dramatic gasps and whimpers. "I especially loved watching surgeons. They really seemed to know their stuff. I learned later, however, these shows are hardly realistic. Take scalpels for example. The way these shows make it sound, there's only one kind. You always hear them asking for a 'ten blade' for every single surgery. So inaccurate."

I moved the case from the table to my lap. "It turns out scalpels come in all shapes and sizes, as you can see. Size ten is one of the smallest and used for most general surgeries and then the sizes and styles go higher up the size chart. There's even special, thicker blades designed specifically for performing autopsies." I picked up the knife with the curved tip and held it up. "This one, for example, is a twelve blade. Doctors use it to lance abscesses. It's one of my favorites since it has such a fine point. The thirty six is almost like a carving knife, but that's because coroners need a thicker blade to cut through dead skin once rigor has set in and whatnot."

"What are you going to do?" she whispered.

Here's how this is going to work. I'm going to ask you questions. If you lie, and I'll know if you are, I cut. The more lies you tell, the more cuts I make. With that said, I'm sure you're wondering the purpose of those blue lines. Those are the approximate locations of the main arteries in each of your limbs. My cuts will start far away from those lines and move closer. Trust me when I say you really don't want me to hit one of those arteries."

I grabbed the pair of latex gloves from the table. "Don't want my hands to get slippery from all the blood now, do we?" I folded my hands in my lap and squared my shoulders. "Shall we begin? What's my name?"

"I only know you as Stephanie Yates," she cried. "Please. There has to be some kind of mistake."

I ran the twelve blade down the length of her left arm. She gasped and cried for several seconds. I scooted closer until my face was inches away from hers. "Wanna try again?"

Her eyes narrowed to slits. "You're Larissa Donovan."

Coming Spring 2025!

About the author

Samara Black was born and raised in Oregon. She started writing short stories and weird poems at age nine. She continued writing as a hobby in college, typing out silly stories with her roommate and came up with the idea for her first book series when she should have been studying for an economics test. After several dysfunctional friendships, toxic relationships, and family entanglements she had enough source material to write stories about characters with messy lives and even messier problems that come their way.

Samara currently lives in Seattle with her family, including several pets who think they're in charge. In her free time, her hobbies include reading, photography, chasing pests out of her garden, and annoying her teenaged children.

Instagram: @author.samarablack

Sign up for sneak peeks and teasers and get a free copy of Mutual Assets: Prequel to The Asset